Hollow Victories

(Volume III of the series *Reporting a War*)

By Emery Buxton

Table of Contents

Dedication

This book is dedicated to the memory of Maximillian Hirsch (d. 1968), father-in-law to the author, who served as a sergeant in the German Expeditionary Force to the Ottoman Empire in 1918. The stories of his experiences were entrancing.

Acknowledgments

"The author thanks the family members who gave advice during the initial drafting of the manuscript, the 'readers' who reviewed the first draft, and the editorial staff at AMZ Publishing Company for preparing the manuscript for publication. All those efforts are appreciated.

The 'history' contained in the writing is based on the lectures of M. Rasjidi and J.A. Williams in their Islamic History courses at McGill University in the 1958-1960 period while the author was a graduate student. The 'Carolina' setting of the two main characters is based on the author's own residence in the Charlotte area in the 1970's. However, the name of the university (Winston Meritt University—WMU) is fictitious, while the names of other institutions of higher education in the "Carolinas," such as Lenoir Rhyne and Davidson are real. The newspaper award at the end of the novel is likewise fictitious. This is a novel after all, not a history lesson, although an attempt is made to be compatible with history.

The cover depicting the entry of Arab troops to Damascus in 1918 comes from an Alamy photo collection and has the permission of that company The maps are from the New Zealand government's collection of memorabilia of the New Zealand expeditionary force to the Middle East in World War I. "

The descriptions of the of sometimes "confused" and narrow viewpoint of university educators, while centered at a fictitious university (Winston Merritt University), reflects the observations of the author at several North American universities as either witnessed by the author or related to him or by his friends and colleagues. Universities are decentralized because knowledge is diverse, so academic responsibilities often follow the same inclinations. While imponderable at times, usually good intentions prevail, but often only through the determined efforts of the people involved. Graduate study is not an easy path."

About the Author

The author was a specialist in international affairs and served in the U.S. State Department and at two major North American universities, researching and writing articles and studies on Islamic culture and its manifestations historically and in the modern era. See *Sultans, Shamans and Saints: Islam and Muslims in Southeast* Asia (available from Amazon Books) Writing under the pseudonym of Emery Buxton he published a series of four novels on the Korean War titled *An Inconvenient War* (available from Amazon Books and on Kindle). He resides in the beautiful hill country of Southeast Ohio where the people are warm and hospitable.

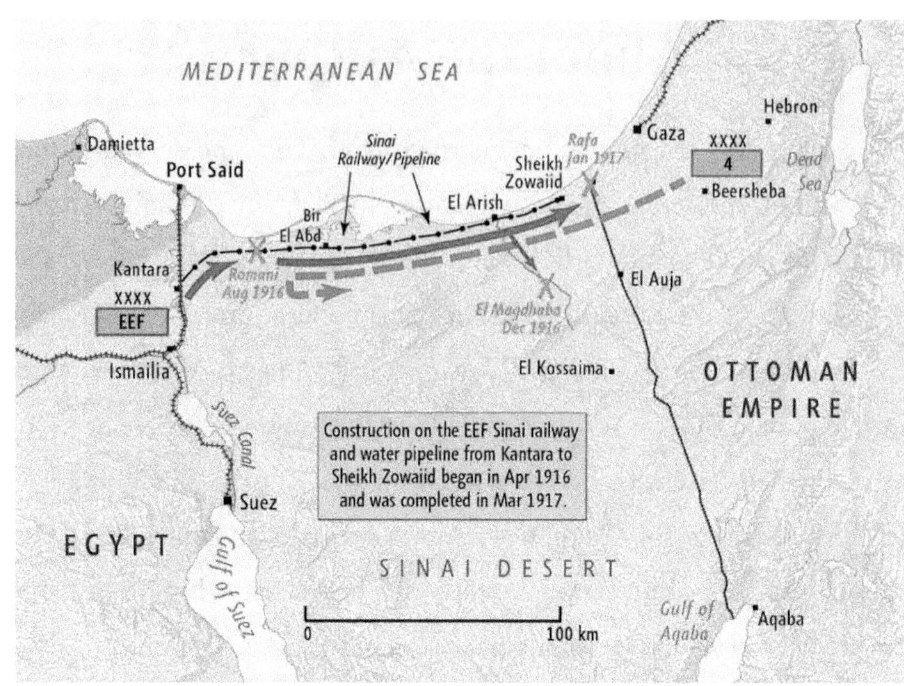

Sinai Campaign [Maps that Explain World War I, no. 23]

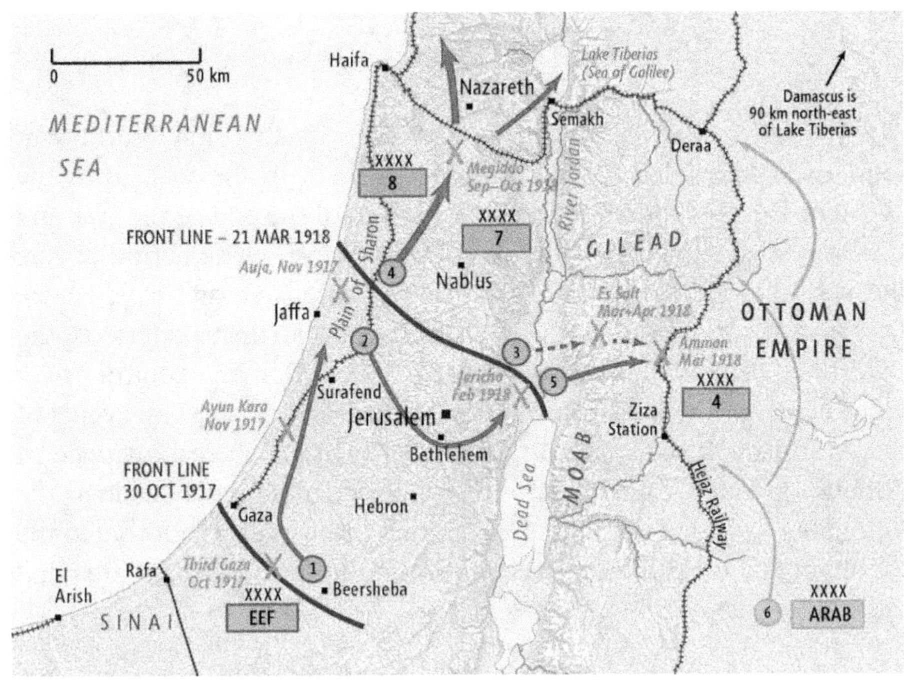

Palestine Campaign 1917-1918 [Sinai Campaign 1916 map at "Images for map of Sinai Campaign nz" second down selection on the right of the page]

Introduction

The first two volumes of this series dealt with the First World War until the end of 1915. This volume deals with the war from the Western Desert Campaign in early 1916 until the end of the war and the Armistice signed at Lemnos in October 1918. The period covers the period when the British went on the offensive and rolled back Ottoman control from the Sinai Peninsula and then undertook the Palestine campaign, which eroded the Ottoman control over Jerusalem, Amman, and the environs. It also covers the key events of the Arab Revolt, which took place in the Hijaz, where Lawrence of Arabia operated, and King Hussein led his revolt against the Ottomans. It ended with the great Syrian offensive, which routed the Ottoman and German units still operating in the Jerusalem area and ended the war.

This was a period of erosion for the Ottomans and their allies, the Germans, in this sector of the war. We see in these campaigns the great reliance the Ottomans had on German military leadership and on furnishing weapons and ammunition to keep the Ottomans fighting. Without that German support, the war might have ended far sooner, as much as six to nine months. At the end of the period, the Ottoman army officers' corps realized that it was not just the war that was lost but the entire concept of an Ottoman political entity. After the great Syrian offensive, the story is told how the Turkish officers and the Arab officers wish each other 'good luck' and go their separate ways, knowing that they will no longer be in a common political nation or empire henceforth. This theme is emphasized in this third book in the series, where a once great empire finally collapses, and an entirely new political alignment arises that is much more aligned with ethnic and racial considerations but is probably no more stable than the preceding empire was. Moreover, it is colonialism that is the winner and not independent states, as many people hoped would emerge. It all ends sadly,

This novel continues to follow the adventures of two international correspondents as they maneuver to get to the various battlegrounds to report the action. The interaction of the two with key figures of the era adds color to the story, and their relationship gives us a story of two young people whose love for one another is challenged but outlasts the conflict.

Chapter 1
A New Theater of Operations

Background

Martin Mintz is an international correspondent with a well-known news agency and became well-known for his incisive reporting on the Ottoman Empire, where he was stationed during the first year of the Great War (World War I). He witnessed fighting on the Russian front, at the Suez Canal, at Gallipoli near Constantinople, and at Kut on the Baghdad front. His colleague, Amelia Caruthers, is also an international correspondent who uses her camera to capture images of the war to accompany her reporting. Amelia centers on the war on the home front and, particularly, the minority peoples who suffer as 'scapegoats.' She collects information on government involvement in relocation schemes against the Greek and Armenian peoples. Both reporters were expelled for their agency's 'treasonous' reporting of massacres, which were linked to Ottoman government actions. After the expulsion, the two reporters visited Paris and were given new assignments in the British sector, which included Egypt and Palestine, where the British were planning offensives to drive the Ottomans from those areas.

Again, Marty is the teller of the tale.

Personal and Professional Adjustments

There has not been an opportunity for me to tell you, my readers, too much about how I view myself, but you need to know something about how I tick. I must deal with so many people in my interviews and in gathering news in general that it has made me conscious of how they see me. As a result, I try to reconstruct my persona to better reflect the individual I want to be. My Aunt Bea, the great counselor in my life from childhood on, always said that "Rome was not built in a day," meaning that good results came from the long-term effort one makes, not any single thing. I worked with that maxim in mind. It pays dividends.

However, there are certain points in life when the long run loses its relevance, and one is confronted with reality so urgent and overpowering that one must concentrate on an issue to the detriment of other matters. That was the case in early 1916 as my colleague and girlfriend Amelia–or Emmy, as she asked me to call her– made our way across the Mediterranean from the French Riviera to Alexandria, Egypt. We were aboard a small, comfortable, and fast cruise ship that plied the route, normally for the tourist trade, but now, increasingly for military personnel moving between the two theaters of war, i.e., Flanders and the Palestinian Frontier. I was on deck the first morning out of port as I was waiting for Emmy to rise from her slumbers so that we could eat breakfast together. It was then that the crisis hit me.

It was a psychological blow that rendered me momentarily inert. There was instantaneously a panic attack, which lasted thirty seconds, followed by a feeling of great dread, which lasted for another thirty seconds. I forced myself to move, in a stagger, from the rail where I had been standing over to the deck chairs, where I laid back and let my senses restore themselves to equilibrium. That took five minutes. During the entire episode, I had no immediate notion of what issues caused the uneasiness, but on only a little reflection, I knew exactly what the causes were: my upcoming job assignment and my relationship with Emmy.

The job situation had three components to it: The working relationship with the local agent in Cairo, with whom I had once had trouble; going into combat situations again, and fear that the British authorities might prevent me from reporting from their war zone. The local agent, Emile Bowdoin, had apologized for our earlier altercation, and he had assured me that he would guard against any recurrence of earlier woes if I came to work for him. However, I had found his earlier 'hands-on approach' to supervision arbitrary and knew I would have to be watchful of him, especially in the opening days of our new relationship. I hoped that both of us had matured in two years and that we would develop a new formula for having a good relationship with one another.

The second matter, going into combat, constituted a permanent dread that I diagnosed would remain with me so long a war was going on anywhere near me. When I was in the forward bunkers for about one hundred days, the Gallipoli campaign had left its mark on me. I did not relish going into a combat zone again. However, I understood that I certainly might be called on to do so in the new assignment. I knew I would certainly go, without any coercion applied to me, when called on to do that. If one wants to be a war correspondent, combat is an intrinsic part of the arrangement.

The third matter, not being allowed to operate in the British zone because I had been reporting from the enemy Ottoman capital, filled me with foreboding. I just had no idea of the reaction I would meet. I might be imprisoned as a spy or on some other trumped-up charge. Or I might be welcomed with open arms. I had no way of telling. Gertrude Bell, the English chief of intelligence at Basra, told me she had no case of espionage to charge against me and that I had a clean 'bill of health' in that regard. But Basra is not the British headquarters in Cairo. I worried about the ordeal of meeting with authorities there to learn my fate.

I quickly concluded that there was nothing I could do immediately to resolve these matters or allay my fears about them. They would best be addressed, one at a time, when the occasion came for them to be considered. In the meantime, it would be best if I placed them on a mental shelf in my mind containing other items that were unresolved.

Then, my mind shifted over to Emmy and the matters that I faced regarding her. Here, again, the precise issues were not hard to pin down. We had been close friends for two years and had only very recently become sexually intimate. On the surface, everything seemed quite good. We were attentive and at ease with each other, but that had been the general state of our relationship for quite a while, even before we were intimate. The only new item was sex, and, so far, only a matter of a couple of weeks, it had been wholesome, fulfilling, and satisfying. Moreover, as sexual partners, we were not shy with one another, and we found that our lovemaking had a place in our ordinary living that did not upset the professional side of our relationship. If all these positives were there, then what was the problem?

Two things, I suspect. The first one was Emmy's former lover, Werner Aussenfeld, with whom she had two brief but intense affairs. He was a German officer stationed with the Ottomans on the Baghdad front. That was hundreds of miles away with difficult transportation links, so he seemed out of the picture. Still, there are any number of scenarios that might bring him back to win her away from me. He had dumped her unkindly, but he had done that before, and she had reconciled with him later. I felt she could just as easily reconcile with him again. I based that notion on a statement she had made to me in an unguarded moment at the time of her earlier reconciliation with him. She said, at that time, that both Werner and I stirred sexual feelings in her, but that, in her daydreams, it was Werner who she visualized carrying her away to live happily ever after. Fantasy, of course, but still telling about basic emotions. On another occasion, she had said of Werner that he was an accomplished and exciting lover. Certainly, that description aces my description of my sexual relations with Emmy being "wholesome, fulfilling, and satisfying." Give me "accomplished and exciting" any day of the week.

I must confess that I did meet Werner in Irbil at the railhead on my transit across Anatolia to the Baghdad front. It was by accident that we were both at that spot at the same time, but we had never quarreled with one another earlier, so our reunion was friendly. He even suggested a hotel for me to stay at, and we had dinner together. At the dinner, after all other subjects had been exhausted, we arrived at the status of Emmy, which is what both of us wanted to talk about from the beginning. He said he was reconciled with his own family and never wanted to leave his children and wife again, but he wanted Emmy to have a happy life. He said he thought she could have that with me. He then said that Emmy was really in love with me and that her constant praise of me when they were together made Werner wonder why she wanted to be with him at all. Werner had concluded with the statement. "Tell her you love her, and she will be yours."

Now, such a statement could be highly flattering, but coming from a rival, I was suspicious. He was feeding me a line to placate me and throw off the scent of him as a rival. I suspected at the time, and still suspect that he was saying, "You can have her for now, but if I want her, I know that I can have her back. I have but to whistle." Now, I think that he might win her back if he tried to do that, but I am not so sure it would be easy. Still, the odds are in his favor.

The second consideration was Emmy's proclivity for 'flirting.' In large part, it was a remnant of her teenage years in South Carolina, where flirting was a pleasant pastime of young Southern men and women and even among some women later in life. She had toned it down since becoming a correspondent, in large part because in the Middle East, it was not understood, and it confused others. Middle Eastern men did not understand what flirting was meant to imply; they did not know how to react.

But Emmy did know how to attract men, and before Werner came into her life, she had several love affairs, including her future stepfather...well, probably. She never found anything amiss about such affairs. While I did not find such short-time erotic sessions wrong or in any way objectionable, I wondered what it entailed for our future. I had my sexual past, but with Emmy around, I did not want someone else. I always feared that her flirting might lead her somewhere she would not ordinarily go. It is not that any sexual activity might be considered wrong, but rather, the matter involved trust in a permanent partner and would cause damage.

I wondered whether our love affair was real and likely to be long-lasting or likely to go the way of so many other romances. I knew I had too much stock invested in Emmy to have our relationship fail. I wanted desperately to find out whether my interests in her were matched by her interests in me. Again, as in the case of my new assignment, there was nothing I could do about this matter. I would have to observe and arrive at conclusions to understand just what the relationship between Emmy and me was and could potentially become.

I sat ruminating on these matters for twenty minutes, during which time my heart rate reverted to normal, and my panic subsided. Still, I was self-absorbed and was not observing what was going on around me. Suddenly, there was Emmy kneeling alongside my lounge chair. She reached across and cupped one hand behind my neck and brought our heads together for a soulful kiss. Then she released me and said, "Good morning, sweetheart. Have you been up long?"

"No, love, I haven't," I replied, with her sweet taste lingering on my lips, "Half an hour. I wanted to wait and have breakfast with you, so I came out here to relax and make sure I did not bother you."

"That was nice of you. "If you are ready, let's go," she replied. "I'm suddenly hungry." Then she switched subjects. "What great thinking did you do this morning? You were in deep concentration when I came out. You were in a trance."

"The usual," I said, "Wondering about the reception we will get from the British authorities."

"You worry too much," she said. "They might make static initially, but they hardly have a case to make. In any event, within a month, they will have forgotten about it. As I said, put it out of your mind."

I agreed, with a shrug, which indicated I would not talk about it at breakfast. I wondered whether I could as easily put aside the part of my reverie about her and the unknown longevity of our relationship. It would be best not to tell her about that part of my panic attack at all. I do not know if our fledgling intimacy could withstand that kind of analysis.

At breakfast, self-served from a well-filled sideboard, we got our food and sat at the sole remaining table not already filled with other customers. Shortly after seating ourselves, a young man, twenty to twenty-two years old, asked if he could join us as all the other tables were full. He said his name was Gerald Gentry from Halifax, Canada. He was a news reporter for the *Times* of London, who had served for six months in Cairo and then had voluntarily relocated to France to cover the fighting there. He was on a quick trip to Cairo to clear up legal problems regarding property he had there. He did not ask who we were, and we did not volunteer that information since he had a lot to say and dominated the conversation.

There were pauses in his conversation since he went back to the serving table several times for more food. He thought we were a couple on our way to Egypt as part of a vacation cruise. The omnibus collection of Jane Austen's works that Emmy toted with her gave him that impression.

During the meal, he segued from topic to topic and finally arrived at Emile Bowdoin, which suddenly made a pro forma conversation into one in which we had a considerable interest. Gerald said he had great sympathy for Emile because he was the best newsagent around. He had an entire string of news agencies around the Middle East that were the envy of all the other newspapers. Most correspondents used the services of those agencies whenever they could. He also had local reporters who could gather news from British handouts and capture the general scuttlebutt floating around an army headquarters. Their coverage of the war was limited, and they often got it all wrong. The other place where his news agencies were not so stellar was the quality and abilities of his international correspondents.

"You would think that with the resources that the *Tribune* is noted to have, he would have led the field, but he was usually near the bottom, largely because he failed to assemble a good reporting staff." Gerald shoveled two small sausages into his mouth, chewed quickly, and washed the mass down with a large swallow of coffee.

Gerald continued, "I drank beer with him one afternoon when he told me he had recruited a young scholar in 1913 who had studied Arabic with a desert tribe and at an Arab university. He knew Arabic idioms like nobody's business. Emile said he thought he was headed for the big time with that kind of talent but lost control of him because Emile, himself, got sick in Sudan, and another *Tribune* agent took control of him. There were complications, and he separated from the young man on bad terms. Emile said that he never was able to find that kind of talent again, even though he had tried different people in that spot.

Mostly, he recruited from the stringers attached to his agency, but none of them ever passed muster, even though he went through at least six of them. None came close to the quality of the one that got away."

That's an interesting story," responded Emmy. "Did he ever try to get the man back?"

"He said he met him once in Persia, where he intended to make amends, but past misunderstandings got in the way of a reconciliation. He also wrote to the man once when the war began, hoping to get him to come back, but by then, he had learned Ottoman Turkic and took a job as an international correspondent for the *Tribune* in Istanbul. Emile said bad luck had been against him the whole way on that venture. Too bad, because ole Emile does deserve a break somewhere along the line. He's too good a newsman to be forgotten without any claim to fame."

"Maybe he lost the man because he didn't treat him right," I said.

"Possibly," Gerald said as he devoured his plate of "over-easy" eggs. "He said he had two Egyptian workers, one a translator, who muddied the waters and convinced him (Emile) that the reporter he liked so much had engaged in unseemly behavior with a woman photographer who had been hired for the project. Emile came to believe that the indiscretion had happened, but it did not. In a confrontation, Emile severely lectured the correspondent and the photographer and thereby ended any hopes of getting the reporter to come and work for him ever again."

"What a sad story," said Emmy. "Did he keep the Egyptian workers after he found out the story they told was untrue.?"

"No," came the response, "When the war started, they got jobs in the Egyptian civil service and left Emile on bad terms, saying he was nothing but a "British spy."

I asked, "Did he ever try to recruit you?"

"No, he didn't," Gerald answered. "He was in awe of the *Times* and did not want to cross the local agent in Cairo. They had frequent meetings where they commiserated with one another about the hard knocks they had during their careers. Everyone in the news business has a hard luck story of some sort.

Emmy asked, "When you worked here, you did not know Arabic. Is that right?"

"That's right," Gerald replied. In the meantime, he had gotten himself a ham and cheese omelet from the steam trays. Between bites, he said, "I paired off with a local Arab who knew English, but I always had trouble because his English was weak, and he fashioned sentences that were far short of what the original Arabic was. Also, I knew he sometimes lost the thread of what the Arabic speaker was saying when the translator would simply make something up. It was not a good situation, and I was glad when I had a chance to leave."

We had finished our breakfasts by that time and had two cups of coffee. Gerald suddenly pulled out his pocket watch, looked at the time, and exclaimed, "My God, it's nine o'clock. I've got to send a message ahead for people to meet me at the dockside. Excuse me!" He got up and left, the omelet only half eaten. He was in a hurry.

We sat on deck chairs during the morning, alternating reading and rehashing the assessment of Emile provided by the reporter. My view was that Emile was a hard-core case and would not know 'reconciliation' if it hit him in the face. Emmy was more charitable and held that, while he was not a reformed man, he had learned a good lesson from the experience and was not apt to repeat it. Reluctantly, I came around to her way of thinking.

We came to the viewpoint that we had to assume the best possible scenario with Emile and go with that approach until proven wrong when we could adjust. Emmy said that if we went in expecting the worst, our negative attitudes might well doom our relationship with Emile. If we went in with positive attitudes, they would show Emile that we wanted cooperation and friendship. We would have to overlook small slights, mistakes, and miscalculations and stay positive for our good intentions to register with Emile. I knew she was right, of course, and I quietly agreed with her.

All my concerns stated earlier in the conversation were merely made so that they would be out in the open so that a reasonable decision could be made. Emmy said it was not necessary 'to beat a dead horse to death' and that a little less 'slopping around in the muck' was necessary. I let the snotty remark go in the interest of harmony. I knew we were going to make love after lunch and that any argument with her about her reaction to my problem-solving style might influence that event. I let the matter slide. That is called 'being pragmatic.'

But, when a day starts with weighty matters on one's mind, those matters continue to crop up throughout the day. So, it was with our sex life. If I was concerned about Werner's abilities ahead of time, I was deeply concerned after the afternoon's session with Emmy. It was a simple side remark that affected me, and I am sure it was unintentional on Emmy's part, but it stung nonetheless. We were in a second round of enjoyment when I attempted to enter her from an odd position that we had not experienced before. Noticing a look on her face that I took to be pain or discomfort, I quickly withdrew and said, "I'm sorry; I don't mean to hurt you."

She said with a touch of exasperation, "Don't treat me like a porcelain doll! I'm much more durable than that! If it hurts a little at first, the feeling on the other end is well worth it."

We finished our lovemaking later, and I must admit, I was satisfied with the results of the session. But Emmy's remark stayed with me the rest of the day, and I took it as a comparison between Werner and me, although I suppose it could be interpreted in some other way. I felt that Emmy wanted our sessions to be a bit more "rough and tumble," and her remarks about Werner had implied that. By evening, my psyche was in shambles over the remark and what it portended for our long-term relationship. It was all I could do to keep my downheartedness from affecting our life together in a small stateroom.

The Cairo Interlude

We met Emile soon after we docked. He was now in Alexandria full-time, where he was close to the British army, which had established deployment centers for its campaigns. Already planned were campaigns against the Ottomans in western Egypt, eastward in Sinai, and to the north in Gaza and Palestine. Emile said, "We'll start here but undoubtedly move northward as the British campaign moves in that direction. But all that is still some ways off."

We talked about his expectations of acting as correspondents, which were not different from what he had told me two years earlier when he first hired me. It was mostly about professionalism, submerged egos into a common team, and whatnot. However, he added, "You two are very mature correspondents now, so I will leave you alone as much as possible to let you get your jobs done. I have seen your writing from Constantinople and understand that the best thing I can do is stay out of your way. Boris has warned me about that. Incidentally, Boris dislikes that you two are no longer working for him. He says you always gave him 'good copy.' I hope that will be true here as well. I will do what I can to help."

Moving on to the war, Emile said that we should go to the American embassy in Cairo and get our passport and visa work updated. "You can also meet with officials there who have expressed an interest in meeting you. Your reporting from Constantinople has reached them, and they want to be sure you are not Ottoman spies." Then, he said, "Afterwards, come back to Alexandria and report to the British army officials here as reporters, and pick up your press passes. While both of you were certified, as of yesterday, the officials here and in Cairo are certain to quiz you on matters they regard as important."

He warned us about censorship and about wording things so that the censors were not prone to ask for change or outright deletion. "You are going to have a more difficult time than many others, I am sure, simply because you are not accustomed to this set of censors. Fortunately, you two are very experienced in your dealing with officials, so you'll do well enough after some adjustment, but remember to minimize your conflict with censors, as differences with them over time can mount up to your disadvantage."

We talked with an Egyptian reporter that afternoon who covered events in Upper Egypt, who was surprised that we wanted to meet with him. When we met him, he said, "The reporters here at the agency have always regarded me as a 'yokel' and wanted little to do with me. I was not even on a first-name basis with them."

We talked for almost two hours about the impact of the rebels on the region of southern Egypt, which he covered. In particular, he told how the local population often protected the rebels, even though they preferred that the rebels move on and leave the local population alone. The reporter said that it was a matter of self-preservation, where British efforts to fight and remove the rebels were usually more invasive than the mere presence of rebels. So local populations tried to get the rebels to tone down their anti-British rhetoric and subversion lest it bring in the British army to crack down on all sides without differentiating normal villagers from rebels. Emmy and I listened closely, as the rebels were from the same group we would be covering in the western desert when the British campaign got underway.

 We ate a meal together at a local Egyptian restaurant, and I picked up the tab, which nearly made the reporter my friend for life. Our predecessors had never treated him to anything. From our vantage point, it was no big thing; we had expense accounts, but our Egyptian colleague did not.

The following day, Emmy and I went to the US Embassy in Cairo, where our office had made appointments for getting us the proper visas, general registration, and 'miscellany.' Our passport and visa work were done quickly, without any difficulty. The *Tribune* office had sent all the necessary supporting documents, so there were no delays or requests for additional information. "Miscellany" involved meetings with officials. The first was with the military attaché. He wanted to know if I would consider an appointment in the US Army as his assistant since the US was trying to increase its presence in the area. "Right now," the attaché said, "I go to meetings with the British and have no idea what they are even talking about since they use so much Arab lingo and military jargon. I am sure you would understand and even thrive in that atmosphere."

He turned to Emmy and said, "You would find dependent housing nice and Egyptian help, mostly from the villages of the upper Nile, honest and hardworking. The women's club has an elaborate program that most of the dependents' wives enjoy. I am sure you would like it here."

I was ready to let his assumption that Emmy was a simple 'homemaker' pass, but I knew that was not going to work because the time would come when he had to regard her as a professional. I decided that Emmy's newspaper life should be recognized immediately. I said, "Sorry, Colonel, but Amelia is not my wife just yet, but perhaps she will be in time. She is a reporter, just like I am, and has been in combat conditions, just as I have. She will be doing the same here in Egypt and the other Arab lands. I say this not to embarrass you but to allow you to regard her in a professional sense and understand that she is not in any way an appendage of me."

He reddened and started to apologize, but Emmy interrupted and said, "Colonel, next time I am in Cairo, I would enjoy meeting you and your wife. I could give you a book of my photographs made two years ago on a trip across the Middle East." That remark blunted the embarrassment. Amelia and I departed the office on good terms with the attaché. I avoided the original question of whether I wanted to join as an assistant attaché in his organization.

The second official identified himself as a 'special assistant' to the British Authority. I knew that my dreads and fears were about to be challenged. Here was the person who was going to decide whether Emmy and I would be reporting from the British zone or not. He was not going to tell us that was his purpose, but both Emmy and I knew from the outset that it was.

He concentrated on Emmy first and wanted to know if it was true that she had been romantically involved with a German officer. When she admitted that she had been, he asked, "How serious was the affair? Did you, for example, contemplate marriage?"

She answered, "It was a tempestuous affair, as most short-term relationships are. We were never 'soulmates,' and both of us understood our affair would last only for a brief time. We carefully avoided any discussion of 'marriage.' I would have enjoyed a little more time with him, but it ended just as I expected it. I enjoyed it, but do not rue its passing."

"It did not bother you that he was German?"

"No, should it?" I am an American, and the United States is not at war with Germany. There should be no stigma attached to me politically."

He paid no attention to the answer but went to her newspaper articles. He noted her coverage of the Ottoman 'home front' and asked if she regarded them as 'pro-Ottoman.'

"Probably," she answered. "I was sympathetic to the ordeals the common people were experiencing in a society at war and trying to provide goods and services for both the military and the people left at home. It was not an intentional bias, but one crept in, certainly."

He asked about her reporting on minorities. "Why did you report on the matter when you certainly were aware that your reporting would rile the officials and have your newspaper suspended."

"I did not feel that would happen," she answered. "I wrote to inform the Ottoman officials and public what was happening so they could do something about it. I always felt that the Ottoman censors would only pass on information they were willing to share with the rest of the world. They always did. The *Tribune* was not suspended because of my reporting but for the unauthorized reporting of another reporter who fled Ottoman territory and reported an uncensored story. I followed the rules precisely, just as I expect to do here."

"What you are telling me," He answered, "Is that every story on minorities that you sent was cleared by Ottoman censors?"

"That is correct," she answered. "I had no other choice since that was required of all of our reporters."

"I see!" he said emphatically. "I was unaware of that."

He turned to me. "Mr. Mintz, do you always use censors?"

"Usually," I answered, "But I was often in areas where there were no official censors. Then, I used high-ranking Ottoman officials, such as the minister of war or a theater commander. At the Gallipoli battlefield, I used the public relations officer."

He said, "The Basra intelligence office says that one report you sent right after you entered British territory had to be withdrawn from transmission because of its sensitive nature. How do you account for that? If you would have used a censor, that would not have happened."

"The public relations officer volunteered to let me use his machinery to file the materials, and I asked him specifically if I needed to find a censor first. He stated that he had read the materials and that they were acceptable. I was in his custody at that point, so I assumed he had the authority to act in that capacity. It was several days later that I met a member of the counterintelligence service who informed me that the article to which you referred had been retrieved, but she never said I had violated any protocol."

He changed subjects and asked, without any warning, "Did you have any sexual liaisons with women from any country of the Central Powers[1] during your stay in the Ottoman Empire."

"No," I answered. "I did not."

He asked, "Did you share previously unpublished information about the Ottoman Empire with British authorities when you arrived? If you

---

1 The Central Powers during the World War I struggle consisted of Germany, the Austrio-Hungarian Empire and Italy. Several other countries were allied with it, including the Ottoman Empire. It was opposed by the Entente Powers consisting of France, Great Britain, and Russia. The United States was later a part of the Entente Powers.

did, doesn't that break your code of neutrality that a reporter follows?"

"I answered. "I shared many things with the Basra counterintelligence office, but none of them were clandestine, except for the one sensitive message the office itself classified as such. No, I am not guilty of any infraction of the newsman's code if the vague wording of the code does imply that."

The officer closed his notebook, put his fountain pen away, and stood up. We stood as well. He shook each of our hands and said to wait in the anteroom. A decision on whether we would be allowed to operate in the British zone would be made immediately, and we would be informed at that time.

In the waiting area, Emmy and I were alone. She said, "He shook hands with us, so I regard that as a good sign."

"The Europeans shake hands with everyone, even their enemies. It's a habit that means nothing," I countered. "But on the other hand, he asked so few questions, I think he was just running through a drill to say he had examined us."

"His questions of you were that way," she said. "But he got into my personal life."

On that sour note, we sat back and waited. It took less than ten minutes, and a young man came into the room and had us each sign a form saying we would protect the document that we were receiving and report its loss or theft to British authorities immediately. He then gave us documents with a hard-black cardboard cover with a single document inside, stating: 'Press Pass. British Zone of Operations, Near and Middle East, with a set of signatures on it and an official embossed seal. We accepted them, shook hands with the clerk, and left the office.

Outside, I said sarcastically, "I never doubted in the world."

Just as sarcastically, Emmy said, "Neither did I."

Emmy and I stayed overnight in Cairo to have dinner at the American Club, where we had not been since before the war began. It was changed because the membership was different. There were almost no vacationers as before; they had been replaced by American businessmen providing services or supplies to the British armed services.

I had never seen the dining room so packed. We had to wait to be seated, so we went to the bar for drinks in the meantime. The *(London) Times* correspondent, who was the guest of American acquaintances, recognized who Emmy and I were and came over to introduce himself. He spoke highly of Emmy's writing, especially her pieces on minorities in the Ottoman Empire. He was not surprised when Emmy said that she had been too absorbed with the subject since she had been exiled.

"Not to worry, Amelia," he said. "All of us, sooner or later, must stand our ground on principle. It's a price a good journalist always knows could face him any time he picks up a pen or pencil to write an article."

I asked whether he knew what became of the *Guardian* correspondent I had known in the early days of the war at Constantinople. He did and told me, sadly, that the correspondent had been killed in action while covering trench warfare in France. It put a pall over the rest of our conversation. I realized that I worked in a dangerous profession, but I shook the mood as soon as the *(London) Times* correspondent left us.

When we finally got to our table, Emmy, uncharacteristically, turned the subject to the Carolinas and home. In looking back on the incident, I can only surmise that our change of relationship created a reaction in her or, at least, led her down lines of thought she had not examined before. I recognized the same unsureness in her that I, myself, was experiencing.

She asked whether I was going to be a correspondent all my life or whether I would be content with returning to North Carolina and getting a teaching position.

God, I thought to myself, this is like listening to Janet, my former girlfriend, who always started a serious conversation about the future with such an inquiry. I had to remind myself that it was not Janet with her possessiveness but Emmy, who I regarded as considerate and non-invasive in my personal life. Still, I reverted to form and took my time answering the question, waiting for clues from Emmy on what my answer should be. I wanted to be solicitous, and I did not think, at this early point in our relationship, that any answer I would give would be engraved in stone.

But as I ruminated and thought about the possibilities, I understood that this was a serious conversation. Emmy wanted to know how I saw us together in the post-war era and felt that I should share with her the feelings I had about it. I arrived at the answer that I would go home to North Carolina when the war ended. "All the juice will be gone from this correspondent's job by then," I concluded.

That seemed to satisfy her, but then she threw out the question I suppose all women want to know about. She asked whether I had strong enough feelings for her that I could see marriage in our future. That one took me completely off balance, given all the doubts that had been occupying my thoughts every day since departing Paris a week earlier. She was unsure of what was facing her in our new relationship. But I was unsure whether she was asking to be certain that I wanted marriage or because she wanted to scotch any such feelings. Her wording was vague enough that the matter could go either way. It put me in a quandary about how I should answer.

My God, I thought, we were now having regular sex together when previously we did not! What was that a step toward, if not marriage? I thought she was asking a redundant question, but then I thought of the woman I was with in Greece, with whom I had sex, but certainly knew that we would never consider marriage. Emmy had sexual relations with Werner, but they had never thought about marriage seriously, either. Or so she had told the British examiner. So, I concluded that it was a realistic question to ask, but, Lord, this was not the woman from Greece, but Emmy, whom I adored and for whom

I would do anything. Surely, she would know that I wanted marriage with her sooner rather than later.

All my stewing the past several days came to mind as well, and, in a trice, I tossed them aside. If she was serious about the question, there was nothing to be jealous about, and she did not prefer him to me at all.

But this was a question that, once asked of a person, cannot easily be swept aside. Neither can the person answering it be in any way equivocal. One's future relationship with the asker of the question rests on a clear and committed statement. I had to announce immediately whether I wanted her or not. It was that simple.

 I was about to let my mind quickly play over other answers and choose a qualified answer, but I knew immediately that was not necessary. There was only one answer. I said, "Of course, I'll see you in my future, you dumbbell! As my wife, of course! There has never been any question about that matter ever since I met you here in Cairo over two years ago. Why do you even ask? Hasn't it been clear to you how much I love you?"

She dropped her fork in apparent surprise, and it clattered on her plate. She had not been expecting such a strong statement of commitment and love. Then she looked at me intently, almost staring. She said, "Why, then, did you let me go with Werner?"

"Because I didn't know I had a choice, and you had already entered the affair before I even knew what was happening. I could only endure it and let the affair run its course. When we stood on the dock in Smyrna, as we were about to leave, and I saw the closeness of you with him, my heart nearly dropped out of my chest. It took everything I had to make it appear that everything was all right."

She merely looked at me and hesitated before saying anything more for a few seconds. Then she asked, "How did you feel when Werner turned his back on me at the hotel in Constantinople when his wife came to get him? Were you happy and relieved that Werner had been removed from the scene?"

"No, of course not," I responded. "I don't want bad things to happen to people I like or love. I thought it a tragedy, even as I think his reconciliation with his wife was last year. But all that doesn't enter my deep feelings of love for you."

She picked up her fork and slowly began eating again but was silent. I was at a loss whether to continue the conversation or to change it. I did neither, and we went through the remainder of the meal, some ten minutes, eating silently. I wondered whether I had offended her but guessed I had not, or we would not be finishing our meal together. Then she rose, excused herself, and went to the restroom. When she returned, she said, "Just one more question, if I may?"

"Sure," I answered. Before I could think what the question might be about, she asked, "I know what you said to the official, but let me ask again and more specifically. Have you slept with anyone since the ambassador's daughter in Teheran?"

The question annoyed me, considering her all-consuming affair with Werner. Why did she ask it? Was she making comparisons of my shortcomings with her own? I put the slight resentment down and said, almost immediately, "Yes!" I vacationed for ten days with a woman I met in Greece. while I was on recuperation leave." I felt justified in excluding knowledge about the Austrian woman whom I befriended on my trip across the Atlantic, who had gone to bed with me to show her appreciation for my kindness. To even mention her was to open an incident in my life that she knew nothing about, and I regarded it as a personal and closed matter that concerned me alone.

"Do you write to one another?" she asked.

"No," I responded. "I don't even know her last name, and we did not exchange addresses. We have not corresponded and have no real means of doing so."

She wanted verification, "Are you sure?" she asked.

"Hey," I retorted, showing annoyance. "You asked a personal question, and I answered it, but I will not have you pick at the answer. Leave it alone! If you think I'm lying, then walk out of here right now.

I will not be badgered!" I was heated, and it was apparent that she felt the passion of my statement.

There was silence all the way home in the taxi, which made so much noise a conversation in it was impossible in any case. We went into our suite, and she disappeared, so I sat down to read the most recent *Tribune*. Midway through the paper, I noticed Emmy had not returned, so I went into the bedroom and found her lying on the bed crying. I took her in my arms and asked softly, "What's the trouble, Emmy."

"I'm such a ninny," she answered. "I should have never confronted you about marriage, and then, to question you about your sex life was low of me. I know you just hate me."

"Well, I am a little perturbed about it all and wonder what has gotten into you to suddenly go off on me. I don't think I did anything to deserve it."

"You didn't at all, but I am sometimes so unsure of how you feel about me that I could hardly believe your feelings regarding me were true. It took me by surprise, as I never realized you felt so strongly about me. I thought you just regarded me as a pal. When you said what you did this evening, I immediately realized that for you to know that I was with Werner must have hurt you very much."

"Well, people are more resilient than we often realize," I answered. "I waited for the time when you would no longer be with him. Sometimes, I can be patient, and I had no choice but to be that during those times. But I can tell you, I was not at all happy about it." Of course, I did not tell her about my more recent jealousy and unsureness about her relationship with Werner. It seemed less relevant now that I understood she was just as unsure about her relationship with me as I was uncertain about my relationship with her.

She started crying all over again, and it took me several minutes to get her out of that funk. "What is it?" I asked repeatedly.

She finally said, "I'm sorry I asked you about other women, but I'm so jealous that I imagine you with other women any time a female comes your way. I nearly fired Cynthia because you teased her like you do most other people you know, and I interpreted it as 'flirting' and a prelude to going after her sexually." Cynthia has been the assistant office director in Constantinople.

"Well," I said, "Cynthia is a nice-looking woman, but she was a colleague and off-limits, or so I believe. I don't mean to be a recluse, but no available and appealing women have passed my way. Somehow, they didn't find their way onto the battlefield at Gallipoli. Worst luck! Somehow, I've been content just sleeping with you without sex. I don't think that our sleeping together that way was a very psychologically healthy thing to do, but somehow it sufficed and kept us close, whether you recognize it as such or not." The two Arab women in the shay on the way to Irbil crossed my mind, but they didn't belong among those women who had tempted me. It was they who wanted me as a marriage partner; it was not me who wanted them.

She was silent for ten minutes, and I lay there with my eyes closed, listening to her breathe. Finally, she said, "Marty, there is something more I want to raise with you while we are dealing with sexual matters. Will you hear me out on this one and listen patiently until I am done? Then, you can say what you want in response.

I immediately wondered what other set of circumstances was coming my way for which I was not prepared, even as the foregoing discussion had been. I did not think I was going to like what was coming my way, but I felt now was as good a time to face the issue as any. "Of course, my love. I will say nothing until you have had your say."

"I don't know why you are so concerned about Werner that it affects you the way it does. Especially when we are making love, I don't suspect it is jealousy, only that you somehow think that I prefer him over you and would leave you if he came back on the scene. It is the remark I made about him being the 'man of my dreams' or some such thing. Today, when I told you I wasn't made of porcelain, I could see you saying to yourself that Werner would not have made that mistake. Don't deny it, you did! I know you too well to miss your facial features and body language, just as you know mine."

She continued, "Marty, you aren't like Werner at all, especially in bed. Sex with Werner was like exercising with the troops. It was done with precision and orderly performance, with each part of the sex act broken down into segments that were undertaken intently. We arrived at the finale together, and he did not finish until I had finished. Afterward, we smoked a cigarette together. We might do that once or twice and then find something to eat or drink. After the third time we had sex together, I could have told you just how many minutes and seconds it took. It was that regularized. But, on the bright side, a woman does not complain when she has two or three orgasms in an afternoon."

I listened but could find nothing to say in response. She said, "In contrast, our first encounter lasted about a minute, followed five minutes later by a second set of orgasms. Since then, we have been much more relaxed and exploratory. Our sessions last between twenty and thirty minutes, and we both are satisfied one or more times. We stop when we have had enough. I find myself fully satisfied afterward. I sense you are, too. It is not regulated in any way."

Again, she paused and seemed to search for words to continue. Finally, she said, "But I know at times you are trying to compare your performance to that of Werner. Please don't do that anymore, as there is no need to do so. Be yourself, as I enjoy it ever so much when you are.

She continued yet again, saying, "As for thinking that our present closeness is likely to be upset by a sudden return of Werner, I can tell you that you have nothing to worry about. For many reasons, I will not fall for him again. I hope I never have to show you how he will exert no control over me, but if he returns, I will reject him. Put Werner out of your mind, and don't bring him into the bedroom. That space belongs to us, not to him."

She stopped talking, so I waited a minute before answering. I said, "Thanks for your clarification. That could not have been easy. I have been concerned about Werner, and I do fear he will someday take you away from me. But, with your clarification in mind, I will try to rid myself of the dire feelings I have in that regard. Instead, I will concentrate on you and win you totally to my side. That's all I have to say."

We waited another ten minutes and then went to bed, where we had our first "make-up sex" waiting for us.

On the train going from Cairo to Alexandria, Emmy and I sat close together. It was much closer than is normal in a country whose attitudes about the proximity of men and women are puritanical, and appropriate distance is usually observed. But we were Westerners, and while Muslim travelers may have wished we had observed local customs better, we were drawn to one another as only new lovers are. If we had become intimate in Switzerland several weeks earlier, we became real lovers because of the revelations made by each other in Cairo. Sitting close was our way of expressing the newfound knowledge of one another gained in that city.

Emmy told me later, on the eve of our first daughter's birth, that after I blurted out my confession of love, my actions towards her earlier made sense. She said that she could trace my love for her in the trials and tribulations, especially in the Constantinople years when she underwent a crisis of identity. She said she always had wondered why I had stood by her then and allowed her to redeem herself. She said she never doubted my love for her after that.

Likewise, I was surprised that Werner's confession in a hotel in Irbil months before had been accurate, to wit, that I was the one that Emmy loved. Her confession in the hotel in Cairo, that she never knew where she stood with me, amazed me. I had always wanted her love and was surprised that it was always there for the taking. I had but to say I wanted it.

The remarks Emmy made about sexual styles were also enlightening. Her remarks put into perspective what we had together and told me that Werner and his style of lovemaking had its limitations. Werner was never in the bedroom with us again. He disappeared with Emmy's explanation. Her explanation of contrast in styles was a bit exaggerated—I am sure it was—but it worked well enough to assure me that all as well. Whether the mental picture she drew in her explanation was true or a fabrication does not matter. She was astute to recognize the problem and set my mind at ease about the matter.

Also, the Cairo trip resolved one part of our work problem. The authorities had permitted us to operate in the Egyptian area. There might still be difficulties in having that license recognized in practice by military men on the line, but we were both convinced that, with time, the reluctance to see us as part of the operation would evaporate.

As we pulled into the station in Alexandria, I realized that the issues that caused my panic attack on the ship from France had been addressed. The only one yet to be resolved was the relationship with Emile. There, first impressions suggested a good start had been made. We would see whether that was true or not in the next few days.

Chapter 2
The Western Desert Campaign

Preparing for the Sanusi Campaign

The day after we returned to Alexandria was given over to dealing with the British army. We were busy getting our credentials checked, our bureaucratic forms filled out, and attending three different briefings. We were the only correspondents still in Alexandria, as the others had already moved over to the western Egyptian frontier, where the strike force was preparing to move against the Sanusi.

I remembered the Sanusi from my early days as a reporter for Emile when I saw a diorama in the Cairo Museum showing the Sanusi village organization. Later I talked with several sources about the sect and discovered that they were one of several different groups in the Sahara and sub-Sahara from Morocco on across to Egypt. The sect emphasized righteous conduct according to early Muslim masters, combined with mystical practice among some of the males and a few of the females. They were desert folk who believed fully in the Lex Talonis, i.e., the law of retaliation, where all strangers were suspect and carefully built loyalties were the only ones that mattered. The Sanusi were prominent in the Hijaz, across southern Egypt up into Cyrenaica, in what is rapidly being called Libya.

I also knew from keeping pace with the war news that the Sanusi had been infiltrated by the Germans in the pre-war years and subjected to propaganda that urged loyalty to the Ottoman padishah as the rightful ruler (*caliph*) of the Muslim world. With the advent of the world war, Sanusi leaders declared a holy war (*jihad*) against the Entente powers. Since then, the propaganda had increased, with a sharp anti-British slant, and German submarines had been used to bring in weapons to them, mostly machine guns and Mauser rifles.

As early as 1914 small unit action had been taken against groups that were not in accord with German war aims. In 1915, Sanusi irregulars had captured villages and settlements along the Egyptian-Cyrenaica frontier. German officers had arrived to assist the Sanusi, but they were few and mostly ignored. The Sanusi constituted a desert army and did not ordinarily fight in formation or with accepted tactics common to European armies.

As I thought about the problem of covering them as a reporter, I wondered if modern technology was useful to the British in this campaign. I knew that railroads extended out along the Mediterranean coast towards the areas that the Sanusi occupied, and I knew from the Gallipoli campaign that airplanes could be used for reconnaissance. At the same time, I felt sure that infantry and cavalry would have to be used in going after the Sanusi, as I was not sure that the few armored cars that were in existence were developed enough to provide much of a mobile strike force. I was anxious to know what the British had.

I remembered a British captain from Kent, who was on the same ship as me when I left Basra, who knew something about modern desert warfare. He had broken ankles that were healing slowly but gave him great pain. I often medicated him at night when the orderlies were not available, so we became friends. To pass the time until the medication took effect, we talked about desert warfare, among other things.

He said that fighting in the desert was more advanced than it had been. Aerial reconnaissance helped a lot but was limited by the short range of planes that could fly only twenty or thirty miles, as carrying fuel was a problem. He said that at the Mesopotamian front, planes had been at a distinct advantage in locating the enemy forces and determining their deployment. "But they were only effective when the weather was clear and, unfortunately, along the Euphrates in the rainy season, planes had been unable to observe much."

He also said that there were now mobile armored units that used cars and trucks with armor plating over them, placed at a slant so that bullets ricocheted off and allowed the car or truck carrying a gun to get in close to a target. Usually, they carried only a machine gun, but sometimes a small cannon. They could travel long distances in a comparatively short period; However, they needed smooth surfaces, preferably improved roads, and were often limited in distance because of that factor.

Horse cavalry was limited because of the need for forage, which often could only be supplied by notoriously slow camel transports, and the camels ate as well. And, of course, in arid areas, most water had to be toted in, which was a concern for all commanders. At Kut on the Mesopotamian front, all these things were daunting. My colleague suspected the campaign against the Sanusi in Egypt would run up against the same problems. "Get set for a long and frustrating campaign," he concluded.

Emmy and I met one French reporter who was in from Algiers. He told me, in French, about the long campaign against similar desert groups who fought against French authorities there. "They are tenacious," he said. "Defeat them in one place, and they simply move ten kilometers and repeat the process." His warning was like that of the officer on board the ship.

Commenting on the upcoming campaign, the reporter said that a success would be to drive them out of Egypt and keep them from crossing the border again. "Chances are; however, they will merely move south in Cyrenaica, beyond the southern patrols, and then move across the southern flank, causing British troops new difficulties in the south. But that would be at least six months away. It takes time for them to move, but that is what will happen, mark my words."

I also talked with a British officer who had been on leave and was about to go back to the frontier to assume command of a battalion of cavalry. He said that there was a delay that was expected to last at least another week before the campaign against Sanusi would begin. The reason was that there was not enough forage for animals in the forward areas and that all horses had been evacuated and camel trains were sent in with enough forage for a return of the horses to undertake the campaign. The horses could only go back to the forward areas when stockpiles were enough for a campaign of at least a month.

The talk with the British officer unleashed a line of thought. I explained that thinking to Emmy, and together, we hatched a plan that was designed to get us to the front where we might have a vantage point unavailable to other observers and reporters. The first step was to get old desert robes that we could wear to infiltrate the camel drivers that were taking forage to the battle site. We went in search of such wear and easily found what we were looking for in a nearby bazaar (*suq*). It included head wrapping for me that looked like a turban and head shawls for Emmy. We planned to use stains for our faces to bring color more in conformity to the people of the area, although my long exposure to the sun at Gallipoli had me looking dark. We stuffed the clothing in our kit on top so that it would be easily accessible.

All the while we were shopping, we talked about how we would file our reports. We would be miles from any telegraphic station, except for British field units, which would not be available to us. The reporters accompanying the main force would have the same problem but would have a pooling arrangement that would get their reports back to some point in the rear, where they could be censored and transmitted. Some reporters would have to go back as well to argue with the censors, so it was not an ideal arrangement, and it would take time.

If we were going to use the camel caravans to get us into the area, we were going to have to use the same caravans to get our reports out. We could only do that once we had arranged with some family or overseer to assist us. At the railhead, we could rely on Emile to take over the further transmission to his office in Alexandria. There, the entire prep work of developing the film, getting censor clearances, and transmitting the final reports could be accomplished. Our system would be no more difficult in time and effort than that used by reporters attached to the British forces.

I called Emile, who happened to be in the office and explained the situation. He was positive about our entire scheme. He said that communication from the railhead to Alexandria was no problem since he regularly sent items, papers, and even people along the railroad in a very efficient process. He gave me the name and location of his agent at the railhead, who a messenger bringing our reports could contact and even be paid for that service. Emile recommended payment upon delivery of the report to that office to ensure that there was a financial motive for delivering it. "If you pay ahead of time, the reports are likely to become part of the litter that is found on all caravan routes." I agreed.

We slept in the open that night but were up by five a.m. when we began a three-kilometer trek to where the camels were assembled for the thirty-kilometer trek into the Bir Tunis combat area. In our just-boughten robes, we passed easily for local people. We even stopped at a small food stall and ate bazaar-style chicken and beans. No one took notice of us. At the field itself, where about five hundred camels were being loaded and assembled, we ambled through the throngs, looking for a camel driver to approach to allow us to accompany him.

We noticed the young woman simultaneously. She looked like she was sixteen years old. She was alone with eight large camels already loaded, but she looked perplexed and uneasy. Emmy nudged me and said, "Leave this to me." She walked over and engaged the girl in conversation. As told to me later, the young woman was worried, as her family had loaded the camels the previous evening and told her to wait until unattached drivers came through, when she could hire two of them to assist her in the drive south to Bir Tunis. Other than us, no unattached people had come by, and she was afraid no one would. The woman assumed Emmy was from a Syrian tribe and did not speak local Arabic, which accounted for her peculiar accent and failings in grammar. "Can you and your husband help me?" she asked.

"We are not skilled at this sort of thing and are merely looking for someone to accompany us to the south, where we have some family business," Emmy said.

"It's not hard to do," the young woman said. "The camels know what to do and stay in line very well. One only needs a switch to remind them. I can teach you. Please help me; I'll even pay you a switcher's wages."

Emmy declined the wages but struck a deal whereby we would help her move the camels south, and her family would help us on our way afterward. The girl was meeting up with her family in Bir Tunis, who were guarding goods brought down earlier.

The trip took a day and a half, and there were only minor incidents. The girl herself, who was an accomplished 'switcher,' knew how to move camels into line when the line sagged and individual camels started to stray. I was uncomfortable at the beginning, but as I became accustomed to the gait that was needed to walk alongside the camels, I soon mastered the chore of keeping the camels in line and moving. I lost track of time and steadily gained confidence. The camels, once started, were relentless animals. They tended to stay in motion until they stopped late in the day when they mostly wanted to rest and chew their cud.

The young woman, named Aminah, was just shy of sixteen and talked mostly of Iskandar, whom she was to marry when she (Aminah) was sixteen. The two families were close and operated a camel transportation business together. Aminah assured Emmy that Iskandar would be at the encampment in Bir Tunis and that Emmy could then see just how handsome, wise, and able he was. Emmy, in turn, assured Aminah that she had been blessed by God with such a fine prospective husband.

Aminah also said that being left in charge of the camels, with responsibility for getting them to Bir Tunis, was a sign of great trust placed in her and only came her way because the two families needed all the usual help at other places just then. She had been scared about it initially and felt she nearly failed in her responsibilities. "I would have, except Allah himself chose to send you and your husband to me at that crucial moment when I had nearly given up hope."

When we arrived at Bir Tunis, there was only Aminah's mother and grandmother at the small encampment. All the men had departed that morning for the return trip to Marsa Matruh for another load of supplies. The unloading of the camels fell to Aminah, her mother, Emmy, and me. We had to take the camels to an open-air storage area, where the grasses and grains we had brought from Marsa Matruh were placed in large piles on the ground and covered with tarpaulin. It rained often at this time of the year, and covering the forage was an absolute must lest it become moldy and unusable.

There was an overseer who asked me what tribe I belonged to, and I answered that I was from the Rwala near Syria. He said, "I thought so. You speak differently than we do, but it is apparent that you are a bedouin, as you do not fear the camels, and you carry yourself with great dignity."

I laughed and said, "Great dignity indeed! I have been most unfortunate in my business arrangements, and I am reduced to camel driving to carry me over to more opportune times."

"Allah tests us all from time to time," the overseer answered. "Be true to Him, and he will bless you in time. Patience in all things, brother." He moved on.

In the evening, after a meal of beans and barley prepared by Aminah's mother, I was shuttled off to one side while the women talked. Aminah's mother wanted to know from Emmy just what business we had in Bir Tunis. Emmy told her the truth about our mission, which did not at first register, but then, slowly, mostly through Aminah's understanding, who had basic schooling, the concept of a reporter and his job emerged. I was proud of Emmy. She brought her Arabic together enough to explain it all, even though her explanations were long because she lacked enough grammatical construction to be precise.

Once the idea of what we were doing was perceived, it was Aminah's grandmother who dominated the conversation. Well, it was a conversation between the three Arab women while Emmy and I listened. Aminah's grandmother saw the best possibilities lying in the use of two camels that had been brought along as transportation for her and Aminah's mother. These could be rented to "the two Rwalas who will pay a good fee," plus board and a place in the encampment while we were there. If we wanted to work as switchers on the way out, that could be arranged and would be preferred, but otherwise, there could be a fee for being our guide.

After a long and thorough discussion, Aminah's mother said that all this was subject to the men when they returned. Aminah's grandmother said nothing, which seemed to suggest that she felt that she was the negotiator and that any deal she recommended would be accepted by the men, even her son, who was the nominal head of the family.

Seeing Battle Preparations Up-Close

But the plans of the women were changed by events the following morning, the day when the men would return with the next camel caravan. The overseer, who had spoken with me the day before, suddenly showed up at our encampment alone on a camel with an extra camel on a rope. Seeing me, he gave out a loud "*As-salam alaikum,*" and I immediately responded with "*alaikum as-salam,*" which is usual for two Muslims in a meeting. He then said, "I have a busy day and need an assistant. Are you willing to serve in that position today? You'll get wages set by the British, which are reasonable."

"Certainly," I responded. "It beats staying here and unloading camels."

He laughed at my remark and said, "I can believe that. The loads are heavy, and the animals are sometimes unruly. There's nothing as nasty as a camel that spits with disdain on a person."

"Let me inform my wife that I will be gone for some time," I said and ducked into the tent where Emmy and the grandmother were working on a small loom together. I told them where I was going. They were so absorbed in the color combinations that they barely paid attention to what I told them."

The overseer watched as I brought the camel to its knees and boarded, pulling him upright after I was aboard. "I love to watch a bedouin board a camel," said the overseer with considerable admiration in this voice. "It's all so effortless." He tossed me a notebook with two pencils inside the cover. "I need to file a report today, so I need you to keep notes for me. You can write the lingo, can't you?"

"Of course," I responded. Then we swung out and toured the larger encampment of the British supply dump, stopping occasionally to talk with workers or fellow overseers. I was introduced as Ibn Tayyim, which surprised no one. Everyone was affable and there was considerable goodwill as the buildup of supplies was going well. It had not rained very much, and the supply caravans had gotten through on a regular rotation, so there were no delays that could cause dissension.

At the neighboring British cavalry camp, which abutted the forage 'dump' for logical reasons, a British lieutenant colonel stepped out in front of us and said, "There you are, Sulayman. I hoped I might see you today. Dismount and come in out of the sun so we can talk. I have something important to raise with you. Bring your assistant if you like since I know he's the one who keeps your record."

We dismounted, tethered our animals nearby, and joined the colonel beneath a tent with its sides up so that the air moved freely. There were glasses of squash ready for us, which I found particularly welcoming. The colonel, meanwhile, immediately raised business matters. "The action that is likely to happen here later this week is going to raise hobs with the mounts," he said. "The mounts will arrive in a day or two, and many will be lame, so they will need attention. Then, when the major action occurs, many of them will be wounded, some lightly, others severely. We are bringing in a team of veterinarians drawn from the camel corps of the Sultan of Darfur, who keeps his mounts in tip-top shape. He has loaned us the vets for two months. They are all Arabs, mostly from Sudan, but trained in Cairo under the British, so they will know their stuff. Do you have the picture so far?"

I nodded, and overseer Sulayman said, "Yesss," in English.

They will be bringing their tents, equipment, and so forth, but they need locals to set it up. Also, they will need locals to help as orderlies in the operating rooms. Often, women do that. Can you help provide me with such?"

"Yesss, Colonel Effendi," said the overseer. "Much surplus men and few women available as supply trains finished."

"Good, have a team of ten men ready tomorrow to set up the clinic and a team of ten women ready to learn duties in the surgeries," said the colonel, obviously not aware of the job it was going to be to recruit such a staff to begin work on short notice. "Let's say, ten a.m. for the men and noon for the women. Yes?"

"Yesss, Yesss," confirmed Sulayman. I concluded that Sulayman was such a British sycophant that he would agree to almost anything so long as the request came from a British officer's mouth. But I stayed quiet and left with Sulayman as the colonel was finished with us.

Once mounted, we moved out away from the British camp. Sulayman was at first deep in thought about how he was going to provide the labor that he had been requested to provide on short notice in a place where labor was notoriously short. He finally turned to me and said, "Your wife can help us. I am sure that the wife of such a capable man as yourself has enough standing that she can call on others on short notice to help us."

I was not about to tell him about the tenuous assumption he had just made, but I did agree that Emmy could work wonders at times when called on to do so. "Why not?" I said, leaving Sulayman in a quandary since I had used an American colloquialism rendered in Arabic. "Let's go ask her."

But Sulayman had no intention of dealing with a group of women. He begged off and went back to his encampment, telling me to join him there when I had solved this labor problem.

It was simple. Aminah's grandmother mentally produced a list of families in the camp who should be contacted. Almost immediately, she calculated how much each family should pay for this privilege. Good salaries on the British pay scale were being offered. Some money should be given to Aminah's family, who were arranging it all. I left half an hour later to tell Sulayman the good news and assure him the labor would be there when he needed it.

He was not surprised, nodded to affirm my information, and raised the subject of the camel caravan, which was due to arrive shortly. He said that every camel driver had to present the bill of lading given to him at Marsa Matruh when the cargo was loaded. It was checked against the actual cargo delivered. It took us three hours to do the job, and I had only one incident in that time. The partner of Aminah's family was short one camel, although the goods were redistributed among the other camels that the family-owned. It was explained that the animal had expired during the journey. I discovered I had the authority to deduct the entire cost of the missing camel, and the family would receive nothing for the cargo. However, I listened to the pleas of the family and decided, almost immediately, that they were due the payment since the cargo was delivered despite the loss of the camel. I did not report the incident, and I concluded that Sulayman committed far more serious offenses in his inspections.

That evening, Emmy said that there was an opportunity to test our 'report delivery system,' as Aminah wanted another trip to Marsa Matruh to help bring back another load of animal feed. This time, Iskandar's family would be nearby, so she might have moments with him without supervision, which was an exciting prospect for the two would-be lovers. Aminah was willing to deliver our package of reports–she felt any such favor was perfectly understandable-- and would have done it, even without the pay she would receive. Emmy sent two reports on our movements and the role of women in the campaign, along with three rolls of film. I sent one report on the layout of the camp and a roll of film.

We were anxious to know how well the delivery system worked and how well the office in Alexandria managed the censor problem. We found that it was successful. There were problems with film development and transmission, but the censoring of reports was swifter and less intrusive than what the office experienced with previous reporters, who had relied solely on military censors.

Sulayman liked my notetaking, saying that it was so legible that I could be a religious cleric (*imam*), but I laughed at that, saying, "I did have training in Islam as a child. I guess the knack for forming a good script was developed then. Unfortunately, I don't practice good writing enough anymore."

My precise notetaking made a great impact on Sulayman's trust in me. He decided that I should do the daily rounds alone so that he could sleep in and drink coffee with his friends. I was free to go where I wanted and see what I wanted.

The lieutenant colonel at the cavalry barracks liked me as well and always expected me to spend about ten minutes with him. I did not say much and always spoke to him in slow and simple Arabic, which he liked, imagining he was a linguist. He told me where the upcoming battle was to take place and even suggested some sites I might go to when it occurred so that I would get a good view of the battle as it unfolded. He was not able to bring many of his descriptions into Arabic, so he used English for this phase of our talks. He never suspected how much I understood, or he would never have been so forthright.

"The artillery always leads the way. Much depends on where the enemy's strong points are, but they are 'there,' 'there, and 'there,'" he said, pointing to three locations on the hills nearby where the Sanusi were known to be. "Artillery explosions are frightening," he said, "especially when they fall close to one, and the debris they throw up can be difficult to survive. After that, the armored vehicles move in, whose machine guns and small artillery riddle an area with bullets and shells that are difficult to withstand. Then comes the infantry, with the cavalry coming in at a crucial moment when the Sanusi come out of their fortifications to engage in hand-to-hand combat. Undoubtedly, many of them will ride their camels." I surreptitiously took a photo of the makeshift map he drew on a notepad that he always carried.

On the first day of the battle, I stationed myself at one of the points suggested to me. First, the overseer joined me, and then Emmy, also mounted on a camel, came by. It had rained the previous night, and, consequently, the roadways and the fields were very wet and difficult to navigate with any sort of vehicle, motor-driven or animal-driven.

Consequently, the usual attack plan did not run true to form. The artillery pounded the enemy positions longer than usual, which was followed by a cavalry charge and then an infantry attack, which gained a small plateau in front of the enemy positions. The armored cars and the horse-drawn artillery could hardly move because of the deep mud over the entire landscape. Sanusi machine guns barred the way, and it took most of the day for the Australian infantry to encircle them and destroy them one after the other.

The cavalry charge demanded that Sulayman and I leave our vantage point and go to the surgery, where a great deal of work was being done on the wounded horses. One of the vets said the situation could have been worse, and he estimated that by the following morning, another charge would be possible with about four-fifths of the horses participating. The lieutenant colonel, who was there when the statement was made, said that about matched the number of troopers who would also be ready the following morning.

When I went back to the vantage point three hours later, I found Emmy had moved to our second location. She said she had a clear view of the Sanusi withdrawal to the south. It was slow but steady. Mostly, the Sanusi rode horses and carried rifles, but sometimes, there would be a camel with a rider as well. After observing that for some time, we moved back to the first position and saw a camel charge by the Sanusi using machine guns mounted on camels. The firepower of the machine guns momentarily drove the Australian infantry away. However, British artillery zeroed in on the attacking force and drove them off with a large loss of human life and camels.

Then, the Sanusi force melted away, seeming to withdraw to the west. I suppose the British could say they won because they were still on the battlefield, and the Sanusi had left it. But it was also clear that the Sanusi forces had not been decisively defeated. I was sure there would be a follow-on battle somewhere to the east. I remembered what the French observer had said, 'Beat them, and they move ten kilometers, and you have to fight them again.'

Emmy and I decided we needed to get new reports to Alexandria to cover the recent fighting. Aminah was not yet back from her trip to Marsa Matruh, so we were unsure how to manage this situation. The caravans had stopped running since the battle had been joined with the Sanusi, so we had to modify our communication system.

As luck would have it, spare parts were needed for two armored vehicles, so it was decided to send a motorcycle with sidecars to get them, which would take about a day for the round trip. The lieutenant colonel asked me to go along, as he needed someone with good Arabic to talk with the ordinance people so that the right parts were sent. Emmy and I finished our reports, and I left with them the following morning.

We had no problem with either the parts or with sending the package to Emile. I had a chance to talk from a railhead phone, and Emile assured me the last reports had gone out as planned. He said he was relieved that new reports had been submitted. British announcements stated that the British had won a great victory and that the Sanusi threat was nearly finished; only mopping up was necessary. I laughed and said, "Well, that's one way of seeing it, but the British are going to have to fight again to finish off the Sanusi."

I briefly described to Emile the delivery system we had and how fragile and unreliable it was. It was likely to be much the same as the British forces shifted to locate the remnants of the Sanusi. Emile was upbeat and said we had done remarkedly well so far and to stay with the present setup until it collapsed. I agreed. What else could we do? I got in the sidecar and rode back to Bir Tunis.

It took five days of patrolling to locate the Sanusi at Aqaqir, which was much closer to the coast and slightly opposite Marsa Matruh. But to prepare for battle, the forage and other supplies that had been brought south to Bir Tunis had to be relocated to a site near Marsa Matruh. It took over two weeks to do the relocation, using the camels again, except the routes were shorter by half a day. Every day, a caravan could be sent instead of every other day.

Sulayman relocated on about the third day, and the lieutenant colonel only on the fifth day. I stayed until the tenth day, at the instruction of Sulayman, who wanted someone responsible in charge at Bir Tunis, lest looting get out of hand. Except, by the eighth day, it was out of hand, and no one was there to stop it. The British had departed by then, so I tried to put order into the pillaging of goods, and, for two days, I succeeded in preventing bloodshed over the division of spoils. But order was breaking down fast on the tenth day when I mounted a camel and started my northern trek. Emmy had left with Aminah's family on the second day, as the family wanted a good spot in the new encampment.

Emmy was relieved that I had arrived because the following morning, she was going to go with Aminah to the railhead to send a news package; she had promised Aminah the payment given at the office where the package was delivered. Aminah had discovered the payment system on the last trip but had little idea of its purpose. She simply saw it as hers for the taking. Emmy did not want to disabuse her of that notion as it allowed the messages to get there faster than otherwise.

The trip was a day's travel round trip by camel; Aminah was tickled to ride a camel that far. My photos showed the annihilation of the Bir Tunis camp, something I believed the British would not let through the censors. I found out later that the photo did clear the censor and that the *Tribune* did print it a few days later.

When I appeared at the new encampment, a runner came to me to tell me to report to the personnel office, which I did not know existed. I found it, and a wizened old Arab with a short, cropped beard said that I had a check for the previous month's work. He held it in his hand and said, "It is customary, yeh, even obligatory, for an assistant to the overseer to sign his first two checks over to the overseer for getting him the job. "It is regarded as proper since the overseer then allows the family of the new assistant special privileges in hiring and other emoluments." I understood immediately and signed the check over to Sulayman. The payroll master sighed and said, "You are a good person and know how the world works. You will always be prosperous." Since I never expected to be paid at all, I was not in any sense aggrieved.

Then, I realized fully how the system worked. The overseer got money from me; I was expected to get it from my 'family,' and my family got it from the people they employed for the work the overseer wanted done. What was I getting from the family? So far, room and board and the use of a person to send messages back to our office in Alexandria which was paid for with a delivery fee in any case. Oh, yes, the family did furnish a camel for Emmy to use on occasion. Was I being compensated enough? Probably not enough, I decided.

I found Emmy, who was out with her cameras taking pictures of the newly organized British camp that was preparing for the upcoming battle. She turned aside from her work when she saw me and ran over to give me a clandestine kiss. "I'm so glad you're finally here," she said. "Did everything go all right? My, you look beat out, so it must not have been a picnic."

"Naw, it was as disorderly as one can imagine, and, in the end, I lost control of it. But then, I think the British expected that to happen and did not care," I replied. Then I told her about my meeting at the personnel office, and there was immediately a frown on her face. When I had finished, she said, "I think I have some negotiating to do with Aminah's grandmother, who asked me to pay for the use of the camel at Bir Tunis and also our lodging." We found a place to sit in a lean-to erected for storage, which was not yet in use. We did rough calculations and determined that Aminah's family had not been total skinflints, but that they were far less than generous in getting us the benefits we might expect.

In the final analysis, we were generous with Aminah's family, only insisting on our room and board and the use of a camel for short periods. Aminah's grandmother wanted to go into recriminatory negotiations over the matter, but Aminah and her mother saw it differently. They liked the arrangement and particularly the involvement of Aminah in the transmission of messages where she featured herself as part of the news-gathering process. They liked us both and, particularly, Emmy. When Aminah's grandmother wanted to contest any adjustment in the family responsibilities, the two threatened to involve Aminah's father. The grandmother knew that if that happened, she would lose the case and damage her standing in the family. She backed down, and Aminah's mother set the terms. She said we could have a settlement once the arrangement came to an end.

The Battle of Aqaqir

The battle of Aqaqir was anti-climactic, as the Sanusi forces were eroded since large numbers of fighters had left after the battle of Bir Tunis. Australian forces easily overcame the small forces that confronted them. The Sanusi side had the misfortune of two leaders failing to stay connected with one another during the battle. When one chose to withdraw, he left his fellow commander to the mercy of the Australians. The Australians ended the battle with a cavalry charge, which decimated the remaining Sanusi fighters and took their leader, an Ottoman major, into custody. The other force eroded and moved back into Cyrenaica, and the British cleared remnants of the force along the coast to the border with Cyrenaica. That took another ten days. I went along with the colonel, two veterinarians, and five of Aminah's people to work in the horse surgery, as the animals needed attention from the rough handling that occurred in chasing down rebels.

When we got back to Aqaqir, the camel handlers were gone, and only Aminah's family was still there. They were waiting for their family members to return who had gone on the clean-up operation. They departed only an hour later, after fond farewells between Aminah and her mom with Emmy. Later, Emmy told me that in settling accounts, a sum of two hundred US dollars was due to us. Emmy took Aminah and her mom to the suq at the end of the old railhead and purchased two gold ankle bangles for Aminah's wedding, which accounted for the remaining money. Aminah's mom was ecstatic about the gift, and even the grandmother was seen wiping away a tear when she discovered Emmy's generosity. The bangles would become part of the dowry Aminah would take to her husband's family when she married, so it was not an inconsequential gift.

While at the railhead, Emmy talked on the phone with Emile who said to return as soon as we were able. There was another campaign occurring, this one in Yemen, that he wanted to send us to as soon as we had some rest. Before leaving, however, I tracked down the personnel officer and signed my last paycheck over to the overseer. That covered all the expenses we had incurred on the trip. All told, we came out even, which meant that the *Tribune* had paid no expenses for our foray into Sanusi territory, a most unusual circumstance.

Chapter 3
Action in the Sinai and the Hijaz

The Failed Ambush at Romani

One of the best things about having Emile as director of the *Tribune* office was his knowledge of current political happenings and the state of the war in the Middle East. He had a reputation for fully briefing his reporters before they went on assignment. Consequently, they went into an area fully aware of what they were facing, and they knew the background of the problems they had to address. It was no different when he called our hotel on the third night of our break and asked that we come to the office at eight o'clock the next day for a briefing. Emmy and I knew immediately that our four-day 'vacation' was at an end and that there was a new assignment awaiting us. I said, "Yemen," and Emmy said, "Sinai."

It was the 'Sinai,' so Emmy was right. "We should have bet on it," she said.

"You always say that after you've won. Never when the issue is still in doubt."

Emile found our teasing an annoyance and said, "Pay attention, children," which was his way of reminding us that there were serious matters afoot and that we were required to pay heed. "The British have the Suez Canal to defend and, while they have been concerned about that obligation, they have not put a full effort into driving the Ottoman forces out of the Sinai and the western Hijaz that could raid the Canal. As usual, a British buildup necessary to undertake a campaign to drive the Ottomans out of the area is impossible, while all excess troops are sent to France for the never-ending trench warfare there."

He paused and then said, "But you know all of that. What the British have done, and which is not generally known, is that they have, with minimum attention, moved inland from the Canal and established a series of small outposts at oases. There, they place caches of supplies and munitions for quick use to counter any aggressive moves against the Canal. Closer to the Canal, the British have been building a railroad among watering holes so that troops can move into the area without running out of water during a drive. The goal of the railroad is to support a campaign to close entry points to the Sinai and keep Ottoman troops north of the Palestine border. That would greatly protect the Canal."

Emmy commented at this point, "I'm surprised that the railroad has not drawn the attention of the Ottomans. After all, news travels fast in the desert with tribal networks contacting one another and, probably, the Ottomans as well."

"Amelia," resumed Emile. "At the beginning of the war, German Colonel Kress von Kressenstein was given command of the Ottoman forces in the Sinai. He led Ottoman troops against the Canal but was stopped by an Indian contingent. Now Kress is supposedly on the march again, this time to disrupt the building of the railroad and, if he is able, to threaten the Canal as well. He picked up the information from the tribal networks and probably from his patrols, which routinely check on British activity east of the 'Canal.' As I recall, Marty, you filed several stories from the Ottoman front on that occasion."

I did and Emmy was with the photographic unit providing films of the action. I paused and then asked "Who's guarding the railroad? British troops or Anzac troops?"[2]

"Anzac (Australian-New Zealand) troops," answered Emile. "People you've seen before, at Gallipoli and in the western desert."

"The immediate question is how we gain access to the areas where the military action will occur," said Emmy. "We obviously can't use

---

2 Anzac troops. Military units raised in Australia and New Zealand, who fought mostly under British officers. Soldiers from Australia were also known as "Aussies" and those from New Zealand were called "Kiwis" after the name of a bird native to New Zealand.

the camel caravan ruse here since the railroad moves all goods and people. What do you suggest we do, Emile?"

"I think you can be rather straightforward about it," he answered. "Your reports did not elicit any comments from the British authorities, military or civilian, so I think you are regarded as 'safe' and 'sympathetic' enough that the authorities will allow you to use the railroad, telegraph, and other facilities as other reporters do. It would be difficult to isolate reporters from the action the way the British military did in the western desert."

He continued, "As for clothing, the rags you wore last time won't do. How about something like the Anzacs themselves wear, which are shorts, tunics, and floppy hats? They also wear heavy-soled boots and knee stockings. Will that work for you, Amelia?"

"Well, it will give me a 'boyish' look, but I can't think of anything much better, and I will not stand out too much in such garb." Emmy smiled broadly.

"We can get the outfits this afternoon and have a tailor do whatever fitting is needed right away," said Emile. "I expect you'll be on this adventure in about two to three weeks. The German commander is always in a hurry, and I suspect that he is alarmed enough about the rate of construction of the railroad–about four miles a week,-- that he will want to hit before too much more track is laid."

Two days later, we were on our way to the front near Qatiyah in the Sinai Peninsula, where over 15,000 men of the Egyptian Labor Corps were feverishly extending the railroad. We rode up to that station on a flatbed car loaded with boxes of supplies on pallets. There were spaces between boxes so that some shade was offered, and air flowed among the crates and boxes. The spacing spared us some of the glaring sun. For a good part of the trip, there were three of us together: Emmy, me, and a British captain assigned to the news and information branch. He had seen the labels we had sewn on the front of our shirts, which read "Correspondent," and sat with us without asking as if he was entitled to do so without question.

Perhaps it was the new outfits that gave him the wrong impression of us. He thought we were new to the correspondent's game, as he made comments about the trip, the troop units we ran across and about filing reports. For example, he took great pains to explain that the small cavalry patrols we saw every few miles were there to serve as an early warning system against Ottoman troops as if it were not obvious. He told us a mechanized company of Australians was from New Zealand; I guess anyone could get that wrong if one did not know what kind of uniforms each army used. He said that censoring was a necessity but that good reporters did a lot of self-censoring because "we do not want to give information to the enemy."

I am always polite and do not contradict people or point out their errors, so I was mostly quiet. Emmy grew weary of the cant after a time and responded with tongue-in-cheek remarks. On one occasion, he said, "Indian soldiers do not do so well in the Sinai since they only know jungles at home and have trouble adapting to the aridness of the desert."

Emmy responded, "I liked *Jungle Book* because it portrayed India so well. I liked the tiger, Shere Khan, the best. How about you?"

The captain said he had not read the book.

When he said that many of the Anzac units had fought against the 'Turks' at Gallipoli, she said, "Amazing. Is that the same place where Darwin developed his theory of evolution?"

"I believe it is," the captain answered. "It's amazing how small the world is, isn't it? I wonder how many of the men who fought there even knew Darwin had been there ahead of them."

"Wait a minute," interjected Emmy, "I think the place that Darwin was at was the Galapagos Islands, which I think are in the Pacific." She nudged me and said, "Why didn't you say something, Marty? You let me confuse two places when it was not necessary. The captain will think I'm stupid."

None of this fazed the captain, and he kept making 'helpful' remarks until we reached Qatiyah. He grabbed his kit and quickly hopped down from the flat car. He said, as a way of farewell, "I hope I have been able to help you orient yourselves to this front. I know that you will not stay newcomers for long but will learn the duties and responsibilities of correspondents rapidly. If I can be of assistance, please find me, and I will do what I can." He disappeared.

After he left, I said, "What a crock! Why did you encourage him?"

She responded, "He's harmless, and the trip would have been boring without some sort of conversation." I realized, not for the first time that my girlfriend had a cruel streak at times.

That afternoon, we were searching for a place to pitch our tent for the night and came across an encampment of Australian infantry. We engaged several of the men in conversation and soon had ten or twelve of them gathered around us, bragging about their role in the war. "You should have been at Gallipoli said one. I'll bet you didn't cover that one?"

"Sure did," I responded. "The artillery would drive anyone bonkers."

"How about the western desert?"

"Right in the middle of it, mate," responded Emmy. "Bir Tunis was the worst because it was in such a god-forsaken place, and it was so hard to get to. Camels were the only things that survived out there."

"If you were in the middle of things, how come your clothes are so new-looking?" asked one skeptic.

"Wore the other ones clean out, so we had to start fresh. We had to peel off the old ones because they were so worn and crusted," said Emmy with a wink.

A wit in the group quickly responded, "I wish I had been there for the unveiling!"

"Don't you though! You would have fainted from the beauty of it all," Emmy teased with another wink. Everyone laughed at that. Everything she said made a hit with them. They could hardly believe that an English-speaking, white woman was out in the middle of the desert talking with them as if they were all on a verandah back home.

We stayed with them for half an hour and told them, in the end, that we would write an article about them from what they had told us. We would see that the article got forwarded to a prominent Australian newspaper. That seemed to please them, but I doubt if most believed us at all. They had heard too many promises with no real follow-through.

The following day, the Ottomans, led by Colonel Kress von Kressenstein, arrived and a battle occurred that lasted over a day in length. The early round went to the Ottomans, who had crossed the desert undetected, bringing with them some artillery pieces so that when they made their assault, they had some muscle. The raiding party was sizeable, with about 16,000 troopers, which is a nasty force to repel in a small space.

The advance units of the Ottomans hit the line at Romani when a cavalry patrol was returning, and gates were temporarily open. Ottomans stormed the open gate and got into the supply depot and much of the road-building machinery. As it was early morning, the Australians had only a few minutes of warning that the enemy was already there, and they ran pell-mell to pre-established bunkers and formed up in infantry formation. The surprise attack gave the Ottomans the advantage and allowed them to seize the high ground. In the early going the Ottomans took prisoners and decimated the Australian cavalry that initially held the position.

However, the British reacted quickly, flooding the area with reinforcements from nearby Qatiyah and, for almost over a day, forced the invaders out of the area, killing some 1,500 Ottoman troops and capturing another 4000. British losses were 900 wounded and 200 killed. The battle turned when the Ottomans became exhausted from the fighting, and their water gave out. Still, they left with their guns and outran their pursuers. They managed to arrive safely back at the Ottoman lines on the Palestine border. There was only weak pursuit by the British and Australians because of the lack of organization after pulling troops together from various locales. It was considered enough that the Ottomans had been repelled; chasing after them was regarded as tempting fate.

The attack occurred relatively close to where Emmy and I had pitched our tent. For our part, we woke to the sounds of the Ottoman batteries pounding the area they were attacking, which was less than a mile distant from us. We quickly secured our gear in an unused railroad shed and moved at double time alongside the railroad track nearby to where the battle was taking place. We found ourselves on low ground, but I had brought a small collapsible spade and dug a ditch that would prevent gunfire from striking us. We stayed there for most of the day, watching as the Australians and British forces, on foot, made attack after attack against the high ground until they were successful.

At first, the Australians were slightly disorganized and panicky, but within an hour, unit commanders took over and set up defensive perimeters that allowed reinforcements to be integrated into the units already there. Several Australian counterattacks took back ground from the Ottoman forces, and it was only the last one, held late in the day, that drove the Ottomans from their positions on the small ridge that dominated the field.

 It was very apparent that the Australian counterattack was done with consideration of the soldiers themselves, and every attempt to move forward used lots of covering fire. Undoubtedly, this concern for casualties rested on previous battles, particularly Gallipoli, where fighting had been done without concern for casualties and losses were high. There seemed to be a conscious effort to prevent such carnage from happening again.

We were not able to see the end of the battle, except when the Ottomans were out in the desert retreating when we finally gained the high ground where the enemy had been earlier. We could only see that the Ottomans were withdrawing in good order to the northeast. They left a sizeable number of attackers dead on the ground, and many more were captured.

For the next two days, we interviewed officers, troops, and prisoners to fill out our perceptions of the battlefield and what went on during the scuffle. Emmy got some grand pictures of the battlefield itself and some small unit photographs. The Australian officers gave us the most clear and accurate accounts, perhaps because they were responsible for relating everything in their after-action reports. They tended to downplay heroism and grand moments for the steadfast actions of many troops who pushed the Ottomans relentlessly out of the area.

The least accurate accounts were told by the soldiers who did the actual fighting because they were absorbed with the dangers of the advance and exaggerated every moment when their own lives were in danger. I calculated near the end of our interviews that, if all the statements by the enlisted men about the casualties they inflicted were true, the figures would exceed the total the Ottomans sent into battle in the first place. Still, despite the notorious exaggerations, these interviews told us what went on in combat and the great dangers involved in the battle.

The German and Arab prisoners were considerably different in their interpretations of what occurred. I interviewed an Arab non-com and three enlisted men from near Aleppo, while Emmy interviewed a German lieutenant and a sergeant. In my interviews, all four Arabs took pride in their accomplishment of carrying out a raid across an open country against a formidable enemy. They believed they had been successful in disrupting the building operations for some time to come. They exhibited high esprit de corps, asserting that their battalion had been specially picked for this task and had performed well beyond what ordinary armies did. They found it sad that they had been captured, as they would have liked to be back in their camp at al-Arish for the victory party they believed would take place.

On the other hand, Emmy found the two German prisoners despondent over their capture. They believed they would be sent to a prisoner-of-war camp and that the chances of parole were small, so they would miss the remainder of the war. They believed the strike force had succeeded in its mission, and they were proud of their role in the attack. They praised the Ottoman soldiers that they had commanded and said they were every bit as good as German troops. "They would be exceptional," said the German sergeant, "if they had been taught to read and write. What kind of an army is it that has to have all its order given orally and where only officers are literate."

Emmy also asked if either knew Colonel Werner Aussenfeld, but neither had run across him. She was relieved and disappointed, hearing those answers. She only asked the question when she did not think I was listening. Perhaps she thought I might be jealous if I heard or that I would find such inquiries on her part to reflect an attitude of not being true to me. I guess all of us must have some matters we keep private, entirely to ourselves.

When we filed our fourth-day reports, we received a telegram from Emile, which said:

> amelia and marty stop return immediately stop new action in the hijaz stop come to alexandria for refit and departure immediately from port said stop emile

I wanted to protest, as I did not think the campaign was over, and I was sure that the Ottomans would make another raid sooner or later. Why move when we would only have to come back? But I knew that Emile had a better grasp on the overall military situation than I did, so I did not say anything about my feelings on the matter, even to Emmy.

The Sea Battle at Jiddah

Accordingly, we were in Alexandria for only a few days to change some items in our kit, particularly desert robes, which Emile said we would probably need if we did any traveling in the area. My own Rwala robes had been lost somewhere in my travels, so I bought new ones, as did Emmy. We thought we looked quite handsome in them.

Emile gave us a rundown about the Hashemite clan that traditionally ruled Mecca and its sizeable backcountry called the Hijaz. It encompasses most of the Western Arabian Peninsula. I had only recently visited with Sharif Hussein and discussed his ambitions for uniting all Arabs in his scheme of a wide Arab federation. But Emmy did not know much about it, never having been there.

As Emile described it, Hussein had been in close contact with British authorities since the war began and sought an alliance that would aid him in becoming King of the Arabs. Hussein assured the British that he would be able to deliver the entire Arab world to the Entente side in the war in exchange for assistance in moving against the Ottoman army. He pictured the Arabs as oppressed peoples who were waiting for an opportunity to rise and throw off Ottoman control.

Early investigation disproved that claim of loyalty. A British agent, Captain T. E. Lawrence, had traveled throughout the area and concluded that support for Hussein was far from universal and was limited almost entirely to the Hijaz. That assessment, regarded as true by British officials in Egypt, was not openly known, so King Hussein was regarded by many, including most of the press, as having considerable political strength. Despite their negative assessment of his overall prospects, the British still supported Hussein because they wanted an Arab group to confront the Ottomans in a vulnerable part of their empire, and the Hashemites were best suited to perform that role.

A tipping point had occurred in Syria only a short time earlier when the governor there had executed several young Arabs for 'treason' because they publicly agitated for a change in the way the Arab part of the Ottoman Empire was governed. Prince Faisal, the son of Hussein, who was a 'hostage' with the governor at the time, had spoken on behalf of the accused and was, accordingly, deemed suspect by the governor. But through a ruse, Faisal had left for Madinah, ostensibly to raise a force to support Ottoman actions on the Sinai border. Once his son was safe again in the Hijaz, Hussein decided to openly oppose the Ottomans.

Emile suggested we use a tramp steamer that would carry us to Jiddah to catch the sequel to the story of Faisal's escape and further adventures. "It will probably unfold rapidly, or else, die completely.

But I have a hunch, and you need to be there to cover the story, either way."

The trip took only a few days and was uncomfortable. The food was bad, the toilet facilities primitive, and the ship was teeming with rodents and bugs. I suffered in silence, but Emmy embraced the questionable conditions, finding in them a new source for her camera work. "I've never taken pictures of rodents and bugs before," she said on one occasion. "They look so insignificant on film because they appear so small. I think I must get my camera closer to magnify their size. If I could get the antenna of the cockroach or the whisker of a rat, perhaps I could make something meaningful of the shots I take of them." By the third day, she had given up on that project and complained about such wildlife until the end of the trip.

When we arrived at the roadstead off Jiddah, the ship's captain was told to 'stand off,' so the ship simply anchored and waited for permission to land. Eventually, a boat came out to us, and an official told the captain that the city was under siege by Arab tribesmen. Ottoman defenders were holding them at bay. "Settle yourselves. It may take a few days to decide the matter," the official said.

The captain was unhappy about such a wait, as he had about one hundred people who were bound for Jiddah, mostly pilgrims going to Mecca. He was inclined to simply keep going and unload us at some other port further along the coast, but there was an uproar from the passengers for even thinking of such action. Finally, the passengers met and a consensus was reached in which the passengers asked for five days in exchange for the equivalent of One Hundred US for each day. I paid for the first day, and two other donors took care of two more days. The captain grumbled but took the money.

I learned later that the action at Jiddah had some planning and coordination ahead of time since the British Royal Navy was active in the engagement only a short time after hostilities began. The action had begun when a bedouin force of 4,000 from the Harb Tribe, which was allied with the Hashemites, led an attack against the 1,500 Ottoman soldiers in the port city. However, the Ottomans had machine guns and artillery pieces, so the attack by the Bedouins was easily repulsed. The carnage had been bad enough among the attackers that some bedouins broke off action altogether and fled the scene. But enough bedouins stayed to keep the Ottomans trapped in the city.

But the wait was not long. Shortly after we arrived, a large British ship arrived as well, one I had seen off the coast in western Egypt that served as a 'mother ship' for seaplanes. The vessel was no sooner anchored than it had its seaplanes flying. There was a long series of reconnaissance flights when the planes circled and tried to locate the places in Jiddah where Ottoman troops and fortifications were located. Shortly afterward, two British gunboats arrived and took up positions near the port but outside the range of the port's guns. Then followed a series of consultations between the officers of the ships and, later, between officers from the ships and tribesmen on shore. Emmy and I watched much of this activity with our binoculars and observed some long conversations, especially with the meetings on shore, which took place close to the water's edge.

In the late afternoon, the bombardment began. The gunships fired countless salvos into the city, apparently aiming at the gun emplacements. This was followed by more reconnaissance flights and then by bombing runs using airplanes. As I watched, I felt it was a cumbersome and inaccurate process and wondered how many of the bombs were doing any damage. The bombing runs were intermittent, and it would have been possible for the Ottoman forces to relocate themselves after every run.

My time in battle zones has convinced me that artillery is probably the biggest waste of war material, as shots often, if not usually, miss their target, and when they do find the target, it is usually only a peripheral hit, causing limited damage. Direct hits are rare unless saturation bombing is undertaken. It took three more days of bombardment and reconnaissance flights before the battle was over. The Arab tribe never tried to storm the defenses after the failure the first day but went quickly into the city to begin the looting once the hostilities ended. The Ottomans were low on food and water, which forced their surrender.

The captain of our ship was anxious to get underway and had us landed with his small boats, even before there were any clearances for such action. No sooner had we been put ashore, a short distance from the city, than the small boats went back to the ship, and when we next looked, the ship itself was moving off into the distance.

No one bothered us, and the entire group found its way to the pilgrim reception area, where there were a few officials present who gave us all permission to use the dormitories set aside for pilgrims. I searched out the Javanese representative, who happened to be the same one I had met in 1913. He had little to do, so he took time to get us tea and biscuits. Then we enjoyed a chat about local conditions. Emmy joined us.

He said that people in and around Mecca generally expected Hussein to declare 'Arab independence' from the Ottomans just about then. To mark the occasion, Hussein had symbolically, fired a rifle in the direction of the Ottoman force to announce his declaration of war. He then mobilized his local garrison in Mecca and went after the Ottoman forces in the city and the nearby area. Fortunately, there were not that many Ottomans there just then since the major force of 17,000 was located some days away at Madinah.

Prince Feisal had raised somewhat less than 2000 bedouins, ostensibly to aid the Ottomans in reinforcing the Sinai front against a prospective British invasion. Instead of using it for that purpose, Feisal turned the tables and used it to bottle up the Ottoman force in Madinah. That left Hussein free to handle the weak Ottoman forces in the area of Mecca.

The Malay representative said that he was torn between which side he favored so long as the pilgrimage activities would continue without interruption. He said he liked the professionalism of the Ottomans and their concern for clarity and order. On the other hand, he admired many of the Arabs for their politeness, sense of style, and friendliness. He feared the Arabs were not much accustomed to rule and might not be very adept at it, although he did have to admit that Hussein had been a good ruler of Mecca.

He also said that the Arabs were now moving on to the neighboring city of Ta'if, an original city of Islam, where the Ottomans had a garrison of some 4000. It was out of the range of naval gunboats, so the battle might not go as easily for the Arabs as at Jiddah. We talked about prospective battle sites, and we both concluded that the most promising one for reporting would be at Ta'if. He then said he could furnish one of several 'packages' to make the trip safer and more pleasant than going without adequate safety preparations.

He said it was essential that I have an armed guard of at least one person, but up to five. Then transportation to and from Ta'if, along with side trips, would require a camel for myself, another for Emmy, and one or more for supplies. A tent larger than the one he believed we had from looking at our kit, should be taken along and, naturally, some water and foodstuffs.

We discussed the issue, and Emmy was the main bargainer. What was sky-high at the beginning began to diminish with every offer and counteroffer that was made. Ultimately, we decided on two armed guards with rifles and camels, who would also pitch the tent, and a boy to pack, look after things, act as a guard when we were not around, and lead the extra camel. Also, we chose a good-sized tent, a second tent for the other members of our party, and two camels for our personal use. The rental was a day rate and did not include gratuities for personnel. We paid an up-front fee of three days in British pounds. I knew that Emile would have a stroke when we presented that bill for reimbursement but would grumble about it a little and then allow the expense.

We stayed out of the city that night because the Arabs were still busy plundering. When that is going on, a passerby is apt to become part of the process and lose whatever he is carrying. Those who plunder are not particular.

We left at dawn. Our guards' names were Mu'izz and Isa, while the boy was called Musa. They were especially polite in meeting us and were efficient in getting everything loaded so we could get underway. It seemed to me we were out of the city quickly, but then I was comparing everything with my last visit when the pilgrimage season was in full swing, and all the roads had been jammed with people and vehicles so that a person could hardly move.

The countryside was simply a desert in that it was mostly arid with some growth of grass and other greenery but went for long periods without rain. Mostly, things were withered and brown. There were some water wells, but we had our supply, so we did not use them, although the camels did on one occasion.

The Siege at Ta'if

At Ta'if, the Arab besiegers were located a considerable distance from the city walls and fortifications because the Ottoman defense rested on the machine guns and artillery pieces that were in place there. Locating besiegers any closer to the city was to invite shots from the various guns the Ottomans had placed along the walls of the city. As well, the Ottomans did occasionally use infantry forays outside the walls, so long as they were covered by the guns of the fort. But they had learned that to go beyond that range was to invite Arab retribution in the form of cavalry attacks when the riders used sabers with great effectiveness. Mostly, however, the Ottomans stayed within the walls of the city. Both sides were waiting for reinforcements which would change the balance of power and give victory to the side receiving such assistance.

The Arab commander's name was Ibn Farid, who was the son of a cousin of Sharif Hussein. The force was under the nominal command of Prince Abdullah, who was, at that moment, in Mecca consulting with his father. I was brought to Ibn Farid to explain who I was, whose side I was on, and what my purpose there was. He was exceedingly polite, even having his concubine get Emmy from her camel and take her to his tent so that she would be out of the sun while the matter of our presence was discussed.

He had a vague idea of what a correspondent might be but could not understand why one would be at Ta'if, so it baffled him. His aides were not helpful, and there was a general feeling that we should be sent away as a general nuisance.

Muizz, the guard, was standing behind me with his rifle slung over his shoulder. He entered the conversation. "General," he said to Ibn Farid, "The *ferangi* (European stranger) and his woman came in with a pilgrimage ship, and he made his arrangements for travel with the pilgrimage officials, who knew him from a former trip. What nobler reference can one have? Also, he and his woman speak Arabic well, showing their respect towards us, and they know about our history and great heroes. He will not be a bother. He will stand aside and observe, and later, you will hear his accounts of the battle as he sees it. Be generous." Muizz spoke like a free Arab is accustomed to doing in the presence of authorities, with little fear of retribution.

Ibn Farid seemed to take no offense that a mere guard had addressed him so brazenly. He said, "If the pilgrimage officials vouch for him, I will, of course, accept him and his woman." To Muizz, he said, "Pitch your tent close to mine so that his woman can visit and do things with my companion." I was unsure how Emmy was going to see all this arranging in her life, but I figured we would straighten that out later.

But Emmy was not born yesterday, and she sized up the situation relatively quickly. She arranged for three of the commanders and their women to share a meal with us, with the men eating first in our tent, with the women serving them, and, afterward, the women disappeared to Ibn Farid's tent to eat by themselves. By morning, between Emmy and me, we knew all the important matters in the camp as well as much of the gossip. Furthermore, although our foodstuffs suffered a hit from the small feast we had hosted, we had shown hospitality and were now accepted as a normal part of the community of the camp.

The one thing that bothered me almost immediately was the reluctance of the Arabs to speak about the original battle that had taken place the previous week. I sensed unease and even shame, so I dropped the matter, understanding that the attackers had probably suffered a loss and did not know how to explain it.

It was Emmy who got the story. Simply by listening to the three women who had adopted her as a companion, the story came out. The Arabs had been unduly sure of themselves and thought that fighting was going to be like the inter-tribal rivalries that they undertook regularly, where showmanship and limited casualties were the norm. Their weapons were the saber and the rifle, and they attacked in disorder on fast horses, and they disappeared just as quickly. They knew little enough about the Ottomans and their military proclivities. The Ottomans relied on heavy weapons, mostly machine guns and light artillery that did a great deal of damage to any force they confronted. They could decimate an attacking group of horsemen in minutes. But beyond that, Ottoman soldiers served on foot with repeating rifles, usually manufactured in Europe, which, with training, made sharpshooters out of the men who used them. Alone, even without heavy weapons, they could repulse an attack of mounted Arabs.

The women told Emmy about the bravery of the Arab attack and how the attackers were relentlessly mowed down by the Ottoman soldiers. The women were indignant with the Ottomans, who, they felt, did not fight fair like champions ought to. They merely used weapons that were outside the normal arms of inter-Arab rivalries. They told of different Arabs who tried to rally their brethren and carry the fight into the camp of the Ottomans, only to become sacrifices themselves.

Then, when the Arabs left the Ottoman encampment, having suffered great losses, the Ottomans had tried to pursue them, only to find that the tables were turned and that fast horses enabled the Arabs to swoop in quickly on enemy gunners and dispatch them with impunity. In turn, the Ottomans left the battlefield, bombarded the Arabs still near the encampment, and settled in for a long siege. Many Arabs, discouraged by the fighting and the huge toll of life that it took, decided they no longer wished to participate and rode away, effectively resigning from any future fighting. It was not what they expected, and they had no desire to repeat the experience.

When I read Emmy's account, I said hers should be sent to Emilc, not mine. I took the sheets outlining my feeble attempts to put together a story of the initial attack and burned them. Now, up to this point in our relationship there was no doubt in my mind that I was the senior reporter and took all the difficult news stories, leaving Emmy with stories 'she could handle, which were seldom very complex and demanding. But I knew that if I were to involve myself in it, I would not have mastered the details and analyzed them faster or better than what Emmy did. So, this report on the Arab attack called for a reevaluation of our relationship. I understood–and, more importantly, so did she–that the 'senior-junior' relationship was not so marked as before and that her status had risen considerably.

Further, if I noticed the change, certainly Emile and the editors in Paris would as well. I braced myself for the next notification of bonuses when I knew that the difference between the size of what was given to her would probably equal what they gave me. That caused me some qualms, even though I was aware that I should not have such thoughts of jealousy about a woman who was certainly going to be my wife and, even, at that moment, was a dear companion.

On the tenth day after arriving at the camp, there was a parlay between the commanders of the contending sides. Neither knew the other's language beyond a few sentences, so I was asked to act as translator. The meeting lasted only about fifteen minutes. The Ottoman commander asked to be allowed to take his force to Jiddah and join the Ottoman forces there, not realizing it had already surrendered. He did not believe the statement at first, but I assured him it was so and had witnessed it. He was perplexed and said he had two gravely wounded gunners who needed medical attention. They would not survive much longer if they did not receive treatment beyond what his basic medical facility could offer. He asked whether the Arabs could assist or at least allow them to be taken to the medical unit in Jiddah. After some thought, the Arab commander said that he would allow that but that the soldiers would not be able to return. The Ottoman commander said that he understood the implicit conditions of such a move.

Then the Ottoman commander asked for water and that was denied.

I volunteered Muizz to take the two wounded Ottomans to Jiddah, which worked in our favor as we had reports that needed to be filed and were running low on supplies. The trip was made without incident, and Muizz brought back a message from Emile.

> amelia and marty stop report on capture of jiddah stirring stop looking forward to siege taif stop situation murky on arab revolt stop if taif falls go to mecca to interview hussein stop emile.

Immediately after this interlude, Prince Abdullah returned to camp and brought two English naval officers with him. They were in camp only half a day and were there only to see the situation on the ground as, presumably, new moves were in the making. The visit of the two officers was almost inconsequential. Mostly, they were surprised that the attack had been made without any heavy weapons and wondered aloud how any modern army would proceed in such a half-baked attempt. Since their 'wondering' was done in English, it made no impact, one way or the other, on the Arabs. But, of course, Emmy and I understood it all when either one of us was close enough to hear.

They made a stop at our tent for refreshments, where Emmy had some lime juice for them and some biscuits. She explained that supplies were rather limited. They barely talked with me but did talk with Emmy for a time about the morale in the camp and whether the Arab force was ready to give up and go home. She said that it was not, and the Arabs felt that they could outlast an effete group of city dwellers from Istanbul (as they called Constantinople). The preference of the naval officers for Emmy over me naturally played on my insecurities about being 'displaced' by her in our order of status.

However, despite my chagrin at being ignored for the most part, I had to admit that Emmy used the opportunity well and got a lot of information from them without it appearing as though it was a formal interview. They felt at home in our tent with English speakers and talked about bringing in a battery of artillery to destroy the Ottoman emplacements and speed up the siege. That suggestion later became a formal part of the discussions with Prince Abdullah, as I understood it, when the informal communique was made outlining what conclusions had been reached during the visit. At that point, because of the complicated language needed, I was brought in as a translator. Emmy and I each contributed to the newspaper report we prepared afterward.

It was another three weeks before the arrival of guns, and it took time to get them up to Ta'if from Jiddah. It was a battery of Egyptian artillery, and the artillerists were not happy to be shunted off into what they considered an Arab 'backwater.' They lamented that there was no entertainment and not even the least trace of modern toilet facilities. Two of them threatened to desert, saying the British had agreed that Egyptians would not be involved in the war. They concluded that they were being kidnapped and, hence, had a perfect right to leave and find their way back to Egypt. But it was all 'talk,' and they, of course, never really considered leaving.

Again, it was Emmy who worked the story, particularly the cultural clash between the Egyptians, from a settled, orderly, and competent civilization, and the Arabs, from a loosely organized and free-wheeling frontier society. The two sides made fun of one another, and hardly a week passed without the calling of names, a scuffle, or an actual fistfight between the more sensitive souls on both sides. Emmy caught this sensitivity, but also the competence the Egyptians brought to their work. It took them time to set up their artillery and to get it properly aimed, but when it was all set up, they set to work on rigorous and thorough destruction of the Ottoman strong points in the city.

After the bombardment began, there was another conference between the two commanders. This time, the Ottoman commander wanted to send out civilians–women, children, and the disabled, particularly. The Arab commander was, at first, not inclined to grant that request, but his council members, who were with him at the conference, convinced him to accept the deal. He said, "The general population are Muslims, after all, caught in a place they don't want to be. They need our help. No good is going to be produced by having these victims suffer in a bombardment." Finally, the leader granted permission and several hundred people filed out, and they scattered to different places–to relatives nearby, to a camel caravan readied to take them to Jiddah, and other places. I was busy with translating, but Emmy caught all the action on camera and in her notes.

A letter was brought to me from Mecca from the Sharif Hussein's secretary, who said that the Sharif had learned that I was in Ta'if and that it might be a good time to interview him again. The secretary said that the Sharif was consolidating his victories and the world would be interested in knowing of his successes. "An article much like the one several months ago where the personality and aims of the Sharif are mentioned would be most apropos in the Sharif's estimation."

Interviewing Sharif Hussein Again

Emmy and I talked over the invitation and decided I should leave immediately while she stayed to cover the siege. I took only Ahmad with me for security, and we rode camels to Mecca. Of course, I carried reports to be sent out from the pilgrimage center, as we had not been able to do so in almost two weeks. There was a further note waiting from Emile. It read:

> amelia and marty stop marty interview hussein stop afterward proceed madinah to cover ottoman attempts to breakthrough faisal blockade stop amelia stay ta'if to cover artillery siege stop get news out faster, if possible stop emile

I chanced a telephone call and did get a clear line to Alexandria, where Emile was at his desk. He was relieved to hear from me, saying, "One always fears the worst. I'm glad to know you are both all right. You really must do something about your communication system with Jiddah."

I assured him I would and then told him I was to meet Hussein that evening, and it was Hussein himself who had suggested the meeting, "so I expect a good interview with him. I'll leave for Madinah tomorrow morning. Reports are that the Hijaz railroad is still functioning, and the Ottomans are still able to get supplies that way. When they have enough supplies, they will assuredly attempt to break Faisal's blockade and unroll the gains of the Hashemite revolt."

Emile responded that was where he wanted me to be. "Good that Amelia is at the siege of Ta'if. It sounds safer than the excursion you're undertaking."

"Probably," I said, "But don't you let her hear you say that. She considers herself just as capable of experiencing combat as I do, and, after seeing her in action in western Egypt and the Sinai, I agree with her."

"I know, I know," he responded. "But I will spare her combat when it is possible to do so. After these sieges are over, both of you will probably have to proceed to Palestine as the British begin their push there. It's still some months off, however, so don't start thinking about it just yet."

Hussein dripped charm when I visited him. We shared a light evening meal, eating from a common platter and drinking date wine. None of his sons was with him, and he allowed only one elderly retainer to stay with us. The retainer did not enter the conversation, but since the interview was in Arabic, he must have understood what was being discussed.

Hussein wanted to know how the world saw his anti-Ottoman crusade. I feigned ignorance, saying that I had been located at Ta'if most of the time and had only witnessed the fall of Jiddah. I said, "I find it telling that you have vanquished Ottoman forces from most of the Hijaz, and those that are remaining are besieged and likely to surrender in time. I am impressed as well by the Arabs who are following you and are taking part in your military adventures; they are devoted to you, Your Majesty."

These statements pleased him. His mood, which was almost sober when I entered, began to be expansive at the mention of such success.

"Then you believe the effort is succeeding?" he asked.

"O, your grace, I am a believer when such questions are asked of me!" I responded. "However, the real answer lies with the Almighty, but it is apparent that He has favored you to this point, so why should He desert you now?"

Even this implied favor by God encouraged the Sharif, and his face was nearly radiant with pleasure. I decided it was time to put some reality into the conversation. But I wanted to do it in stages and not all at once. "Would you say, Your Majesty, that the great distance between you and the capital of the Ottomans is great enough to protect you in some sense?

"I suppose it is," he answered. "It takes time for them to understand what is happening and for a response to be formed. Yes, I believe you are correct in that assumption. In that sense, I have an advantage. They must respond over miles and miles while my decisions can be enforced immediately."

"But haven't the Ottomans also constructed transportation, communication, and military systems that can function over great distances? Just think, the seventeen thousand soldiers in Mecca that your son has beleaguered got there via the Hijaz railroad, which runs from Constantinople to Madinah. In a period of two days, reinforcements, ammunition, and instructions can be sent from that capital to the front lines. That is faster than the distance between here and Mecca when you and your son communicate."

He either did not want to grasp the point, or he denied it. "No matter," he said, "It is the quality of response that is important, not necessarily how rapid the response."

"O, I agree with you," I answered. "Do you want a quick and powerful response, a slower, less powerful response, or no response at all?"

"The rulers in Constantinople have often not taken me very seriously," he said. "They are disdainful of my efforts, and I hope they will not react quickly so that I can deal with the remainder of their forces here before dealing with new units being sent against us. But sooner or later, those other forces will be sent, and we will be prepared for them. In the final reckoning, we must be able to deal with the most powerful strike they are capable of sending."

I moved to my checklist of questions to ask. "At both Jiddah and at Ta'if, the Arab fighters charged into battle and gave a good account of themselves. There is nothing like the courage of an Arab tribesman. But in both cases, they were repulsed by the Ottomans, who had more modern weapons. It was the rifle and saber against the machine gun and artillery. Conditions changed in Jiddah when the British arrived with gunboats and airplanes. At Ta'if, the British were bringing up artillery to end the siege there. Do you think you can always rely on the British to give your forces the heavy weapons they need in this very modern war you are fighting?"

Hussein's face clouded a little. He said, "The Ottomans are effete and must rely on new weapons, as they are no match for the bravery of Arab warriors. It will take time to adjust to the strategies of the Ottomans, and perhaps we Arabs need new ways of delivering the power of our armies against them. But the time will come. Yes, we must rely on the British to assist where they can, but ultimately, we will no longer need them."

Later, I asked him about the future. "You want to build an Arab State. What will that look like? Will it be a state like the Ottomans have, with great administrations, a powerful army, elections, and highly educated leaders? Or will it be like the Hijaz is today, with tribal organization, councils of elders, a monarch, and a law based on religious sources?"

He answered quickly. "O, the latter, of course. We lay great stress on tradition, and the strength such tradition gives us. That does not mean that we will not create more sophisticated councils, perhaps use people with some Western education, and armies with more technical and powerful weapons. But we will keep our tribal ways, our piety, and our love of God as the primary centers of life."

I left the interview not surprised at the answers I received. Neither was I surprised over the next six weeks as the battles around Mecca were fought, for the keys to Arab behavior were contained in the interview with Hussein. But immediately, I had work to do. I wrote up the interview and took it to Jiddah to be sent to Emile. Along with it, I sent a note to him about his latest instructions to me.

emile stop on way to madinah stop sent your message to amelia at taif stop future message every thursday using couriers stop ta'if and madinah probably long campaigns stop marty

I wrote the following to Amelia.

Sweetie: Read Emile's message first and then the rest of this letter.

I interviewed Hussein, and a copy is enclosed. It went well enough, I guess. I can hardly believe the fellow believes his plan will suffice for a government. The British may get him through the war with the Ottomans, but afterward, I doubt whether they will help him very much.

As for Emile's assignments, I am all right with them, but I would rather have you with me, but leave it for you to decide. I don't think Emile would balk if you decided to join me at the Madinah front.

I have outfitted myself with another two guards, an extra camel, and a boy to guard my things. The journey from Jiddah to Madinah will take at least six days, and I cannot risk being alone in the open countryside for that length of time. I am sure to be set upon by thieves and other disreputable people if I don't have security guards.

My suggestion is that you send one of your guards to Jiddah every week to file your reports. I think I can use the Yanbu railway station which will be nearby to where the Arabs are preparing to fight the Ottomans. I wish there were some way we could meet regularly, but that must wait for the future.

Be careful as you always are, and remember that when all this is over, we will live happily ever after. All my love, Marty

Amelia Alone at Ta'if

Emmy decided to stay just a while longer to finish up some projects that were occupying her attention just then. It was only when Emile ordered her to Mecca that she left Ta'if. She reported regularly on the siege of the city, especially the work of the Egyptian artillery, which delivered a bombardment on Ottoman positions in fits and starts. There was a great deal of trouble in bringing ammunition up from the coast, which took time since it came across unsafe terrain and had to be guarded. Further, there was a labor shortage in the area, and finding people who would handle the transportation of munitions was difficult. So, the shells were delivered at irregular intervals, and that allowed the siege to drag on.

The three women with whom Emmy was friendly each had husbands or male companions who had other responsibilities than simply sitting out a siege. One was a tribal elder, and the other two were prominent in their extended families, so they left occasionally and then returned. On three occasions, Emmy was invited to come along for a few days to see how the women ordinarily lived when not at Ta'if. During those visits, she saw family life in bedouin families up close. She saw that there was a significant division of labor and status between men and women. Men oversaw activities outside the family, and women were concerned mostly with the care and welfare of the family itself.

In the family, she noted the roles of women among themselves and how the senior wife of the most prominent male was accorded great respect and authority. If she was kindly and humane, the household reflected her warmth and grace, but if she was jealous, suspicious, or holding grudges, then the entire women's quarter was not a place one wanted to be.

A bedouin household had several generations living together, so women had their places in a hierarchy, usually, but not always, based on the seniority of the males to whom they were attached. The wife of the eldest son of the patriarch had only the wife of the patriarch over her, while the second wife of the youngest grandson was low on the ladder of respect. First wives ranked over second and third wives. Concubines in great favor with leading males were treated extremely well, while those who were not in great demand had extremely low status.

As a guest, Emmy found she was given the status of the woman who brought her into the household. Since she was there only temporarily, she was given dispensations from many duties that might otherwise have fallen to her, but she always tried to do enough that other women would not criticize her. For the most part, the women liked her because of her open, American attitudes and lack of class distinctions. She could be friendly with the highest woman one minute and talk intimately with the lowest-ranking concubine the next.

Emmy was at first confused about the many children that were found in an extended family and initially believed that they were lumped together without much differentiation. Older girls from twelve to fifteen years of age were often in charge of groups of seven or eight children, whom they tended to, amused, took from place to place, generally helped the children pass the time, and learn some basic things. She soon discovered, however, that the children spent some parts of the day with their mothers, their fathers, and their siblings, so smaller units emerged that still retained a role in the larger family.

Emmy was relieved that she was accepted in all three places she visited. Individuals and small groups came frequently to talk with her and ask questions of her, in large part because she was open and answered their questions about herself, her countrymen, and her profession. They asked questions about her appearance, her speech, her somewhat different clothing, the color of her hair, and the shade of her skin. They wanted to know about her children, about her husband, about her parents. One boy, about eight years old, wanted to know about the house she lived in while she was at home in America and whether it was at all like living in a bedouin dwelling. When she got to know people, she was sometimes asked to tell stories about her own land, so she told them about the Statue of Liberty, the White House, and Myrtle Beach. The last was a favorite tale because she made a sound like rolling surf, and she had to retell it many times.

The males all knew who she was and treated her cordially and with respect, especially when she served them at meals. The patriarch of one tribe once asked her, in the presence of most of the male members of the family, whether she missed her husband and 'was he not afraid of her living in such a different kind of society?' "I know he is a city-dweller," the patriarch had said, "and does not much understand such large families."

Emmy said she responded by saying. "My husband is exceeding thankful that I have found a bedouin family to spend time with since he comes from such a large family himself and thinks I could learn much from you. But I feel at a loss without him and count the days when I shall be with him again. After all, at Madinah, where he is with the army, he relies on men and boys for his food and entertainment. Thank you for allowing me to spend time with your family."

"Very nicely said," answered the Patriarch and then to the other men around him, "To think she is an English speaker ordinarily. Her Arabic is good enough to give a particularly good 'thank you.' She must come from an established American clan herself."

Emmy took photos, of course, but she had only a limited amount of 'quick developing' film, so she left only a few photos with them, mostly group photos, which faded within two or three months. She took a limited number of other photos on regular film that she would send back with reports for use in the reports or to be added to the archives.

Each visit consumed about ten days to two weeks of travel time. She had, in every case, to travel back alone, using her escort for protection and, often, guarded part way by males from the tribe she had visited. The males were always very solicitous of her and were careful not to get close to her or to hold any long conversations. She said she always felt safe.

The French Mission and Its Aftermath

Several years after her service in the Hijaz, Emmy told me about her assignment to Mecca to get information on the French mission to arrange assistance to Sharif Hussein. She regarded it as the most challenging of the assignments ever given her precisely because she was a woman operating in a society that allowed little contact between men and women in political matters. Even while she had a modest reputation in the Middle East as a journalist, her work had largely been centered on portrait work, on general pictures of nature and society, and with female society in general. She had never conducted full interviews with men by themselves without me being present. When given the assignment, she was unsure that she would be allowed by the authorities to do it. Even worse, she was afraid of being imprisoned or expelled again, knowing that even Western society would not be very sympathetic to her if that happened.

She told me that she pondered the matter and looked for a means whereby she could conduct the interview and not violate the general rules regulating the behavior of women in society. She knew that women could travel in Muslim society and that they could even contact men for worthy reasons, so long as rules were properly observed. She felt that two conditions needed attention. She had to be accompanied by at least one other female, and there must be a male present who could serve as her protector. Having decided that these conditions could be fulfilled, she now needed someone to assist her in making the arrangements.

She went to the Javanese agent at the pilgrims' center in Jiddah and told him about her needs. He was happy to help–for a fee. He found the name of the hotel that the French delegation would use and got her a room there. The room was in the women's wing of the building. As there were only two days before the arrival of the French delegation, he called the hotel registration desk to learn whether an advance agent had arrived. Fortunately, one had, a man named Jules Montrose, who spoke French and English but no Arabic. The Javanese agent told him of Emmy's desire to meet with one or more members of the delegation and explained who she was. Montrose knew the name and that she represented the *Tribune* and was pleasantly surprised at the request. Montrose was sure that someone from the delegation would talk with her before the meeting with the Arabs took place.

With those arrangements made, Emmy checked into the hotel. With her on the trip to Mecca and during her stay in the hotel, she was accompanied by another woman and by a male security guard, both supplied by the Javanese agent. Coming into the hotel, she was wearing the normal shawl (*chadur*) that Muslim women in the city wore. Since she was properly attired and was accompanied by others in general accordance with legalist rulings, she fit into the landscape and was received with no undue problems. The several proctors in the hotel did not even look her way.

That evening, the day of the delegation's arrival, about eight o'clock, she got the call that the entire delegation was going to eat together in a private dining room and that she was invited to dine with them. She put on her 'Western clothing' that covered her well but was still European in style. There was a long, pleated skirt that reached to her ankles with black stockings and low-heeled shoes. She wore a long-sleeved blouse with a scarf to cover her neck and throat area, topped with a jeweled stick pin. She wore a Tam-like hair covering, under which her hair could be tucked. With this outfit on, she was completely covered according to Islamic dress codes, but those who saw her would know that a Western woman existed beneath the clothing, which is what Emmy wanted to convey to the French gentlemen she was meeting. She had her escorts accompany her through the hotel lobby to the private dining room and left them at the door with instructions to return in two hours.

Inside, she found the delegation of five men and Monsieur Montrose, who all stood as she entered the room and looked intently at her, perhaps admiring such a well-dressed woman. She first removed her scarf and headwear, and when those items were removed, her medium-length blonde hair fell to her shoulders. She involuntarily shook her head to let the hair fall naturally. It had an appealing effect on the men, although she probably did not intend for that to necessarily happen.

All the men were in their late thirties or early forties, and all had mustaches, and one had a beard. They were well-dressed and exceedingly polite. They all came to her with friendly greetings and considerable charm. Two of them kissed her hand, which reminded her of Werner, although these diplomats were ever so much more genteel. It was apparent that they were all impressed by her clothing, which was different than normal women's clothing in the West and gave off an aura of mystery. As a result, they were attracted by her and were inclined to see her as a friend and, probably, something more intimate. The spokesman said that everyone knew who she was, and they all looked forward to dining with her and answering the questions she had. They sat at a round table that was a little cramped but was 'cozy' as a result.

The early part of the session dealt with ordering food, complaining about the relative lack of alcohol–there was date wine, which hardly satisfied any Frenchman's palate–and making general comments. Emmy told them about the siege of Ta'if and her visits to bedouins, and they made lots of comments about her remarks. Emmy said that all the men kept their eyes on her when not on the menu as if expecting the apparition to leave before they had enough time to look at her. She said that this was not unusual as men in other settings had often concentrated on her that way. It was a handsome woman. She did not encourage it, nor did she seek to discourage it.

When the food arrived, they talked for a while about its different tastes and whether they liked this dish or that. Then they got to their work. Without hesitation, they said they were there to keep the British 'honest,' that is, not exceeding the agreements made between Great Britain and France about territories each claimed in the Middle East. They said that two earlier efforts had been made by the French to assist Sharif Hussein. Reconnaissance units, artillery batteries, airplane squadrons, and even small naval units were under consideration to assist the Hashemites, but the matter of where and how they would be used needed to be decided. The French spokesman at this point said that the Arab leaders had little understanding of such matters, and he wondered whether the Arabs could use such esoteric military units at all. Another member of the delegation commented that he wondered how the Arabs had gotten as far as they had without such units.

To this point, Emmy had said almost nothing, but she had used slight facial movements, modest body movements, and other physical indications of when she agreed or disagreed with the statements of the various speakers. But during the latter part of the discussion, she began asking questions and making comments about some of the answers that were given to her.

They moved over to matters of strategy and coordination, and it was noted by one member of the delegation, who had said little to that point, that the Arabs cared little for the problems of colonial powers like Great Britain and France. The member pointed out that the Arabs did not understand allotments of territories, the construction of colonial states, the types of rule that different societies used, and such matters. He said at one point, "They are like little children who have little concept of who the 'mayor' of their city is and cannot conceive of how a city relates to a nation. "So, when we talk about French control over a certain section of the country to bring it into contemporary times, the Arab shakes his head and says, 'so long as no one interferes with the customs and grazing areas of the clans and tribes. It is frustrating.'"

The conversation drifted until the dessert and coffee appeared, and then there was one last attempt to round out the French presentation that would be made the following day. It concerned an earlier conversation with the Hashemite delegation about "modernity," in which it was suggested that the Hijazi Arabs did not have enough artisans to support an updated, technical civilization. Lacking were draftsmen, blue-print readers, foundry workers, and wheelwrights.

At the earlier meeting, it had been assumed there were such people in the French colonies of Africa, so information about the matter had been sent to colonial administrators, who sent back replies that there were a few such people, and those few souls mostly worked for French companies. However, there certainly was not a surplus but a shortage of such people in all the French colonies. Those colonial administrators suggested that the delegation contact the British to furnish such people from India as a place more likely to get such skills.

Emmy said that at the end of the session, the men had become accustomed to Emmy, and her allure lessened as they got deeper into their argumentation. They did not forget that she was a woman and a desirable one at that. It was that they could keep that in the back of their minds for later enjoyment while dealing fully with the subject matter at hand. The member of the delegation discussing the point about foreign Muslim assistance for the Arabs said that Indian technicians were out of the question if the purpose of bringing in such people was to increase French influence. They would probably Anglicize matters instead.

Along with this matter of technicians, the related question of obtaining military volunteers produced a somewhat similar response. However, the objections to using French Muslim volunteers for service in the Hijaz centered on bad climate, low pay, and unfavorable working conditions. Language was a major impediment, despite the supposed common language of Arabic, which, on closer examination showed a variety of different styles throughout the Near and Middle East.

During this last discussion, the six Frenchmen slowly lost their interest in the subject and were ready to move on to the other events of the evening. After some inane remarks, they decided to end the meeting. Three of the five members of the delegation departed for their rooms with the promise to meet two nights hence, when they might have another pleasant conversation about the meetings with Arabs.

The remaining two each seemed to be trying to outlast the other one so that only one would be left with her. She realized the game that was part of being played with herself as the intended prize, but not being particularly aroused by either of them or, remembering her ties with another man, excused herself. Her escort had returned, and she joined them and left. If the two gentlemen were disappointed, they did not show it to one another. They wandered together out into the concourse of the hotel, looking for something else to do for the remainder of the evening. Emmy spent the evening writing a report on what had occurred.

There was no follow-up meeting. The delegations met for a single session lasting until three o'clock the next day and the leader of the French delegation decided that, since they had their ship waiting for them, they may as well leave for Alexandria that evening. He said that waiting until the following morning was a waste of time. He was oblivious to the half-hearted laments of at least three members, who would have liked a more time with "that delicious reporter" from the *Tribune*. They, too, wanted to be on their way.

The delegation leader did, however, leave a note at registration for Emmy, saying how much the delegation had enjoyed meeting with her and talking about the situation in the Hijaz. However, they had other commitments, and a further meeting would not be possible that day. But, if they were all in the same city sometime soon, perhaps it could take place then.

The sudden departure of the French delegation left Emmy with only half a story. Certainly, what she had learned from the French was significant, and Emile would certainly not berate her for turning in just that material. But she considered herself to be a superior journalist and decided to confirm the French story and, if possible, learn what the reaction of the Hashemite negotiators had been to the negotiations with the French. Accordingly, she went, with her escort, to the palace and found the office that dealt with public information, except its real purpose was something quite different. Historically, it was an office where Arab subjects petitioned the Sharif for redress of a grievance, such as a bad land deal, over-taxation, or a guilty verdict for a questionable crime. But with new times it was the place where some public relations matters were handled as well.

As it turned out, the office did not handle the press releases of conferences. Supposedly, those press releases were handled by the secretariat of foreign affairs, so she was sent to that office. There, the officer in charge said he could not help her, but she might try the secretariat of the cabinet, which did know what the matter was all about. She had to state who she was and whom she represented. Then she waited for nearly an hour but understood that she was asking for something that this government probably had never been confronted with before. It was not usual for a reporter to ask a government official for any sort of information about its policy-making role.

At the fifty-six minutes mark, she was taken, with her female escort, into the office of Prince Abdullah, whom she had met briefly at Ta'if, where he was the nominal commander of Hashemite forces. He asked her to sit and then asked how her husband was and whether he was likely to return from the Madinah front soon. She replied that it was not likely, as the fighting was continuing, and the *Tribune* editor always kept people at a site so long as there were hostilities. She said there was a possibility that she might join him there.

Prince Abdullah then turned to the results of the meeting with the French delegation. He said that, overall, the results were somewhat disappointing. It was apparent that the French were more interested in keeping tabs on the British than helping the Hashemites. Did she think this was true?

Emmy did not want to give away what she had learned from the French but did not believe she should lie about the matter either. She said, "Well, from an independent view, I can understand why you might think that. The French are, after all, a colonial power and are known to compete with the British at times. It would be strange if that attitude did not surface in other places, such as your negotiations with them. I suppose what you want to know is whether they are true and reliable with you, even while they protect their colonial interests elsewhere."

Abdullah's eyebrows arched when she said that. "Really," he said, "I had not looked at it that way, and it calls on our side to reassess our discussions with them. We were looking at the matter only from our viewpoint, not so much from theirs."

Emmy said, "There was concern among the French, as I recall from other reports, that they could supply workers to you who were Muslim, understood Arabic, and could perform technical functions. I was doubtful that, even if the French had them, they would part from them. Can you tell me about that matter?"

Again, the prince's eyebrows arched. "You are well informed! They said that the results of the search they ran for such people were inconclusive, and they would continue to search. However, it appeared that the number was not great enough that the French wanted to release such people, particularly since their expertise was needed at home."

Emmy was encouraged at this point and said, "Was the matter of modern weapons and their integration into Arab warfare discussed? That has been a matter the British have raised, as I recall, so it probably was with the French as well."

By his body language, Emmy knew she had surprised him again, even though he controlled his eyebrows and did not raise them this time. "It is always the same theme with the French and British, he said. "At Ta'if, I knew when we attacked that unless we were very quick in overrunning the city and capturing the Ottoman defenses, we could only hope for a long siege. I wanted modern weapons desperately at the time but had to content myself with what we had. The question is whether we can integrate such weapons into our armies. Probably, but until we get them, we are never going to know. The British and the French do not seem to understand that. They only blame us for being backward."

So, Emmy went over the entire French report and got the Hashemite side. When she was finished, the prince thanked her for helping him understand the very meeting he had attended, and she had not. Emmy was aware of this, but the prince probably was not, which indicates that her interview was a success from a news-gathering perspective,

When Emmy and her female escort left his office, the prince's wife, whom Emmy had not met, was there to take her first to her apartment in the palace, where they had fresh fruit and coffee. She met the children and was shown around the apartment, with pleasant talk the entire time. Then, the wife took her to the palace entry where Emmy's guard waited, and the three members mounted a horse-drawn vehicle resembling an Irish dogcart, which took them to the hotel where Emmy was staying. Emmy thought, as she ascended the steps of the hotel, that the afternoon had been a real success, and to think, that three days earlier, she had been in doubt about ever gaining the information she needed from such supposedly reluctant sources.

Gertrude Bell Redux

As she picked up her key at registration, there was a tug on her sleeve. She looked and saw a woman with Western clothing but with a desert head cloth covering her neck and shoulders. "Amelia Caruthers," the woman said. "Do you have a moment to talk?"

Emmy recalled hearing my report of my meeting with Gertrude Bell, so she said. "Certainly, you are Gertrude Bell, if I'm not mistaken. You talked with my colleague, Marty Mintz, last year in Basra."

"That's right," came the answer. "He helped provide information on the Ottoman Empire," said Gertrude, "but was adamant about not undertaking a mission for us."

"Good for him!" Emmy answered.

"You say that with such strength," said Gertrude. "Do you not care for Great Britain?"

"No, your assumption is incorrect. I don't have animosity towards the British and have good relations with many of their officials, as you well know. Rather, my colleague is a reporter and a future professor without any training in espionage. I don't want him sent on missions where his life would be put in needless danger."

"Well, I think that point is clear," said Gertrude, just a little put-off. "Rest assured, I will not ask you to do anything like that. I think I already know the answer. I need some information, if you have any, on the French delegation that was here the other day. Can you assist me?"

"Perhaps, but not here in the lobby," Emma answered. "Can you give me an hour or so to bathe and change clothes? I smell so bad that I can barely stand myself. I get accustomed to it when I'm in the desert, but here, where there are bathing facilities, I like to pamper myself.

Can you come to my room? I'll order some supper for us if that is all right with you."

Gertrude smiled, the first time that had happened since first approaching Emmy. "I would like that very much. May I have your room number."

 They met an hour and a half later. There were kabobs, hummus, falafel, and pita bread, along with a bottle of red wine, already laid out. When offered a glass of wine, Gertrude said, "I would not have thought you could get that in Mecca. Did you bring it with you?"

"No, one of my guards found a source yesterday and told me about it. He knew I liked it, so he purchased two bottles. It's an unknown brand, so it's probably far from the top of the line, but I think it will do us well enough tonight when there is no other choice."

While they ate, Gertrude asked about Emmy's stint at the siege of Ta'if. Emmy described that operation and then told her about the visits to the homes of several of the women that she had undertaken. They fell into an easy conversation about bedouin life and, particularly, about the lives of the women in the camps. They had similar experiences and understandings of what life in the camps was all about. It was apparent that Gertrude did not realize the extent of Emmy's experience in the Middle East, and she soon began to see her as a kindred spirit.

Then Gertrude asked whether I (Marty) was as close to bedouin life as well. She said, "I have seen him ride a camel, where he is quite accomplished, but that tells me nothing about his ability to adapt to living in the desert."

Emmy answered. "Marty may sometimes give the impression that he is an effete, know-it-all from the city, but he is quite at home in the desert, as he is just about anywhere he goes. His parents exposed him to lots of different social situations when he was young, and he has built on those experiences. Right now, he is in Yanbu, living in a tent as a member of Faisal's retinue. He says he has barely spoken a word of English since he got there and seldom eats anything that resembles

Western-style cooking. He thinks he has lost a couple of pounds, but that is because he operates in forward areas and does not eat regular meals.

This led to a discussion of Gertrude's own experiences in crossing the Arabian desert several times and in visiting out-of-the-way places that called for outdoor living of a rigorous nature. They finished an entire bottle of wine and had started on the second one before they even got to the subject that Gertrude had come to talk about, namely the French mission to King Hussein.

"I have already filed the report, so there is no reason why you should not have a copy of it. Also, you may want to review my notes. There are a few references there that would add to a specialist's overall knowledge of the visit and what they were after." The two women moved to the sitting area and got some lamps working properly so that Gertrude could read. She looked at everything and then asked Emmy questions about the delegation. She wanted, especially, to know who was there and who said what. It took almost an hour to finish that discussion. Gertrude was disappointed that there had been no follow-up meeting.

At that point, Emmy told her about visiting with Prince Abdullah to get the other side of the story and to understand better what happened during and after the meeting. "You must understand, Gertrude," Emmy said, "That I have not filed this story yet. It probably will go out late tomorrow, so you must not release it to others before the weekend. I do not want another reporter to "scoop" me on this, as I have gone to a lot of trouble to get this story."

Gertrude said, "I understand completely and will not betray your trust."

Emmy then told her about the meeting with Prince Abdullah and answered all the questions that Gertrude asked about it. They both then wrote reports and did not finish until after midnight. Both bottles of wine were finished by that time, and their only lament was that they did not have a third.

At the door, as she departed, Gertrude said, "I am only sorry that I never got to meet you and Marty earlier, but we were always in different places. We certainly would have become fast friends. I have met several people who understand the bedouins, but few enough who retain their good sense about their experiences with them, as you and Marty seem to have done. I like to think I have done that as well. Please give your regards to Marty when you see him.

The following morning, Emma filed her reports at the Pilgrim Center, paid for the use of her escort, settled her accounts with everyone there, and left appropriate gratuities. Then, with her original guard who had been with her at Ta'if, she reported to the caravan leader that she was present and ready to proceed to Madinah with the rest of the travelers going there. She looked forward to being with me again and thought of the erotic reunion we would enjoy.

Chapter 4
The Wasteland at Yanbu

The Journey to Yanbu

It was a long camel ride to Yanbu from Mecca, over five days, and, at that, we–my guards and tent boy-- took the coastal route, which is slightly longer according to some travelers. No caravans were going north at the time, so we could move at a good pace without worrying about stragglers from other parties. At the same time, there was concern among my guards that we were all alone in a hostile country and that brigands could accost us. They moaned continually about the lack of pilgrims to visit the tomb of the Prophet at Madinah as providing additional security that could have benefitted us.

There were two incidents, both minor, although both had the potential to become major if not handled right. The first one involved our encounter with three young bedouins who were on another track parallel to us, about three hundred yards away. They were moving at about the same rate of speed as we were. Ibrahim, my lead guard, noticed them first and gave a warning. We talked about who they might be, and it was Ibrahim's view that the group was a messenger group sent by one clan leader to another, where a group of three was sent for reasons of safety. Ibrahim said that so long as we were not being led into an ambush, we would be all right.

The group stayed parallel for some five hours until mid-afternoon, when we halted for a break, especially to drink some tea, which my entire guard seemed to regard as a daily rite. Ibrahim kept a close watch on the other group lest they should use the occasion to attempt to close with us. They did not but kept going so that, by the end of our brief refreshment interlude, the other group was completely out of sight. All of us were relieved that we no longer had to be concerned about them.

But about an hour from sunset, when Ibrahim was scouting for a place to camp for the night, the group was directly in front of us, apparently waiting for our arrival. We approached them with caution, and my two guards spread out to guard both flanks. We were in open country with good views in every direction and could see no places where a larger group could be waiting to spring a trap on us. All three of the strangers stood in the open with rifles unsheathed but not pointing at us directly. Ibrahim went forward to talk with them and, after a short while, returned.

He said, "They make a claim to be from a nearby tribe and have been sent to locate a smaller group known to be operating in this area but have not found them, and all their water is gone. They ask whether we can give them some until they can reach a wadi about twenty kilometers from here, where there is a spring. I said I would consult with you about it."

"What is your assessment as to their condition? Do you think they are telling the truth, or are they a danger to us?"

"They are young, probably no more than sixteen or seventeen years of age, and are frightened about the situation they find themselves in, Effendi. It could be a ruse, but I think not. I suggest we give them some food and water, for goodwill, and even let them stay with us for the night. They could even ride with us to the waterhole (*wadi*)."

I brought the other guard, Isma'il, and the tent boy, Ahmad, together to discuss what should be done. Isma'il listened to Ibrahim's story and said, "I have been in that situation and know how upsetting it can be. I agree that they do not pose much of a threat, although one of us must be on guard all night long. Ahmad listened, with his eyes almost bulging from his face with excitement at this turn of events. He nodded affirmatively at Ismail's remark. He probably felt compassion for the young travelers.

I ran the problem over in my mind and made one last sweep of the horizon to make sure there were no confederates nearby. Then I said, "You have given me good counsel, so we will do as Ibrahim suggests. Let us make camp, invite them to eat with us, give them some water, and settle in for the night. The three of us can rotate on guard tonight. Tomorrow, we can take them to the wadi and hope that they can find some trace of their relatives." As it turned out, Ahmad had some lamb he was saving for a special meal, so we divided that along with the endless supply of beans he carried. It was not a sumptuous meal but better than most meals on the trail. The three visitors were ravenous and ate everything available.

I stood guard on the second watch from about midnight until around three in the morning. It was cold, and I wrapped myself in a blanket. I looked at the stars, which were so clear in the cool desert air. The Milky Way was the center of it all, and I do not remember ever seeing it so bright and glorious, like a great dotted white blanket in the middle of the sky. I was almost sorry when Isma'il relieved me. The three visitors did not stir at all during my stint of guard duty. I guess they were tuckered out and felt safe.

After a short breakfast at six in the morning, we were on our way with the three visitors out front so that we could keep an eye on them. Ten kilometers down the way, we encountered the group of bedouins that the young boys were trying to locate. The group was as cautious as we had been and sent out a speaker when Ibrahim went forward to talk with them. There followed a rather lengthy conversation, and then Ibrahim returned.

He said, "Effendi, they claim to be the family that the boys were to meet and wondered what had happened to them. They will take the boys as soon as we release them. But they want a fee for passing through their area, as they claim they have the right to demand that of travelers. They want the draft camel led by Ahmad as the price. I pointed out that the passageway belongs to the Sharif of the Hijaz and that it is open to all travelers. He laughed and said that the Sharif was not here to enforce that concession, so the fee must be paid. He said that you might want to make a claim on the Sharif when you see him next. Effendi, I counted twenty rifles to our three, so fighting our way out does not seem to be an option."

"Thank you, Ibrahim, for your efforts. You are right. We cannot force our way through here. But we can try something a little different. Please return to their speaker and tell him that I would like a short audience with their shaykh to discuss his fee further. I am sure he will agree to that, and you will accompany me when he does. The speaker will ask who I am, and you are to tell him I am a notable from Beirut who is traveling to join Prince Faisal in his battle with the Ottomans at Yanbu."

Ibrahim and I met the *shaykh* a short time later. I brought the three boys along with their gear and passed them over as the first item of business. The boys dropped to their knees and thanked me for my hospitality, a small rite that was not lost on the *shaykh*. Perhaps, I thought, that might cause a twinge of conscience, even as the reference to Prince Faisal and his war might. The *shaykh* brought forward no refreshments, which labeled him as a difficult man, so I called for Ibrahim to give me and the shaykh water from my canteen. The *shaykh* declined the offer, but I drank fully.

I said in my best al-Azhar Arabic, "So, you want one of my camels as a fee for passing through 'your' territory. It is a fine camel, and I depend on it to carry my cooking supplies, so it would be a great inconvenience to lose it. Perhaps something else will do. I moved my rifle, which was a fine gun not often seen in these parts and was used for sport more than for defense. The shaykh's eyes caught the gleam on the rifle barrel as I moved it. A look of revelation and greed briefly crossed his face. He could hardly contain himself. The camel was forgotten as the gun became the center of attention.

"Perhaps your rifle, which is unusual, might substitute for the camel" he suggested.

"Hmm," I vocalized, "The rifle, you say. I had not thought about that. I suppose I could go without it a few days until I return to Beirut and get a newer model." Then I paused and said, "But it is a sporting gun, and I never give away a sporting gun." I saw his face drop a little. "But I will wager it on a sporting competition. I'll tell you what. Why not have a competition wherein we both move out into the open space and wait for the hawks to fly past? The first one to bring down three hawks wins. If I win, we go through without the fee. If you win, I give you the rifle."

I did not know how good the *shaykh* was with a rifle, but I imagined he was rather good. On the other hand, I was a junior skeet shooting champion of central North Carolina. So it would probably be an even match.

The shaykh was excited by the offer and could think only of the rifle he would win. He did not evaluate his competition or, if he did, he only saw an effete city dweller from the west coast of Syria with limited skills. The competition did not last long. I took the first two birds out of the sky immediately before he was able to even get a shot off. I held back and let him shoot at the next three when he bagged one. Then, I ended the competition with a difficult shot of a hawk flying just over ground level. The shaykh threw his rifle down in disgust and repaired to his tent, where he remained, refusing to even wish us well on our trip out of his camp. The three young boys we had befriended, however, did come to us as we departed and gave us their good wishes.

The second incident occurred two days later, as we came up to a water well that was marked on our maps. It was indicated as open to all travelers, but a bedouin group had established a camp there and refused to let others use the water because they were watering their livestock. We would have to wait until they were finished. When asked when the watering would be complete, Ibrahim was told that it probably would not be before another day or two. Everyone around the speaker laughed while I watched from ten feet away. I simply said, loud enough for the speaker to hear, "Tell your shaykh I wish to speak with him. I will have tea ready in half an hour. Perhaps he can join me then.

I had Ahmad unload his needed utensils and, using our water, made tea for our group. When the shaykh and two retainers arrived, they were given cups of tea, along with some biscuits, which were passed among the group. We all ate slowly and deliberately, with my retainers, each consuming about four biscuits apiece. Following their lead, the shaykh ate that many himself. "These are good biscuits," the shaykh said, "Where did you get them?"

I answered, "They come from the pilgrims' store in Jiddah, where there is a special bakery that puts them into tins so that they do not become mangled and crushed. It's one of the few pleasures my group enjoys on such a long journey as this."

"Where are you headed?" the shaykh asked.

"Prince Faisal is preparing to meet the Ottomans near Yanbu, and we are headed north to meet him there." I was taking some chance that the shaykh might not feel kindly toward the Hashemites, but I thought that it was a safe bet that this shaykh was probably a staunch supporter. He was and was delighted with my answer. He said he had four of his followers already in the Yanbu camp. Could we possibly take some small supplies to them? I assured him we would, and then we talked about the Hashemite cause and its prospects. He knew little about the war beyond the Mecca-Medinah area but was enthusiastic. By this time, Ahmad had cleaned up after refreshments and brought a biscuit tin with ten biscuits still in it, which he passed to me. I showed the shaykh the interior with the biscuits and said, "Maybe your women might like a treat this evening." I closed the lid and passed the tin to him. He accepted it with a big smile, which was nearly a grin.

Then I said, "Perhaps tonight, when your animals have had enough water, my followers could take half an hour to water our three camels and replenish our drinking supply. Would that work?"

"Of course," he said without hesitation. "The animals will have had their fill by then, and in any event, my followers need some sleep. There is no reason why you can't water your animals, then. After all, it is well open to travelers." We went to bed early, rose in the middle of the night, watered our animals, and left with full canteens. Another disaster had been averted.

Listening to Paroled Ottoman Officers

Immediately after we arrived at Yanbu, I found the telegraph office. I sent a brief message to Emile saying that I had arrived safely and that this telegraph office would be the one from which I would file reports until the military situation changed. I received a brief acknowledgment of the message but no instructions. I also left a message at Jiddah for Emmy, figuring it would be picked up in a few days when one of the guards deposited her latest report. I told her that I missed her, particularly since I was in a strange place and longed for companionship.

There were no hotels or other living quarters in the city where I might stay, so, with my travel companions, we moved outside the town center, where we found a tent city where we pitched our tents. There was a modest fee for pitching the tent there, which supposedly included security, but I was still warned to "watch your things as there are a lot of thieves about." It was late afternoon, so I waited until after sunset and evening prayers, a time when people relaxed, and conversations with officials at their leisure might happen.

I went back into the central city and found an old run-down building that probably once might have been the living quarters for a prominent official, which had been divided into rooms and apartments. It had a verandah, and on it, I recognized a group of Arab officials, all speaking Turkic. I knew instantly that I had stumbled onto a group of former Ottoman military officials from Arab provinces that had been captured–most probably in the Mesopotamian theater. I had heard in Egypt, while I was still there, that some officer prisoners were being allowed to exchange incarceration for freedom to aid the Arab Revolt. Most of those on the porch were in uniform without identifying patches and insignia of rank, while a few were in desert robes. They were in small groups of three to five people, with a total of probably thirty-five to forty people in all.

I thought for a moment about the scheme to incorporate such captive Arab officers into the Hashemite 'army,' with the very personalized command structure that existed, which seemed to center on the whims of King Hussein and Prince Faisal. From what I had seen, both were capable people, but both operated based on personal allegiances. Both expected their 'chosen' commanders to have their favorites and to have the loyalty of a group of men who were willing to be their soldiers. Little training was undertaken, and what did occur took place within the tribal system, where leaders taught their followers' basic maneuvers with a horse and how to thrust and parry with a saber.

The paroled officers from the Ottoman army came out of a professional corps, where all had gone to military schools. At the schools, they had mastered the use of a great variety of weaponry, had studied battle tactics and strategy, and had mastered the art of leading various-sized units into battle. They operated with troops who had undergone specialized training, who would not rely on enthusiasm and elan but, rather, on grit and a solid command system that translated orders into meaningful military action.

I understood that a fusion would be made between the two groups but that it would be a difficult process with lots of frustration on both sides. In the beginning, the paroled officers would be a disgruntled group of professionals, knowing they had lost their careers in a truly professional army and would experience great uncertainty in the new world they were facing. They would not like it, so I expected to hear a great deal about it in my upcoming interviews. Well, 'interviews' was probably not the correct term, as it implied some questions by one side and answers by another. I simply intended to listen.

I boldly walked up onto the verandah and sat down at a vacant table, and soon, two paroled officers joined me and started a conversation. I nodded as if I knew them, and they nodded back and took their seats. We were served some weak tea by a waiter. No one identified themselves, but each person seemed to believe that everyone present belonged to the group. One said, "Well, Nuri is wrong if he thinks that Hussein will give us positions of responsibility in Faisal's army. Faisal seems to have his favorites, and I doubt whether any of us can replace them." I was to learn that Nuri al-Sa'id was rapidly becoming a leader among the parolees.

"I agree," said the second officer. They both looked at me, and I nodded my head. He continued by saying. "But it goes beyond the positions that would be given us. Do we want to be part of a country that uses camels and horses as its main means of transportation? Where are their staff cars, trucks, tractors, and trailers, their artillery, and their machine guns? This is not a modern army and cannot lick any of the major armies of the world. None of us would be here if we had faced off against the Arabs, but we had the misfortune to fight against Anglo-Indian forces, who do have all the training and necessities for fighting a modern war."

"I asked a sergeant where the ammunition depot was, and he told me it was that crate near the bottom of the hill, where there were a few boxes of cartridges," said the other one. He continued, "This is too primitive." He turned to me and, noticing my desert robes, asked, "Have you had a chance to go inland?"

"Yes," I said in Turkic as well. I have less of an American accent in Turkic than in Arabic. "It's a land with not much in it except bedouins and their tents. There are a few small cities, but few are any larger than this one, except maybe Mecca and Madinah. It is rural, meant for bedouins, not farmers."

He hardly paused when I finished talking but said, "There you have it. Why should we join such a country? It has no army, no cities, probably little government, no railroads except the one running down from Damascus to Madinah, and no real roads. I would rather stay with the Ottomans, who have all the things the Europeans have and who keep working so that everyone in the country has those things as well."

His compatriot said, "Yeh, I suppose, but we may not have much choice, as the Ottomans seem to be taking a slow beating in this war and are being overwhelmed. Then everything will be divided up among the victors, and there will be no more Ottoman Empire."

"I cannot believe that," said the other. "The padishah has always managed to prevent that from happening. I think he will rescue us all again."

Just then, a man, who was Nuri, who had been mentioned at the beginning of the conversation, joined us and, without introducing himself, entered the conversation. After all, he knew the other two and thought he knew me because I was with them. "I heard the remark about all the things this place lacks, but that is a narrow perspective. There is the entire Syrian area that the *Sharif* wants to annex. That area is richer, has many more facilities, knows what modernization all is about, and would make sure all parts of the country are brought along. If you see things with Damascus, Aleppo, Beirut, and Sidon all included, the place looks a lot better. Some of the people in my barracks back in Cairo were from Beirut, and they say that all the new hotels are wired with electricity. That's probably ahead of most parts of Constantinople."

I stayed for two hours while the group at the table changed people several times. The central theme changed over time and, more and more, centered on what kind of assignments the paroled officers would be given. Most thought in terms of 'companies,' battalions,' and 'regiments,' which were terms European armies, including the Ottomans, used. Most wanted to command 'battalions' and 'regiments.' I thought they were not being realistic about the units that existed in the Hashemite force or the uses the paroled officers could be expected to perform. Not even Nuri, whom I found to be the most reasonable and insightful among them, was anywhere near the truth of the matter. I thought the most they could expect was to be advisers to Faisal's picked commanders without any direct command functions of their own. But I said nothing, lest it bring the wrath of the group down on me for revealing the truth of the situation.

I made only three or four comments all night, just enough to stay associated with the group I was with at the time. All were at sea about whether to throw their lot in with the Hashemites, and they were not any clearer about it at the end of the evening than they had been at dusk when I arrived.

Becoming a Member of Prince Faisal's Camp

The following morning, my retainers packed up, and we went west into the highlands, where we discovered the main Arab camp. The Hashemite banner flew over an enclosed area with several large tents, so I calculated that it was Prince Faisal's center of operations. I went directly to it and was surprised that we got to the roped-off area before anyone stopped us. Even then, it was done politely. "Effendi," the guard said, "This is the area of the prince. Others may not enter without his express permission. Do you know him well enough for that?"

I was not entirely sure Faisal would remember me, but I thought he might, so I gave the guard my card, which puzzled him. I said, "Please give this to him and ask if I might see him for a moment. Tell him I will not be long."

The guard was gone less than a minute when he returned and said, "Effendi, he will see you immediately. However, your guard must remain outside, perhaps to the side over there." He pointed to a nearby area.

"Without comment, I walked into the tent, and there was Faisal with an aide. Faisal gave me the Muslim greeting, and after I had replied, he said, "So the crows gather for the feast, eh? I was wondering how long it would be before you arrived. I heard that you were in Ta'if and that you visited my father last week. What can I do for you specifically?"

"I'm here to observe and to write news reports, as always," I said. "Will you give me permission to operate in your forward areas?"

"Of course, you may. You may want to pitch your tent down among the staff tents where you will be out of the way of fighting units." He sounded cheerful and gave his permission without reservation. "But, of course, I shall use you just as you use me. The British are sending agents to examine my units and my staying power. They will want to talk to those outside my establishment, so you can be one of those people. Are you willing to speak in support of me?"

"Of course," I answered. He certainly expected that answer and smiled when I gave it.

He said, "You may see my chief of staff this afternoon at the officer's briefing when he tells of the upcoming campaign. I will have him informed that you will be there." He went back to his duties, and I exited the tent.

Having the Prince's permission to pitch my tent in the staff area gave me a clear status in the camp. I was no longer an outsider but a member of an intermediate group of people who served the prince as his retainers in an administrative sense. It was much like that of a regular general in a modern army, which undertakes communication, supply, and manpower duties, only this one was quite simple and highly personalized with great loyalty to Faisal himself.

It was expected that my retainers would have the same loyalty, which I immediately recognized and discovered that my retainers did as well. They felt as though their status had risen greatly as a result of being included in the staff area and being accepted as such by the other inhabitants. Over time, we figured out who the key people on the staff were and what gifts were appropriate for them. I erred on the side of generosity, but not overly so, because I did not want to be labeled as 'profligate,' which can be just as bad a reputation as 'tight-fisted.' I did not find it difficult, probably because of my upbringing, where my father was a master of walking 'a tightrope' between conflicting social values.

I did go to the briefing that Faisal had mentioned and found it to be revealing, although it probably was not intended to be quite as transparent as it was. The audience consisted almost entirely of tribal shaykhs who had brought groups of fighters to aid Prince Faisal. They wanted to know where the other shaykhs were with their fighters. "We can never beat back the Ottoman devils with the puny force that has been assembled so far," said one outspoken leader.

The spokesman tried to quell such open criticism by saying, "They are coming, they are coming!! You yourselves know that preparing forces of the size we need takes time to organize. We have two confederations from the interior who have committed to sending fighters, and we expect the first contingents to arrive within days."

"Has Ibn Sa'ud agreed to send anyone?" asked a fighter from near the open flap of the tent in which we were meeting.

"Ibn Sa'ud has been informed that we face a grave test of our Arab fortitude, and he has been asked to send as many fighters as he can. He has replied that there must be clarifications on the leadership of the fighters and the command structure of the assembled Arab hosts. He will send troops as soon as those clarifications are made to his satisfaction." It did not sound like Ibn Sa'ud was likely to send anyone. Others around me groused at the reply, probably arriving at the same conclusion that I had.

The spokesman, apparently believing this discussion was going the wrong way, sought to change the subject. He said, "On the other hand, we have support coming from the Khedive of Egypt, who is sending a battery of artillery, which will undoubtedly square off against the artillery of the Ottomans and even give us an edge." I realized that the Arabs besieging Ta'if had just been stripped of the battery to aid this effort. I wondered how long that would lengthen the siege at Ta'if. Emmy would get word to me about that development.

"One battery, only?!" said an elderly Arab shaykh near the front. "That's not enough. We need at least a battalion of them. Over 15,000 Turks are coming after us. The small number of guns that a battery has will hardly have any effect on their advance."

Another person said, "I agree. The Turks are notorious gunners, and it is almost as if they feel with their hands where their shots should go. They train so many gunners and have so many guns that it is nearly impossible to counter them. A battery will never do. Tell the khedive that he does not fully realize the threat here and that he might well consider many more batteries if he wants to help us."

That subject received several more caustic comments, and then the issue of the captured officers who were being allowed to serve in Faisal's army was raised. None of the Arab shaykhs wanted them on their side in battle. "They were the enemy once, and now they are nothing but turncoats who cannot be trusted," said one shaykh who had not spoken before. He continued, "But even if we were to accept them, what good would they do us? Can any of them lead a charge that our warriors are accustomed to doing? I doubt it very much. They are accustomed to infantry attacks and coordinating them with cannonade fire, which is almost lacking in our forces to date. At most, we can use four or five of them for staff officers, but that will not do for them. They feature themselves as leaders. Well, we already have leaders. Let them go back and help the Ottomans!"

Then, with the impulsiveness I had noticed in bedouins, the shaykhs rose and departed the tent, apparently feeling that enough time had been spent on discussing such matters. I was the only one who remained sitting on the ground in the middle of the tent. The spokesman came and sat opposite me. "You must be Effendi Marty," he said. "The prince asked me to be sure to talk with you after the meeting was over. I hope all the negative remarks did not mislead you as to the devotion of the shaykhs towards the *sharif* and toward Prince Faisal."

"Not at all," I answered. "They were merely letting loose of their frustrations, as bedouins are famous for. Their courage in battle, however, offsets their doubts."

"I'm glad you see it that way. By the way, your Arabic is superb and much better than I was led to believe was true." He was not above a little flattery to bring me around to his way of thinking.

"Thank you, major. I have had plenty of opportunity to use it and perfect it," I answered. He then brought forth a map with the major roads and traces through difficult terrain. I studied it and saw, almost instantaneously, that there was no practical way to get Yanbu to move against Mecca.

The spokesman said, "This is the logical place to arrest the Ottoman force, and it is here, without a doubt, that the dream of an Arab state will be assured or will be doomed. It depends on the ability of the Arabs to hold this line, which will be difficult for a desert force which is accustomed to open spaces for maneuverability rather than the hills, the canyons, and the uneven terrain of this place."

"Will you have enough men to do that?" I asked.

"Probably, but to be successful, this campaign has to be a long one, or otherwise, the Ottoman force will not be decimated over time to the point where they cannot go further. But Arabs do not like to fight for that long. We can only hope for other tribes to send fighters at different stages. If that happens, we can outlast them."

I turned to the problem of the paroled officers. "Can you use them, or did you take them merely to please the British?" I asked.

"Mostly to please the British, of course, but there are other considerations," he answered. "Those officers may be of limited use to us now, but in the future, they will be indispensable. Eventually, we will need to build some infantry and artillery units, so we can use officers who can do that for us. But, more importantly, we will need governors of settled areas, and these officers have the requisite skills to serve admirably in such settings. They are trained in administration, they know how to make decisions, they speak Arabic and they are professional in the modern sense. Our bedouin leaders cannot do those jobs without a great deal of retraining or experience."

"So you will allow them to sit around and breed discontent while you wait for the liberation of Syria?" I asked.

"O, I doubt that," the spokesman said, "Faisal has plans to begin using some of them in the defense of the area as the enemy attempts to invade it. It will take a lot of planning to anticipate the enemy's moves and to counteract them. These paroled officers will be useful in that regard, and loyalties may grow as a result of the adventure." I had to agree that he made a good point. It was one that I had not thought about.

Preparing for the Ottoman Advance

I spent the next few days on a camel, examining the terrain where the Arabs were to make their stand. Like Faisal, I concluded that it would be a formidable task for the Ottomans to move through unscathed if the Arabs attacked relentlessly while the Ottomans were on that terrain. There were many vantage points from which the Arabs could mount harassing attacks on the larger force of the Ottomans. Much depended on the Ottoman commander and his willingness to take significant losses to get through the terrain. Once through it, there was little to stop the force from proceeding along the entire coast to Mecca and Jiddah to the south.

I understood that no commander likes to see his strength eroded in battle. There is sort of a law of military conservation, that battle losses erode the strength of a unit until enough losses are suffered that the unit loses its military integrity. Then, the military force no longer has the strength to do the job the unit is assigned. It is, of course, simple common sense, but military commanders, even flamboyant ones, seem to grasp this principle and guard against it.

The battle then was going to revolve around the ability of the Ottoman army to move through the terrain, as difficult as it was, while taking as few casualties as possible. The Arab army's task was to slow the Ottoman advance and inflict significant casualties on the enemy so that it would lose its military integrity. It was going to be difficult for both sides to perform their roles so that they would achieve success. Given the experience, the odds lay with the Ottoman army.

My bodyguards were intrigued by my explorations and, after some time, began to make observations of their own, so we talked about the Ottoman advance through this area. When they understood what was to happen, they were more interested than they had been initially, and they, too, wondered where the best places for me to observe would be. Elevated spots were preferred, but the enemy and the Hashemites might want those spots as well because they afforded a good overview of a section of the battlefield. Well-hidden spots, of course, usually lacked clear viewing. Places to the side of the main enemy force were most sought after, but we had no real way of ascertaining just which route the enemy would take through the area. We could guess, but nothing was certain. We fretted over the problem while undertaking our explorations but noted perhaps ten key locations, which I entered on my writing pad.

Then, the British delegation arrived. Well, it was not a delegation. It was simply a group of officers on an inspection trip to ascertain whether the Arabs were ready for the battle that they were surely going to fight. With them was the well-known T.E. Lawrence, a captain who had gone into many tribes in the past year trying to raise support for an Arab uprising against the Ottomans. He had limited success in that endeavor, but he was well-liked among bedouins because he used camels and horses well and spoke good Arabic. I had nodded to him very briefly in Baghdad the previous year, where he had been unsuccessful in extricating a British force being besieged at Kut on the Euphrates River.

When we met in Faisal's command post, he did not seem to remember me at all, and I did not remind him of the previous encounter. After all, we had seen each other only across a crowded room. On this occasion, he paid only occasional attention to me, seeming to dismiss me as inconsequential, possibly because I was a correspondent, not a military figure. Overall, he was not very talkative in the small reception that was held to welcome the inspection team. However, the head of the team saw me differently and took me aside to ask about my perceptions of the Ottomans in the Arab environment. "I understand this is your third battle on Arab soil–in Sinai, at Ta'if, and now here. What is your assessment of their strength and capabilities? he asked.

"Each battle was different," I answered. "In Sinai, it was a highly organized raid led by German commanders that aimed at destroying the railroad that the British were building. The Ottomans performed well and left in good order, with all their guns. At Ta'if, a sudden attack had left a force isolated in a difficult city to besiege, and they defended it well. They did not seek a way out, which may show some lack of initiative among the leaders, as they were content to wait for relief. This fight promises to be different. The Ottomans come from a well-supplied base with numerical strength. They face a rag-tag, undisciplined army. They have modern weapons and numerical superiority. They ought to win handily, but they have terrain against them, and they must get by the gunboats that I know the British will eventually furnish."

"Good analysis," he responded. "It's nice to hear a realistic assessment. The Arabs certainly never give me one, and the British commanders exaggerate everything from Ottoman strength to Arab failings. "But do you think the Arabs will hold?"

"Somehow, they will, I think, largely because you won't let them fail."

"So," he asked, moving on in his questioning, "Is Prince Faisal the man to command the upcoming battle?"

"Probably," I answered, "He's a favorite son of the *sharif*, so you don't have much of a choice. You are going to have to live with him. But beyond that, he has brought together enough of a force to hold a superior Ottoman army at bay two hundred miles from the goal in Mecca. That is impressive. Moreover, he is getting the tribal shaykhs to honor their commitments to assist in the operation and probably, will have them filter their way through here throughout the campaign. That is a real accomplishment. Maybe Ibn Saud could do it, but I have my doubts, and besides, Ibn Saud's strength is on the other side of the Arab Peninsula. The Hashemites are where you can use them. They are probably the better bet."

"You've given me something to think about," came the reply. "Anything more?"

"Yes," I responded. "Faisal knows the terrain, and I don't think many other people would have chosen this stretch of hills and rough places for a defensive war. For several days, I have ridden through it, hunting for vantage points from which I could observe the fighting. The selection of the site for an area to defend shows a real understanding of warfare. I think Faisal does know what the war is all about."

"You have ridden through it?" came the disbelieving query. "How did you do that? On horseback?"

"No," I replied, "On camel. I had my two outriders with me for protection. One can't be too careful in these places."

"So the desert robes you wear do not just show with you then?" said the officer.

"Well, they do make me appear 'desert-savvy,' I will admit," I responded, "but they are also very, very practical."

We did not have much to communicate after that, and he soon excused himself and left me standing by myself.

The following morning, I watched from a distance as the inspection team made a reconnoiter of the probable battlefield and discussed it among themselves afterward. Prince Faisal was with them and, near the end of the tour, signaled for me to join them. I rode over, and he came forward out of the group. He asked whether I had been on the Ottoman side at the siege of Kut. "I was a correspondent passing through that area last December," I said. I have never 'fought' with the Ottomans, even as I have never 'fought' for the Arabs. I am an American and a journalist and, therefore, do not fight for anyone."

"Did you meet Captain Lawrence during that trip?" he asked.

"Yes, I did, Your Grace, I replied, "He was with a group of English officers waiting to go into a meeting with some Ottoman officers who were talking about getting a besieged English force out of that city. We did not speak, as I was on my way south to Basra at the time since I had been reassigned to the Cairo office of my newspaper." It was not quite an accurate rendition of what happened, but it was close enough to the truth to handle this small crisis.

"The captain wondered whether it was you that he saw there," said the Prince. "So, it was?"

"Yes," I responded. He said nothing more but turned and rode to catch up with the rest of the group. I briefly wondered whether my days in the camp were over, but reasoned that, if he was willing to have paroled officers from the Ottomans in camp, my case was minuscule in comparison. It was not worth the bother of doing something. Besides that, I knew he liked my reporting and would not willy-nilly put an end to that. He would realize that getting good press was not always easy, so why jeopardize what he has?

That afternoon, there was an assembly to greet the British inspection team, and all the British officers wore their uniforms except Captain Lawrence, who appeared on a camel wearing the wedding robes of a bedouin groom. The camp erupted in cheers as he appeared, and a great fuss was made over him. He spent some time with groups of Arab fighters who all regarded him as a great fighter and hero. I could not but wonder whether my earlier conversation with the British commander might have played a role in the selection of Lawrence's wardrobe on that occasion.

The following morning, as the inspection team was about to depart, Captain Lawrence came to my tent. He said, "I did not mean to put you on the spot yesterday, but it inadvertently came out that you and I might have been in Baghdad about the same time. The prince wondered why you were there. I think you straightened it out with him, didn't you?"

"I think so," I answered, "But then there was little to straighten out, as I was there as a reporter. I did my job and moved on. There is no reason for anyone to think otherwise of me, so I do not mind explaining it. Are you satisfied?"

"Yes, of course," he answered. "I never had any doubts. On another subject, you were there when I rode the camel into the camp to please my supporters," he said. "I only wished I wore desert robes as you do and rode a camel with the ease you do. How did you master those things?"

"Long practice," I guess. "I was out here in 1913 and have not left since then, so one masters many things in that period. I use trains when I can, but they are not always available to the places I need to go."

We shook hands, and he departed.

When the Ottomans finally came, they were cautious and moved slowly into the nasty terrain. Their commanders were careful to clear areas slowly and not to be caught in ravines and cul de sacs. What would have taken them a day ordinarily now took them a week. They cleared areas ahead of them slowly, using artillery when they felt they had to and never allowing the Arabs to lure them into traps. Whenever the Arabs congregated for an attack, the Ottomans dispersed the gathering with artillery, and they kept persistent pressure on the front.

But the Arabs effectively surrounded the Ottoman force and pecked at it from the sides, rear, and front. The long supply line back to Madinah was a special target, and after losing several wagons to the Arab raiders, the Ottomans armed the small caravans with rifles and, occasionally, with machine guns. Resupply went on, even though there were frustrations in getting the materials through. No one went hungry, and there was always plenty of ammunition. But tension and frustration rose with the difficulty of the attack over such wretched terrain.

But an army on the march, particularly one that is harassed, suffers from health issues and morale breakdown, and so it was with this Ottoman force. By the time the Ottomans were halfway through the rough terrain, the wagons returning to Madinah were carrying back increasing numbers of the sick along with limited numbers of wounded. Attrition was apparent, and the law of military conservation was at work as well, where units were being eroded of their strength.

During this period, I stayed relatively close to the front and, using field glasses, watched the relentless advance. I used some of the vantage points I had discovered earlier, but I found others as well. I had to move often, simply to gather enough information about the advance to write meaningful stories. I would get out to the 'line of resistance' early–about six a.m.– as the days were getting shorter as autumn wore on. I would move two or three times during the day and return at about six p.m. Twelve-hour days were a snap after the grueling regimen of Gallipoli. Well, not really!

I went alone most of the time, but sometimes, I went with an officer or a group of enlisted men with definite reconnaissance goals in mind and stayed with them until our purposes took us in different directions. I drank sparingly and ate lightly. My guards did not go with me. After all, their contracts did not specify that they should take part in warfare. But they were always concerned about me, and they would meet me as I came out of the combat zone. They accompanied me back to camp, where there was nearly always a meal awaiting me.

Yanbu itself was not too far away, so I sent reports three times a week but seldom received any instructions during the entire campaign. I was captured once when I was spotted by an Ottoman scout who directed a rifle squad to encircle me. I ceased wearing desert robes when I no longer rode my camel, so I was wearing tan pants and a cargo shirt with a floppy sun hat. In other words, I was not wearing anything that could be called a uniform, but I was close enough to a uniform that the Ottomans who took me decided I belonged to some enemy force, probably the Australians.

I was not roughly treated, and no one asked who I was as they moved me quickly back behind their lines. Then, a sergeant said to me in broken Arabic, "Who are you?"

I replied in Turkic, "I am a war correspondent. Please take me to an officer so I can show him my papers."

The sergeant disappeared and, after a short time returned with a major. The major said, "If you are a correspondent, you have papers. Let me see them." I passed them over, and he said, "Martin Mintz of the *Tribune*. Why are you with the Arab rebels?

"Just a convenience," I said. "For the first two years, I was with the Ottomans, but since January of this year, I have been in another zone where the British operate, so I have been permitted by them. The Arab rebels, as you call them, are the British allies, so I can operate here."

"What is your country?" he asked.

"American," I answered. "See on the form it is marked USA for the United States of America."

"America is not in the war, I think," he said.

"That's right. It remains neutral and has relations with the Ottomans."

"Does it have relations with the Arab rebels?" he asked.

"No, I don't think so, but regards this territory as disputed between Ottomans and Great Britain, I think." I shrugged my shoulders.

"Why do you speak Turkic so well? Are you a spy?"

"Because I lived in Constantinople for over a year," I patiently answered, "No, I am not a spy, but a newspaper reporter."

He took me to a covered wagon drawn by two horses that reminded me of a Conestoga wagon from Western movies. He disappeared inside and then called for me to join him. Inside, in the light of a kerosene lantern, sat a colonel with his arm in a sling. The colonel said, "We don't see many correspondents around here. There were some at Gallipoli, I remember. Did you know any of them." he asked.

"I was one of them," I responded. "My God, what a campaign! I went in right after the invasion occurred and stayed there until the Australians left."

So we talked for about fifteen minutes about the Gallipoli campaign, and then he said, "It was nice to meet a fellow survivor of the Gallipoli campaign, and, under better circumstances, I would invite you to stay for supper, but food is rather short these days. Perhaps you will have better luck on the Arab side. The sergeant outside will see that you get back to the front lines. Be careful and do not get shot running across to the Arabs. O yes, better move back because we're about to start an offensive." He laughed. "Tell the Arabs that in any case. It may make them scurry around for a while."

I passed through the lines without difficulty and went back to meet my security guards right on time. It was as if I had not been gone at all. After eating, I went to Prince Faisal's tent and was admitted to him without any question. I told him about being captured and passed on the information, probably fake, that an attack was imminent." He agreed it was probably a fake report but wanted to be on guard, just in case. As it turned out, the attack did occur in one sector of the battlefield but was not anywhere as serious as the colonel had made it out to be.

I continued my observation of the Ottoman attempts to take the wasteland with minimal casualties. I also saw the Arab efforts to change tactics from cavalry charges over to static defense and operations on foot. It was a challenge for both sides, and each suffered setbacks as they proceeded with tactics with which they were not always familiar. There was one day that was particularly costly for Prince Faysal, for example. On that occasion, an opportunity for a horse charge was possible along an old road where the Ottomans had placed considerable equipment and troop replacements. It was not well protected, nor was it organized. Moreover, it was open from one side to the open countryside where an Arab horse charge might be possible.

Faisal's military staff noticed it and decided to attack almost immediately. Faisal's new advisers from the paroled Arabs wanted one of their number to have command, but Faisal believed that such a charge would be better left in the hands of a bedouin chieftain who knew about quick charges and immediate withdrawals. He named Tariq al-Aziz, a 54-year-old leader of a prominent clan, to head the operation. Not only was his pedigree right, but he was the presumptive nominee for the position of governor in the area where the battle was taking place. It only lacked Sharif Hussein's signature for the governor's warrant to become final, and the courier carrying that warrant was on its way to Mecca.

Tariq knew his stuff and organized a swift attack that struck with great surprise. Enemy troops were quickly driven off, and the supplies that were located alongside the road in great abundance were set on fire, mangled, or otherwise made unusable. It would set the Ottomans back by two weeks to replace it all. For good measure, Tariq pursued the retreating Ottomans and forced a sizeable skirmish. Over a hundred highly trained Ottoman infantrymen were killed, and another fifty were taken captive, all at a loss of only ten Arab fighters.

Unfortunately, one of those lost was Tariq himself, who, in the spirit of great bedouin leaders, led the final charge against the cornered Ottomans. He was cut down by a machine gun that had just been set up as a last-ditch effort to stop the Arab attack. Tariq's body was brought out by his youngest son. The victory was highly celebrated in the Arab camp that night, and Tariq was accorded great adulation and high praise.

I went into the battle on a borrowed horse and saw most of what happened. There were huge bonfires from the gasoline, oil, and lubricants. There were dead bodies from the skirmishes, and there were the pell-mell advances of the Arabs as they tried to keep the Ottomans from establishing lines of defense, which everyone in the battle knew would change the battle over to an advantage for the Ottomans. I saw Tariq lead the charge that killed him and admired him for his bravery, but somehow, I felt in my insides that his charge would take his life. When he fell from the saddle mortally wounded, my heart sank.

But the results were just short of catastrophic politically, although the impact was to play its way out over months, rather than immediately. Tariq was succeeded by his oldest son as head of the family, so his two sons stayed in camp. However, Tariq was succeeded in his clan by his older brother, who had quarreled with Prince Abdullah, the brother of Faisal, sometime in the past and took a vow at that time to have nothing more to do with the Hashemites, but rather to support Amir Ibn Sa'ud. When he heard of his brother's death at Yanbu, he immediately withdrew the fighters who had accompanied Tariq. Twenty prime fighters left when the order came, which was not a great setback, but it portended another shift in Arab politics away from the Hashemites over to Ibn Saud.

Faisal was aware of the consequences and tried to distract attention from the political loss. A young warrior named Yunus had distinguished himself in the same battle, and Faisal rewarded him by giving his father the governorship that would have gone to Tariq. The man was not as renowned or as capable as Tariq but was still respected and, with his son's pizzazz, would probably make a worthy ruler of a frontier area. To sweeten the deal, Yunus was immediately betrothed to the daughter of one of Faisal's cousins, giving the family entree to the Hashemite family. The move was popular, as a hero was being honored, and the steadfastness of the hero's father was honored as well. But it was somewhat thin compensation for the costly loss of Tariq al-Aziz.

On the Ottoman side of the line, the commanders of the various units were not idle, and they were coping with the terrain in their own way. If the rough country hindered the movement of their heavy weapons and motorized vehicles, then the Ottomans had enough skill to build a road to allow normal movement. The road was begun shortly after the arrival of the main force and about two hundred Ottoman enlisted men of the engineers detachment went at the task methodically. Considering that they were operating close to enemy lines and snipers disrupted operations from time to time, they made good progress, about a mile a week.

There was an old, somewhat disguised trail along one side of the battlefield that ran along a gully that my camel was able to traverse. About once a week, I made the trip to check on the progress of the road. It was dangerous, as Ottoman units sometimes crossed the gully, and one could be fired on if he came upon an Ottoman unit without warning. But I was careful and only had two or three close calls. Usually, it was as easy as a hike through the woods near Grandfather Mountain in North Carolina on a lazy summer day.

Mostly, the work on the road was done by hand, that is, with pickaxes, shovels, and wheelbarrows, although later, some small trucks were used for hauling. The earth was first smoothed, with small growths taken out of it and roots removed. Fill from the neighboring landscape was used plentifully, and the new roadbed was several centimeters higher than the surrounding area, with a slight crown in the middle of the road. It was raked repeatedly, pounded down, and made stable. Sometimes, fires would be lit at night so that work could go on until midnight.

Certainly, the road was a boon for vehicles, especially artillery wagons, but the infantry also found movement easier along the road and were able to rotate troops with minimum difficulty. As I watched the road progress, I could almost calculate the day the campaign would come to its crucial battles.

Finally, after nearly two months, the Ottomans were nearly through the wasteland, and with one more push, it was obvious that they could break out. Then, they would be able to fight on level ground with room to bring their heavy weapons and trained formations to play. It seemed that the day of reckoning for the Arabs was at hand. But just as I had predicted, the British brought gunships to Yanbu and began to bombard the area where the Ottomans were likely to break out. At night, the ships played their spotlights on the terrain as well, indicating that any attempt to pass that point would be defended.

Everyone in both camps was aware that a big battle was at hand. New trench lines were dug, what artillery the Arabs had was brought forward, and Arab contingents prepared for all-out attacks against the Ottomans. I had moved my tent back to the edges of Yanbu, and my guards were prepared to move into the city the following day. The mood in the Arab camp was one of high excitement, knowing that a great battle was at hand, in which the decision could go either way.

But the following morning, no attack came, and then the second day came, and still no attack was made. Then, Arab raiders came in from the rear and reported a general Ottoman withdrawal in the direction of Madinah. All day long, reports came in about the withdrawal. Faisal did not pursue it but sent scouts to watch the withdrawal proceed. He then declared victory and ordered a day of celebration.

Return to Alexandria

I filed a report that evening but received no answer from Emil. I wondered all night–between the retorts of the Arabs shooting in the air in celebration–just how long it would be before Emil ordered me to another zone of conflict. So, the following morning, I went to the telegraph office to see whether a message had come in overnight. It had, but it was not what I expected. It read:

marty stop great news ottoman withdrawal stop your story superb stop serious matter stop amelia hurt in caravan trip to Yanbu stop marauders attack beaten off by guards stop amelia has head wound broken leg body contusions stop amelia now on ship to port said stop pay off guards stop return to egypt via ship soonest stop emile

I did dismiss the guards, and they and the tent boy were happy with the gratuity I gave them. All three were delighted about their transportation arrangements, which would return them to Mecca via ship. They had never been on a ship before and regarded it as a great adventure they could tell their families. I went to say goodbye to Prince Faisal, but he had departed for Mecca the previous evening, so I left him a message saying goodbye.

There were no ships due for passage to Egypt for at least a fortnight, but I found a windjammer that was headed to the Mediterranean that agreed to take me to the Egyptian coast near Port Said for the normal fare on a regular tramp steamer. The only difference was that I would be let off somewhere on the coastline away from customs officials. Any difficulties with government agents seemed inconsequential to finding needed transportation. I paid the fee and brought my baggage on board immediately. We sailed shortly afterwards.

Chapter 5
Home Leave

Hospital Recovery

I was in Port Said within three days. When I arrived, I called the Alexandria office and was told that Amelia was in the Mother of Mercy Hospital. The office secretary told me I should go there, as Amelia was insistent on seeing me as soon as I arrived.

I went to the hospital expecting the worst and saw immediately it was as bad as I had expected. She was bruised about the face and on her arms, she moved very carefully as she shifted her position in bed, so I knew her torso wounds were bothering her. Her leg was in a cast and elevated. She seemed to be in pain by the sour look on her face. When she saw me, her face lit up and she said, "Thank God you are here. Now I can sleep in peace. I've been worried about you and was afraid the brigands would get you too."

Before I could reply, a doctor came into the room, looked at me, and said, "Sir, you look in bad shape. Your color is bad, you are emaciated, and you look like you are on your last legs." He examined me and ordered me to bed when they began giving me saline solution intravenously and a series of shots. They gave me something to knock me out because I did not wake up until the following morning.

I was given a non-salt breakfast, which almost made me vomit. Then, they gave me a battery of tests, beginning with a urinalysis, a stool sample, and a complete examination of my body. I was not finished with their prodding, poking, and other forms of torture until after lunch. But for lunch, the diet changed, and I was given a good portion of red meat, well cooked and flavored, along with cooked green beans with butter on them, but no fat back. The food made me feel better.

Early in the afternoon, the doctor who had admitted me came by with a chart and told me all the ailments I was experiencing. "You have intestinal worms, which we will go after beginning tomorrow," he said. "Your blood pressure is low, but we probably can get that back up with some healthy food. You are about to get beriberi, so we will give you lots of fruit juices to drink. You have lots of bites and scratches, many of them infected, so we will treat them with ointments. They should heal within the week. Your weight is down and needs a good strong diet of protein and carbohydrates to build it back up again, but it must be done slowly."

He paused and said, "We want you to stay a week in the hospital so we can take care of those worms. You need the rest, in any case, to bring you back to normalcy. However, we want you to be happy, so I am acceding to your wife's request that you share a room. I cannot let you have a bed together, although your wife has suggested that. I do not want you contaminating one another. In any case, if you both behave yourselves, you can leave about a week from now, and you can sleep together wherever you go after that.

He said, "I understand you are both international correspondents and have been in the field for long periods, nearly a year this time, so I understand the poor health you both are experiencing now. I have already spoken with your supervisor who is alarmed at your condition, and I have recommended that you be given at least three months recuperation leave. He agrees with me and says he will make it happen."

That afternoon, they wheeled my bed into Emmy's room. She was asleep when they did it, so I simply lay there and looked at her. God, how I had missed her. I was so happy to be back with her again.

Suddenly, she was awake and looked over at me. "Hi honey," she said in kind of a whisper, "They say you can stay only if we both behave ourselves. If we are found sleeping together, one of us gets kicked out. Talk about killjoys, but what can you expect from a Catholic hospital?" Then she put her hand over her mouth mischievously and looked around to make sure a 'sister' had not overheard her cutting remark about Catholics."

Later that day, Emmy told me about her ordeal near Jiddah. The caravan she was with was not a large one, only about twenty-five people, probably only ten or twelve actual patrons. Emmy said that, at the end of the first day, one of her guards told her that the caravan was being shadowed by a group of several riders. He expected that there might be an attempt against the caravan to take valuables from the baggage and the patrons. The guard warned her to keep her camel close to the main group of riders to avoid being a single target. She said she was aware of the dangers but probably was a bit overconfident because of her long exposure to desert life.

The raid had come unexpectedly. When it happened, Emmy said she had her camel in close to the main column, with her two guards riding close by. In the first rush, two brigands had grabbed the reins of her camel, while two confederates had attacked her guards. She had been dragged off her camel when her leg was broken, and she suffered a concussion when she hit the earth, landing on her head. The brigands had dragged her away to a horse nearby, where they tried to throw her across it and take her away. Her two security guards, --who had first to disable the two thugs who had attacked them– had rushed to her, throwing her captives aside and taking her into the scrubland through which the caravan was passing. The guards had gotten their rifles out and shot at the brigands as they attempted to close in on them again. Emmy herself was in a daze, but there were lucid moments when she knew what was happening.

The bravery of the guards precipitated action by others in the caravan, who put up a fierce fight against the marauders and kept them from taking more prisoners. Fortunately, the bandits were driven off with some effort. The melee lasted about half an hour. Two of the attackers were killed, but most fled, taking several wounded members with them. Two other women were in the same sort of condition Amelia was in, so it was decided to turn the caravan around and return to Jiddah. Moreover, most of the ammunition was gone, so any further travel would have put everyone at risk in the event of another attack.

Emmy was very groggy for over a day, but by the second day, she was lucid again. By this time, however, she was no longer operating on adrenaline, and, as none of her wounds had been treated and her broken leg had not been set, she was in misery. She was transported in a cart, which jostled a lot, agitating the leg a great deal. Further, her experience filled her with great dread, and each time something appeared on the horizon, she thought it was the brigands returning. She said she cried a lot, as did the other injured women. It was an experience that no one in the group ever wanted to have repeated because they felt so abused and violated.

At Jiddah, the pilgrimage clinic diagnosed her, cleaned up her abrasions, set her broken leg, and gave her some painkillers. The two guards who had rescued her came to see her, and she thanked them, although that occasion was lost in the fog of medical treatment that was occurring at the time. The Javanese agent also came to her and said he had checked in all her equipment and billed the *Tribune* for all her costs, including the clinic stay. He had booked passage for her on a ship leaving the following day for Port Said. He asked how much she wanted to give the guards and boy as gratuity, and she named a price. The agent said, add a zero, and it will be more than enough. "After all, they saved your life." She agreed.

Our hospital stays went quietly and without incident. Emmy and I did not talk much, largely because we were both full of medicines that made us sleepy. The swelling in Emmy's leg went down, so she was able to walk with a small cast and some crutches. I left with some de-worming medicine to use for another month. We were invited to Emile's to stay, but we chose the hotel the firm offered us so that we could finally sleep with one another the way we wanted to.

Three days after that, a representative from the home office of the *Tribune* arrived and, with Emile, came to see us. After spending some time asking us how we felt, the representative said, "We have never had reporters who consistently turn in such excellent copy–always fresh, relevant, and readable. We thought it would go on forever, but this incident has indicated that it will not. Both of you have been in the field too long. It's time you both took a long break. The doctors are recommending three to six months, so we are working on a scheme to get you back to the USA for home leave and, perhaps, some time there working on a book signing or speaking tour. We will not let you return to work until one of our doctors signs off on your health.

I have brought tickets for you to leave on the Ionian Princess to Lisbon for a week from today and from Lisbon to New York after that. You both should be able to travel by then. You will have a stateroom on both voyages. I think you will be comfortable with those arrangements."

I assured him it would be. Emmy, with tears in her eyes, merely nodded.

Later that day, I indulged myself by eating a bowl of custard that I had discovered on the room service menu. Emmy had been sitting at the window with her leg braced on the sill, looking out at the passing scene. She seemed deep in thought. Then, without turning, she asked me to be serious instead of making jokes all the time to cheer her up. "Sure," I said, "why not?" I put on a sober face.

She said, "Did you notice that in the hospital we were referred to as husband and wife and that, even here in the hotel, people see us that way? In Ta'if, when you were gone, the other women all referred to you as my husband. What does that tell you, Marty?"

I did not answer because I felt she was about to propose to me. I wanted to see whether she would go through with it. Emmy takes charge when she is called on to do so, and I wondered whether she would feel she had to in this case. I had a feeling she would merely set up the situation and expect me to perform the role of the male who does the actual proposing. But I was wrong; she decided to finish the task herself, even if her wording was not very eloquent. She said, "Well, you're suddenly tongue-tied, which is a rarity, so I'll answer the question for you. It tells us that we ought to be married, dummy!"

"Yes, of course," I answered as calmly as I could. My heart was racing, and my mouth was dry. "Do you want to do it here in Alexandria or wait until we get home?"

She said, "If we were going back into the field, I would say we should get married now, here in Alexandria. But we are going back to the USA, so we may as well let the relatives enjoy themselves celebrating the event. Don't you think so?"

"You're right, of course," I answered. "Aunt Bea would never forgive me if I didn't get married where she could drink some highballs and tell dirty jokes. For us, it does not make any difference since we've been together for the past year when we have the opportunity."

I bought Amelia an engagement ring in the great Alexandria bazaar, with the help of Emile and his wife, as they understood jewelry and the costs of different kinds of stones. We settled on a yellow topaz ring circled with petit diamonds, which made a very striking engagement ring. We also selected a diamond wedding ring with topaz edging that would match the engagement ring. There was also a solid gold wedding band for me. I watched several months of work disappear when the rings were passed to us, and I paid for them. I guess Emile noticed a bit of reluctance on my face as I paid the bill. He said, "You can afford it, moneybags!" Amelia was so taken with her Topaz ring she began wearing it immediately.

Amelia called her mother that evening to relay the news of her engagement and to describe the ring. I called my home the next night and told Aunt Bea about my good fortune. She said, "It's about time. Good God, you've waited long enough. I can hardly wait to tell Janet Everett's mom; she'll have a conniption!" Then, after her moment of exhilaration, she impatiently said, "Now, put Amelia on the line so she can describe the engagement ring. You can't do that, as you would leave the important parts out."

2. The New York Adventure

We traveled to Lisbon with the Levantine steamer, 'Ionian Princess,' which catered in peacetime to wealthy tourists. Now, it handled all sorts of people connected with wartime activities, especially businessmen. We had a comfortable stateroom, but there were few activities on board, and the food service was limited to cafeteria-style cooking. Fortunately, the beds were comfortable, and as both of us were still recuperating, we spent a great deal of time sleeping and resting. We did catch up on our sex life, and its quality improved by the day, to the enjoyment of both of us.

The liner from Lisbon to New York was different, however. There was plenty of space as travel to and from Europe over that route was down. We had a cabin on the port side with two portholes, and we had a seat at the captain's table because we were international correspondents. The other members of the party at the captain's table were self-centered businessmen and their wives, who talked incessantly about the people they met and the importance of those people. After the first night, when some listened to our adventures, they paid little attention to Emmy and me, but the women did admire her engagement ring.

In New York, we checked in at an agency in Manhattan that was first on the list of things we were to do. The agency was in touch with the *Tribune* office in Paris. The agent said that there were preliminary plans for a speaking tour two months in the future. It looked like a four-week tour along the East Coast, where we would be featured as a speaking duo sharing the same time slot. We would be expected to give about twenty-five speeches during that time frame, which was about one a day, although in a few instances, two in a day was not impossible. The entrance fees would cover the costs of the trip, but we would receive our normal pay from the *Tribune* during the period. The *Tribune* would pick up all bills and all profits, although it was expected that this speaking tour would probably break even.

I was somewhat disappointed with the agency, as it seemed to have no one on its staff other than generalists. Most were schedulers, without knowing anything about the persons giving the talks or the subject matter involved. The people with whom we spoke, for example, knew where Cairo was and that the pyramids were there but had no inkling about places like the Hijaz, Baghdad, or even the Sinai. One person had, as a child, been on a trip with her mother's church group through the Holy Land but was quite sure that Constantinople was located very near to Jerusalem and that Christ had met the 'woman at the well' there. Still, the members of the agency staff were polite, competent, and friendly, so we said nothing about their lack of knowledge about the Middle East. But, then again, I could not find my way from Manhattan to Brooklyn, even with a subway map. Maybe we were even after all.

We also spent a morning at the *New York Times* office, where the agency had arranged a question-answer session with the reporters of the international staff. It lasted an hour. Given the reporting load of these people, both Emmy and I thought an hour was a big chunk out of their day. But those who attended were pleased to meet us, as they had all seen material from us that crossed their desks.

One woman writer said to me, "Your writing is hard to condense, as your theme runs across an entire article, so leaving out any part of it begins to destroy the essence of the mental picture you have drawn." Another said to Emmy, "I try always to include your photographs, as they amplify so well what you are writing about. I seldom see other writers who combine photo and description so well."

They asked difficult questions as well. "Wasn't it hard to go into war on a German battleship knowing that probably Americans did not much favor the Germans, even at that stage of the war? Would you do it today when we seem to be on the brink of war with them?" I said I did not give much thought to the problem at the beginning of the war, largely because I was unaware of what was occurring until the raid was suddenly undertaken without any warning to me ahead of time. I was a captive at that point and had little choice, but I do not remember feeling I had been victimized. I continued by saying, "Today, I probably would feel differently about it. Undoubtedly, I would not have gone on board the ship to start with, let alone go into battle with it."

The women reporters, some of whom were sympathetic to the suffragettes of the time, wanted to know how Emmy felt about the limited role of women in Arabic bedouin society. A woman reporter asked, "Here you were, a guest in an Arab home, and you were obliged to take on the role of a servant to the men at mealtimes. Didn't that bother you?"

"Somewhat," Emmy answered. "I come from a well-to-do family in South Carolina where such household duties are done by servants, often Negro women, but I had often, as a young woman, to help prepare food and serve it to the adult members of the family or guests. When I was in the Bedouin households, I simply saw myself in a similar situation and did not resent it, although I would have rather been doing something else. But to the larger picture, cultures differ, and theirs is different than ours, and so, if I want to find out about theirs, I must play a cooperative game, whether I like the hand I am dealt or not."

But, most of all, the staff members were intrigued by our relationship and the love story that was implicit in it. "You both always refer to the other in generous and kindly terms. "Is that real, or put on?"

Emmy answered that question. "Oh, it's real enough. We have always liked one another and tried to assist each other. Friendship has ripened into real love, I think, and what we reveal of our feelings towards one another in our writing is but a smidgeon to what we feel.

A person asked whether dating, courting, and so forth, had special difficulties in war zones and how we dealt with it.

Emmy answered that question by saying, "Well, we were both thrown together so much that there was almost nothing of a private nature we didn't know about one another. Familiarity takes away the mystery that men and women usually enjoy. I remember once in the Russian campaign, we stood guard over one another as we "did our business" in the woods when almost everything of the other person was in view. Maybe it should have stimulated us or discouraged us one way or the other, but it became normal and something one took for granted."

I said, "Courting was difficult because we were with other people a great deal of the time, and finding private moments and private space was rare. But probably most of all, in combat zones, one wants emotional stability, and to upset it with dating practices is not something either of us wanted to do. I think we let some good opportunities pass us because of that. Several times, we had dates with outsiders simply because the events were separate from our every day relationships and could be isolated and controlled. That might not have been possible with one another. Of course, it was different after we were engaged, when we did look for opportunities to be with one another. But I will say that we often 'turn off' our romantic impulses for the demands of work."

Emmy thought it a good time to announce our upcoming wedding, so she said, "We will be married within the month, just as soon as we get back to the Carolinas." There was clapping, hoots, and stamping of feet.

One male reporter blurted out, "Who proposed?"

I responded to that one. "Through our conversations from time to time, we both knew we were going to marry. The only question was "when." When we were given home leave this time, Emmy had that part of the conversation that made it all official. I thought she might leave the final words to me, but I guess she was afraid I would back off, so she completed the thought." Everyone laughed.

We met afterward individually with several editors and key reporters who treated us like visiting royalty. At lunch, we met with a general editor, a publisher, and an owner, two of whom were women. They were interested mostly in our reporting from Constantinople and wondered about the difficulty of working across borders where countries are fighting a war with one another. One editor asked whether I found it easier to place myself in the context of one country and view the war from that side or whether it was easier to try to view it from both sides.

"It's almost impossible to try to see a war from both sides since one loses context. One can only report from the perspective of where one's vantage point is. Sometimes, that allows an overall view where the positions of both sides are apparent, but most of the time, the view is that of the single side where one is located. That does not mean that one necessarily makes judgments that way, only that observations are made that way."

She had trouble following that line of analysis and thought it better to retain a neutral view whenever possible. I thought we were discussing different things, so I did not carry the conversation on that matter any further. She, too, seemed ready to leave the discussion behind.

Throughout all these meetings, most questions centered on the Armenian reports and the Western desert stories. Both allowed Amelia to say a great deal about her work as a reporter, which she seemed to enjoy, as it was seen as more important than her earlier work with photos, which was regarded as less serious and as 'fluff.' Wearing a cast helped her image, as she could refer to the dangers of traveling between assignments.

Our last stop in the building was at the personnel office where we were given tentative job offers, valid for the next three months. The offers would have increased our salaries by a third, along with a series of benefits that we did not enjoy with the *Tribune*. "There is no pressure on these offers," the personnel manager said, "We will not contact you about them, but we certainly hope you will contact us." We left, certainly elated at the kind of treatment we had been given that day.

When we arrived back at our hotel later that afternoon, two people were waiting to see us. The concierge had arranged for us to meet them separately in an interview room. We took them in turn. The first person was a representative of the U.S. Department of State, who invited us to visit the State Department in Washington to talk with the specialists working in the Middle East. He said he hoped that we would be able to work in such a meeting during our homestay. A few days later, I contacted the people planning our tour and told them about the invitation. They willingly agreed to include that speaking engagement in our itinerary.

The second person was a U.S. Army colonel who offered me a job as assistant military attaché in Cairo and Emmy a job as a civilian consultant to the political section of the Cairo embassy. He said that U.S. entry into the war was imminent and that "this would be a wonderful way to serve the U.S. in its hour of peril." I did not tell him I had been offered the same position the year before. In both cases, we said that we were only at the beginning of our homestay and that such matters would have to wait until after we had recuperated some. I had decided not to go into the military. I was not so sure I would enjoy it very much, largely because I would not have the freedom of movement that I think I have as a journalist, even though that may be a matter of perspective. But, since the United States was not yet in the war, it did not seem to me that I ought to be too concerned about the matter. When the time came, I could always choose the other path.

The Difficulties of Marriage Arrangements

At home in the Carolinas, we discovered that our plans to get married had brought to the fore some problems we had not anticipated. Foremost among them were some concerns by Emmy's family. First, there was the issue of religion, and second, there were some concerns about an inheritance problem. Religion should not have been a problem, as both families were Protestant, but I soon discovered that there are Protestants, and then there are Protestants. My family was Lutheran and belonged to the United Lutheran Church. We had been supporters of the educational efforts of the church for years, as well as belonging to a congregation in Hickory, North Carolina. Both my mother and my father belonged to the church, so there was no dispute in the family on that score.

In Emmy's family, it was not so clear-cut. Her father had belonged to the Church of Christ, and her mother was a member of the Calvary Baptist Church. Each thought the other was in gross religious error. The father believed fervently that music in church was anathema and only the human voice could "sing the praises of God," while her mother was more concerned about baptism by immersion and about being 'born again of the spirit.' Both regarded Lutherans as "Catholics in sheep's clothing" and to be avoided, if possible. The Lutherans regarded both the Baptists and Church of Christ followers as incomplete thinkers with little substance to offer their followers. They believed the less said to Baptists and Church of Christ members, the better.

I was not very much concerned with religion. When I was home, I went to church with my parents, who were serious about their religious obligations but very tolerant of the faith of others. Well, maybe that is overstated. Probably, they just did not care what others thought one way or the other. Tolerance did not enter the picture. As for me, I was generally moral and generally followed the teachings of the Lutheran Church, but I was in no way a fanatic about it, allowing exceptions to many issues as the occasion seemed to demand. Aunt Bea had another perspective. She said I lacked any scruples and was little better than a 'heathen,' although I am sure she meant that in jest, not reality.

Emmy had grown up hearing her parents quarrel incessantly over religious belief and practice and had hardened her heart to it. She was simply non-religious and found no reason to follow the dictates of any creed or religious way of life. She was kind, sympathetic, and compassionate, but those feelings did not rest on any religious tenet. Rather she regarded such behavior as necessary as a human being existing in a human society. When I first met her, I regarded her as 'naive' in religious matters, but later, when I got to know her, I found that her position was based on solid thinking. The 'naivete' I accused her of was certainly the result of not engaging in regular discussions defending her viewpoint, which made her position seem less sophisticated than that propounded by regular thinkers on the subject.

Emmy's mother was concerned about any offspring that might emerge from our upcoming marriage, and she cornered Emmy about the matter soon after we arrived to stay at her home in Fort Mill. Emmy was not ready for any such conversation and could only think that all the religious arguments she had loathed as a child were being thrown up before her again. She reacted strongly and said, "Don't go there, mother. I will not have your insistence that religion is only what you believe. I have no idea what religion our children will be if we have any at all. There is time enough to think about that matter when they are children. Don't raise this matter with me again, or I'll leave the house immediately."

Rose, of course, regarded this as a central issue in any marriage. She was determined that her daughter was not only going to answer the question but also that the answer would be favorable to her viewpoint. The child would be a Baptist!

Unfortunately, Aunt Bea and Rose had begun talking with one another, so the gist of this conversation passed over into the Mintz home in Hickory and caused an immediate reaction with my parents. Mother called me and wanted an assurance that our children would be raised as Lutherans. "I thought you were tolerant of other religions," I said, "That's what you have always said. Why are you protesting this issue now? There aren't any children anywhere on the horizon."

I gave the same warning that Emmy had given to her mother. "Lay off, or I'll not visit home." But the issue spread throughout both families. Emmy and I decided a clear statement had to be made that would resolve the issue and put an end to the bickering. Finally, we issued a statement and sent it to everyone invited to the wedding. It said:

Amelia and Martin announce that they regard their beliefs and preferences on religion as private and not subject to the debate of others. Their children, when they arrive, will have religious instruction when they are small in an acceptable Protestant Church and, afterward, will be free to make their own religious choices. This is also not subject to debate, and we two will break socially with anyone who attempts to make it an issue with either of us. The issue is closed.

Emmy's mother was the only one who tried to raise the issue again, but Emmy did not answer her; she merely shoved a copy of the announcement before her and pointed to the words "The issue is closed." The matter was not raised again during the time we were in the Carolinas, but mysteriously, religious tracts often found their way onto the bureau in Emmy's bedroom (we were not permitted to share the same bedroom before we were married), among the papers in Emmy's briefcase, or in the family car when we used it.

The second issue revolved around a gift of $50,000 in stock that would be awarded to Emmy when she was married, which was a bequest from her late grandfather. He had followed the protocol of the time when it was thought that a woman should not have such control and that all money should be placed in the name of a woman's husband. The letter from the attorney stated that this was the case and that the money would be turned over to me as Emmy's guardian. The matter was generally known in the Caruthers household, where there was concern that I would claim the money and spend it as I saw fit. When Emmy became aware of the matter, she told me about it, and as soon as we were married, the two of us went to the lawyer who controlled the bequest. On his advice, I accepted the stocks and then had them immediately transferred over to Emmy with my signature verifying the transfer. That matter was settled in less than half an hour, so it was no longer an issue.

An unforeseen third issue arose just after we arrived home and was debated during the same period as the religious membership of any prospective offspring. It involved national service, i.e., the draft, for all able-bodied adults in my age group. Most people kept quiet about it, but five people spread across the two families believed I should immediately enlist in the U.S. Army to fight against the 'godless Huns." I found the nomenclature of 'godless' rather 'droll' as I knew that Werner Ausenfeld was Lutheran and that Liman van Sanders had said he was Catholic. Most Germans I had met had a religious affiliation. But I still understood the gist of my family's concern: Germans were the upcoming national enemy, and I ought to respond to the call to arms. Immediately after sending my letter to the wedding guests about the religion of any future child Emmy and I might produce, I decided to tackle the 'military issue.'

I called the five critics on the phone and spoke with each for about twenty minutes. I pointed out that I had been to the draft board, where I had been told that my war correspondent duties would mean that the draft board would not call me so long as I stayed in that role. I then pointed out that I had been contacted twice with the request that I become the assistant to the military attaché in Cairo, but, on each occasion, was told that "I would be doing essentially what I was doing as a correspondent." That statement told me what I would be doing if I was drafted. On this basis, I decided that I did not need to enlist, as the military had no role for me other than what I was already doing. At this point in the conversation, three of the five wanted to drop the entire issue, but I would not let them. The other two still held to their conviction that I would be a 'shirker' if I did not go.

I then switched over to their situation. Four of the critics were men, one was a woman, and all were in their forties. I suggested to the four men that they consider going to the enlistment office and 'sign up' immediately so that they could get good assignments in the upcoming war. If they were turned down, I suggested that they relocate and take a job in a munitions plant to serve the war effort almost directly. No one thought I was being very practical, and three of the four wanted to drop the subject, saying that they understood, considering our conversation, that the matter of service was an individual choice. The fourth male said he found me rude and unreasonable and did not wish to speak to me again. I said he had just described what our future relationship was going to be.

That left only the woman critic, who was the widow of a veteran of the Spanish-American war. I suggested to her that she and I should visit her husband's grave, where I could place a wreath of flowers in his memory, and she could tell me some of her husband's reminiscences of war itself. (Actually, he had not seen war in Cuba as the woman implied but did get as far as a navy training camp in Pensacola, Florida). This softened the woman's heart, and we did what I proposed. When Emmy heard about the arrangement, she insisted on coming along as well. The woman had nothing more to say about my enlistment. By the time of the wedding, the entire issue was no longer even discussed–at least publicly.

With these three issues out of the way, wedding fever descended on both households, and we found we had necessarily to take part in the planning. Both families wanted the wedding festivities in their respective cities and were very adamant about the issue. Moreover, the wedding guest list was well over 500 people, with each side demanding that the other side limit the number of people it could invite. By careful coordination between us, Emmy and I gradually whittled down the size of the wedding list and agreed that there would be a wedding ceremony in Chimney Rock, where Amelia's grandfather was once a pastor. Only close friends and relatives would attend, and there would be a light reception after the ceremony. The following two nights, there would be large receptions in each of the two hometowns–Hickory and Fort Mill. The cost of the wedding ceremony would be footed by the bride and groom, while the two receptions were the responsibilities of the two families respectfully. Ultimately, about 100 people attended each of the two receptions.

Then came the problem of the wedding dress and the choice of the wedding party, which was easily resolved. Amelia acquiesced to her mother and wore her wedding dress with a few minor alterations. I wore a tuxedo that belonged to my father, although it was difficult to know whether he had worn it at his wedding. I did not ask, and he did not volunteer that information; he just gave me the outfit. I liked the scarlet cumberbund with fringes all along the front edging.

All these things take time to put into place, which was just as well. Emmy wanted to wait until the cast came off her leg, and she could walk easily again. It came off with a week to spare.

There were two incidents in the days preceding the wedding. At the first one, Emmy's stepfather confessed his love for his stepdaughter at an awkward time when many people were present, all of them relatives. He said he had made love to Emmy while they were alone together once in Cairo. The mother was upset about the confession, and Emmy tried to explain that there had been a kiss between them that had not led anywhere. Emmy said it was inconsequential, and she had forgotten about it. Besides was not her mother happy with her husband, who seemed devoted to her. Since Emmy was not sympathetic with him about the confession, the stepfather decided he had made a mistake and tried to recant his statement. After two hours, the mother searched out the daughter, and they made up, but the husband was in the doghouse for nearly a month until he had acceded to enough of his wife's demands that she decided to be friends with him again.

I was not privy to the incident itself and was in Hickory with my parents. Emmy called and told me about it. "I hope you are not jealous about it or think I have held something back."

I said, "Forget it toots. If Werner doesn't bother me with the crush you had on him, why should I be concerned with what you did with your stepdad before you and I were lovers?" It was probably the wrong thing to say. Maybe I should have left Werner out of the conversation, but I think my lack of denying that anything could have happened in Cairo with her prospective stepdad was the real issue. She was a little upset with me and then said. "Raising Werner at this moment was uncalled for. Why are you raising that issue now? And certainly, you don't think I would betray my mother?"

I replied, "Emmy, don't go making mountains out of molehills. You took me off guard with your information, and I responded without thinking. Everything is all right. You and I never talk about 'old loves,' and I do not wish to begin doing it now. Thanks for telling me what is going on, lest someone try to spring this on me at some unguarded moment, but I am not interested in the substance of it. Let's move on with our lives, okay?"

There was a silence on Emmy's part for a full ten seconds as she quickly thought her way through the mini-crisis that had emerged. I guess she felt the best way out of it was to accept my pleas for peace. "Okay," she answered, but the tone of her voice said she was unhappy with the outcome of the talk. She had expected a great deal more sympathy and understanding from me.

Remembering what I did of Aunt Bea's concerns at the time, I was not so sure that the incident with her stepdad had been as innocent as Emmy described it and that it might have been a sexual encounter. But I accepted Emmy's version as the best way out of an awkward family situation. But, even if my suspicions were correct, I felt that Emmy was a free, adult woman when she did it, in much the same way as I was free and adult when I visited Port Said. It was nothing I wanted to get upset about, and I wondered why others did.

As for Werner, Emmy had come to me as a lover after he left her the second time. She had said, at that time, that 'enough was enough' and that she had no intentions of becoming his lover ever again. That was a clear statement. Moreover, Emmy and I had dealt with the issue right after the two of us had become intimate when I was concerned that he would reenter her life. It had been a tough moment for me, and it was only Emmy's understanding that got me past it. Considering all that, I should not have even mentioned her love affair with him in this context. However, the incident did not die, as much as it morphed into a broader subject of both our relationships with other people. Another issue was to arise that would put the Werner incident into clearer perspective.

When I was in Hickory visiting my parents for a few days before the wedding, Janet Everett tried to contact me by phone, but all three times Aunt Bea answered when Janet called. Aunt Bea decided no good could come from such calls just before the wedding, and she found excuses not to call me to the phone. Janet said she only wanted to congratulate me. She also said that she wanted me to know that her marriage was strong and hoped that mine would emulate her own. That's Janet, I thought. She always gets conversation back to her and her view on life.

There was a second incident involving Janet, who met Emmy at the Belk Department store in Charlotte. Janet must have had a drink at lunch because she berated Emmy for taking away 'the light of my life,' and if Emmy didn't treat me right, she (Janet) would divorce her husband and give me the love that I deserved. No one knew about this incident except Emmy and her mom.

Unfortunately, this meeting came two days after the telephone conversation between Emmy and me about Werner and Emmy's stepdad. The incident took on a greater importance in Emmy's mind than it normally might have. The evening, Emmy called me and related what had happened and asked whether I still carried a torch for Janet.

I responded that I did not 'carry a torch for Janet' and that I had not been in touch with her since her letter over a year earlier when Janet announced her decision to get married. I also said that Janet was given to theatrics and that much of what she said was intended to 'blow off steam' and had little to do with reality. However, Emmy felt she had a cudgel to come back on me for my 'insensitivity' to the issue of Werner and her stepdad. She said she wanted my assurance that I was not in contact with Janet anymore, nor would I be in the future.

When she said that, I interpreted her remark to be that we were on the cusp of canceling the wedding unless I acquiesced. Moreover, we both knew what she was implying. There was a pause as I attempted to find an answer that would satisfy Emmy and defuse the threat to our upcoming nuptials. Finally, I said, "I have listened to Janet and her offbeat message since we were children, but I am tired of it. I am no longer in contact with her. I dated her and enjoyed being pals with her when we were younger, but as an adult, she developed obsessions about me that I did not share. I have never been intimate with her and never want to be."

Emmy was still hot with anger and self-righteousness. "Then why did you go to Hickory for a visit rather than staying in Fort Mill with me? You certainly knew you would run into her. You may have even planned some meetings."

"Emmy," I said. "I like your mother and Dan very much and enjoy talking with them, but they are not my flesh and blood, so I want to see and talk with my parents, my sister, and Aunt Bea some of the time. Also, Hickory is where I have lots of friends, other than Janet, who I want to see. Give me a break! Not everything revolves around Janet. Be reasonable!"

Emmy did not like the explanations, especially after she had given me an edict and wanted me to return to that subject. "Are you going to promise me you won't have anything to do with her in the future or not?"

There was an ultimatum there, but I chose to ignore it. "Emmy, dear, I have just said that I am not in contact with her, that I never have had sexual relations with her and never plan to. That ought to be enough of an assurance for you. I have nothing more to say on the subject."

"Fine," she answered. "When are you coming back to Fort Mill?"

"On Wednesday, as I planned," I answered.

"That's two days away. I thought, considering the conversation we just had, that you would come back tomorrow," she replied.

"The conversation had little to do with my schedule," I said, ignoring the broad hint that I needed to rush to her house to somehow make amends for our falling out. "Dad and I are going to Morgantown for fishing tomorrow, and the following morning, I am going over to Lenoir Rhyne College with Mom to see the new art exhibit. Its theme is 'mountain painting.' I think one or two of Mom's friends have paintings in the exhibition. I'll leave about one o'clock and be in Fort Mill about two hours later."

After the phone call, Aunt Bea, who had overheard the entire conversation, at least what I had said, remarked, "You handled that well enough. You have got to be assertive with a woman, or she'll run all over you."

I said, "You know, Aunt Bea, you really shouldn't listen to other's conversations. Mother would say it's not very polite."

Aunt Bea waved the objection aside, "Your mother says lots of things. Some of them, she believes. But honey, I am always concerned about you. You have become something special, and I'm very proud of you. If I listen in to your phone calls occasionally, indulge me. I'm the best friend you've got."

Emmy was not at home when I arrived, so I went out and chopped some wood for the fireplace, a job that had fallen to me since arriving from Europe. She was there for dinner but only spoke to me when it was necessary. After that, she avoided me for two days, obviously as a punishment for all aspects of the Janet affair, but I decided to tough it out. I did not know how to even begin to set things right when I was unsure what needed to be set right. She did not either. I simply waited for Emmy to get over her snit. She did, two days before the wedding. As I have said before, I can be patient, when it is in my interests to be so.

Everything came together, the wedding went off without a hitch, and the three receptions were held as expected with the usual amount of celebration, joy, and bad will among people who know each other too well. We eventually departed for a two-week honeymoon at Myrtle Beach, where we ate too many crab cakes, consumed too much seafood, and probably screwed too much. No one bothered us, and we returned to the home of Emmy's mother in Fort Mill, where we were making our residence until our speaking tour began.

Not so strangely, there were questions on both sides of our new family about the arrival of children. The women on both sides hinted rather broadly that Emmy might want to consider early pregnancy and then return home to begin the family. Emmy, to her credit, said nothing, except to her mother and mine, that early pregnancy was not in the offing and that she intended to remain a correspondent at least until the war was over. She asked them not to make any suggestions about pregnancy and children while we were in Fort Mill. They heeded her, and the issue was not discussed until we left again for the Middle East.

The Speaking Tour

The speaking tour was both exhilarating and boring. It was exhilarating to interact with audiences who were interested in what we had to say and wanted to engage us in conversation about our experiences in a faraway region of the world. It was boring in that hotels have a sameness, food on the road is repetitious, and travel agents are much the same. But the time went well enough, and both of us felt that the length of the tour was exactly right. The largest crowd was in Baltimore, Maryland, well over four hundred people, where we could only interact through a question-answer format. The most intimate was in Boston, Massachusetts, where only fifteen people were present because of a sudden sleet storm. There, we had an informal conversation in a round-table format.

The most frequently asked question was, 'Why did you decide to go there in the first place,' Emmy and I answered somewhat differently, of course. Another question that was an audience favorite was, 'What was your most unusual experience.' Emmy said it was talking with a grieving Armenian mother who had just discovered that her family had not survived a forced march by Turks from a neighboring village. I said it was helping village boys from Anatolia write their signatures on letters they had dictated to me so their mothers would know that they were still alive. Still, another question was, "What experience would you wish you hadn't been subject to." Emmy said it was being attacked in the open desert by marauders, while I said it was being caught in a firefight between contending forces in the last campaign near Yanbu.

We made time in the tour to incorporate an interview with White House and State Department staffers concerned with the Middle East. There were about 20 of them. They asked mostly questions about the future of the people in the Middle East. Emmy and I had never talked much about this problem with one another, so we were surprised when the answers we each gave were very much in accord with one another. Both of us were loath to see the Ottoman Empire dismantled because it had come so far with modernization and still had much to offer its population. But we recognized that it had done a poor job in recent years in handling its minority people who deserved a voice in their futures.

Further, we were not much in favor of an extension of colonialism to the area, perhaps reflecting our American views on the subject. Still, we believed that Great Britain could assist in guiding the Arabs, Armenians, and Kurds into new states of their own. When asked what kind of a role the US should play, we both responded that more US diplomats needed to be in the region and that US businesses could operate projects of mutual benefit to the countries of the region.

Before we left the State, Army, and Navy Building next to the White House, we shuttled through Austin Creel's office. Austin headed an agency devoted to the dissemination of U.S. propaganda, including the Middle East area. He was not there, but a senior member of the staff talked with us about coming to work for the agency. As we had other job offers, we said that now was not the time to talk about such matters.

The reviews on our tour were all positive and the attendance had been twice what had been projected. We were asked whether we wanted to extend it, but we begged off, saying we had enough. Several months later, we heard that we were to receive a bonus of 500 dollars apiece for our efforts, which came from the profits of the trip after all other expenses had been paid. We reckoned it a success.

We returned to the Carolinas and decided to stay with my parents, who had been miffed earlier when we stayed with Emmy's folks. Within forty-eight hours, we received a call from a physician's office in Charlotte, NC, saying that the *Tribune* wanted each of us to take a physical examination to decide whether we were fit enough to return to work. The tests noted that both of us still needed to put on a little more weight but that, otherwise, we were both healthy and ready to be returned to duty.

We knew immediately that there would be a call from Paris within ten days, asking us whether we wanted reassignment or whether we wanted to leave the firm. We had the other offers to consider, of course, but within two hours, we decided that since there was a war still going on in the Middle East, we wanted to return and see it through to the end. Afterward, we would leave journalism and try to get teaching jobs at universities in the Carolinas. The only caveat was about field assignments. We did not want them to be as extensive and as grueling as the ones we had been on in the western desert, in the Sinai, and in the Hijaz.

The call came as expected, and only it was not from Paris but from Emile in Alexandria, who first congratulated us on our marriage and then asked whether we intended to return. Emmy was on the phone with him, and she did the negotiating, what there was of it. She raised the matter of too much time in the field without a break, and he answered immediately that he, too, was concerned. He said that he would make sure that there was a break every two weeks and certainly no longer than three weeks. "It will not be much of a problem anymore, I think, Amelia," he said, "the fighting looks like it will be in Palestine and Syria in easily accessible areas. The grueling hardship areas that you and Marty experienced are gone, forever, I hope."

Emile said that two young Americans had taken our place but wanted reassignment to the Western Front in France so, as soon as we returned, they could leave. However, they never took on the extensive fieldwork that we had. Mostly, they gathered their stories from stringers who went up to the lines. Also, they got information from the British offices that issued statements about various matters. "I feel you could do a little more of that and put in some of your efforts from time to time, but I think the intensive fieldwork you did earlier is no longer needed to get good stories. But let us try it and see." All our concerns were swept aside once the new campaign started and appropriate times for rest and recuperation were ignored by all of us.

Emile also said Paris had decided that Emmy had earned the title of 'Senior International Correspondent,' that each of us was given a standard pay increase, and that we were each given a $1000 bonus for services rendered during the past year. We were granted two more weeks at home. So, I think we were substantially rewarded and made to feel that we were very appreciated.

British Army Interrogations

On the return to the Middle East, we caught an Italian liner in Baltimore that sailed through to Naples, which gave some variety to our cross-Atlantic voyages. We had a stateroom for ourselves but did not sit at the captain's table, as we did not have a following in Italian newspapers. Nonetheless, we had nice dinner companions in any case. Several had been to Beirut and other cities in Syria close by and had nice things to say about those experiences. One older man was a painter and longed for the time he could get back there to paint some more oils. "The people are so lovely, and the landscapes are exquisite," he said.

We spent two days in Naples and then caught a Levantine freighter with some passenger space, which was 'different' and proved to be a treat. There were no set hours for meals, and when one went to the room where food was served, every meal was made from scratch but made from fresh, good-tasting vegetables and loaves of bread. There was always someone different to talk to, and we used all our languages and, sometimes, reverted to simple sign language to make ourselves understood. We met the captain once, who was there for a tuna sandwich and coffee. He chatted with us for about fifteen minutes and, having finished his small meal, excused himself and went back to the bridge.

Later that afternoon, we were invited to visit the bridge, and we spent nearly two hours there watching the changing Mediterranean and chatting with the captain. The ship was headed straight for Cairo, so we and several other passengers were let off at the Alexandria harbor, with the boat that delivered us to the pier returning to the ship immediately. When I came to Alexandria with the windjammer, there were no customs or immigration officials, so we simply picked up our baggage and found our way to public transportation.

We checked into our hotel, but no messages were waiting for us. I tried to contact Emile, but he did not answer his phone, which meant he was probably out for the evening. We ate a leisurely meal in the dining room and then went to our room and went to bed early to enjoy ourselves. The newness of marriage had not worn off yet, so we enjoyed all the intimate moments we could, understanding that a return to the combat zone was going to bring a halt to such pleasures.

The following day, Emile did contact us. He invited us to lunch at a nice restaurant in the city, which featured separate rooms for private meetings, especially clandestine ones. I had heard about such eating arrangements somewhere in my travels while Emmy remembered the meal with the French foreign office group in Mecca. When we arrived, we were ushered into a spacious room with a large electric fan and elegant furniture. There were three men already there with Emile, two of them in British army uniforms with colonel insignias on them. We were introduced to one another, and then we sat down to eat when there was general conversation. Later, as coffee was served, the conversation switched over to the battles of Ta'if and Yanbu.

Over the next hour and a half, the three men broke down the various aspects of each encounter and asked for our input on nearly every feature of the action. It was analyzed in depth. In the end, we were asked what actions might have been undertaken that would have made any difference, particularly in the pace of gaining a victory.

In the case of Ta'if, Emmy noted that the battle was nearly not a battle at all but simply two armies trying to 'out-wait' each other until reinforcements could arrive. The arrival of the artillery should have been the culmination of the battle, in her opinion, except the problems of getting ammunition to the site were botched badly and prevented a swift end to the campaign. She felt the Ottoman commander had been let 'off the hook' by the Arabs. When the artillery was withdrawn, it was almost as though the Ottomans had won, even though they were bottled up in a foreign city. By that time, all efforts to quarantine the Ottomans had broken down, and they were trading freely with the locals and traveling about the city at will. She said she realized that bringing in British troops was impossible given other priorities, but perhaps Anglo-Indian troops might have been used, where many of them were Muslims who could have related to the Arabs. The examiners liked that suggestion.

In the case of Yanbu, I noted that the Arabs, with minimal British help, had fashioned a victory by their ingenuity and fortitude. The Ottomans had been worn down in rough country and forced to retreat before they could begin an invasion of the southern Hijaz, which would have jeopardized the Arab revolt. I did not think anything at all should have been done any differently. The examiners were surprised to hear that, especially since Captain Lawrence would have preferred more English involvement.

I responded by saying, "Undoubtedly, British assistance was necessary, but I believe Captain Lawrence did his part admirably, and the Royal Navy did its part with the gunboat. Perhaps more assistance might have helped, but I think, in retrospect, the job was accomplished exactly right." There was a little disgruntlement with my analysis, as all three examiners seemed to have already accepted Captain Lawrence's views on the subject.

We were thanked for our input, and we left immediately afterward for the *Tribune* office, where there were all sorts of reports to read concerning political conditions in the Middle East. By the time the afternoon was over, my eyes were nearly 'glassy' from so much reading. When we asked Emile when we would be leaving for the front, he said, "Not for a few days yet. Try to enjoy your preparation time. You'll soon be busy enough with the war."

Two days later, we were invited to British Army Headquarters, and when we got there, we met with the same three examiners. This time, Emile was not with us. The leader of the group said, "When we met earlier, we did not realize that you had been at Bir Tunis and Qatiyah. I hope you will spare us the time to talk about those battles as well. Your information the other day was invaluable, as we discovered when we checked it against other sources we had. Yours was far and away the more analytical and helpful for both battles.

We described what we saw of the battle at Bir Tunis but had to tell them something about our location during the battle, which was fascinating to all three. Through our comments, they saw aspects of the battle and preparation for it that were unknown to them. The part about hiring local camel herdsmen to transport animal foodstuffs and the care given to cavalry horses was new as well. Also, the descriptions of the battle itself, particularly as seen by Amelia, told them a great deal more about the battle than they had known earlier. The follow-on battle at Aqaqir was almost virgin ground for them because the reporting had been so haphazard, with almost no after-action reports finding their way to headquarters. Again, they asked for copies of our reports.

The battle at the Qatiyah railhead was different. Here, they had myriad reports, and what we had to add was minuscule, but they heard willingly what we added. Our analysis of that battle was heard but not found useful, but they were too polite to say so. Suddenly, they excused themselves and left. I thought we had seen the last of them, but two days later, they came to our office and questioned me about the battle of Gallipoli, saying that a view from the 'other side' was completely lacking in their files. They spent nearly three hours going over my memories of that battle. I gave them some copies of pages in my notebook, but most of my notes dealt with the attitudes of Ottoman soldiers. These examiners were interested in the actions of Commonwealth troop units, and my knowledge of them was scattered. Yet they gleaned what they could and thanked me profusely for bearing with them as they asked question after question.

Emmy and I were curious about all the battle reviews and asked Emile to clarify if he could. He said, "Well, I expect that General Allenby is unhappy with much of the reporting he is getting. He gets rosy reports that do not bear up under scrutiny, and he hates sycophants who only tell him what they think he wants to hear. He is looking for other sources of information than the official ones that he does not completely trust. You two are independent observers, not trying to cater to British authority. That probably has meaning for him."

"Somehow, I don't like the sound of all of that," I said. "Are we in danger of being co-opted into the British reporting system? If that happens, we can throw our usual reporting out the window, or we'll become just like the rest of the general's inadequate reporting system."

Emmy and Emile agreed with me, and Emile said, "I make a promise to both of you that I will fight hard to keep this from happening, and I know you will, too."

Emmy said, "If we are co-opted, I think the only sensible thing to do is resign and go home."

"If the general will let you do that," warned Emile. "After all, he has considerable power as commander-in-chief of His Majesty's forces in the Middle East." We all had other things to do, so our conversation broke up on that sour note, yet we knew that the episode was not yet finished.

Late that afternoon, Emile received word that an appointment had been made for Emile, Emmy, and me to meet with General Allenby at noon for a general discussion on 'reporting. Cucumber sandwiches and tea would be served. No clothing was designated.

Emile responded that we would attend and then told us about the invitation, or 'summons,' as I called it.

We arrived five minutes early but had to wait fifteen minutes before we were ushered into the general's office. He had with him a captain, who was introduced as a G-2 officer of the headquarters staff. His name was Alfred Ramsing, and he seemed to see the world as a parade passing in front of him as amusement. He spoke crisp, clear English with an Eton affectation, and it was clear by the way the general spoke to him throughout the meeting that the general found Alfred amusing and trustworthy. My first impression was one of distaste, and Emmy told me later that she felt he could not be trusted. Emile, on the other hand, said, "It takes all sorts of people to make up the world. Don't be so judgmental; he'll grow on you."

There was only one plate of sandwiches, so when the general took four slices and Ramsing three there were only three pieces left for us. Probably cucumbers were difficult to procure in this climate, I thought to myself.

The general went immediately to his reasons for bringing us in. "I would not have believed that civilians would have a good insight into warfare, and my experience in the Boer War seemed to justify that judgment. However, I find that here, in the Middle East, the reporters for the *Tribune* seem to have a special talent for analyzing what battles are all about and how they are fought. I am amazed on the one hand and jealous on the other, but above all, I want to gain from your observations. On the other hand, I do not want to interfere with what you are already doing so well."

I found that statement interesting and certainly flattering, and I expected, at the time, that Emmy had the same reaction. I found out later that she did. Both of us wondered how this was going to be accomplished. The general did not leave us in suspense. "There is no reason why you should not do your reporting as you always do and submit it to the censors as you always do, except you should leave it in two copies, with one uncensored copy to be forwarded to this office, which is a process our good Major Ramsing is going to define. Isn't that so, Captain?"

Ramsing, in his stiff upper lip style, merely answered, "Quite, general, quite! The censor can then review the other copy, go through the procedure he ordinarily follows, and make his changes according to the guidelines he follows. Do any of you see difficulty with that process."

Emile spoke for all of us when he said, "That's a reasonable approach, and I have no objections to providing an extra copy. It's a small inconvenience." Emmy and I nodded.

Ramsing took the conversation in another direction. "Your reporting often relies on special efforts to get to a zone where something is occurring, and it seems to me that you often expend great efforts to get there, which must detract from your reporting abilities. I think the western desert showed how great your efforts had to be to get to the proper locale to even see the battlefield. This complication should be addressed. The Palestine campaign is apt to be done on a fast-moving battlefront or, at least, on a front with several key battles going on at the same time. At headquarters, we would be aware of such things and would like to steer you in the proper direction. Do you have objections to that?"

I commented immediately. "If you mean you will direct us to stories you want rather than ones we want, I do object. If you see opportunities for us that would not ordinarily come our way, I have no objection."

The captain looked at me as if he were looking at a fly that had suddenly dared to land on his kitchen table while he had a fly swatter in his hand. But I could see him change over to regarding me as a person he had to accommodate. I immediately admired his ability to change his persona that quickly and effectively.

He said, "Excellent point, Martin, if I may call you by your first name. We will always have to be mindful of that, and now that you have raised it, I'm appropriately warned. But mostly, I think what we are concerned with is some event that is unfolding that is unknown to you but that you would cover if you knew it was occurring. It might be a parlay between enemy commanders, the storming of a citadel, or some such notable event."

Emmy entered the conversation. "Your clarification makes sense, Captain, and I have no difficulty with what you are trying to accomplish. After several years of trying to make sense of a campaign or a battle, it would be nice to have the input of someone more knowledgeable about the shaping of the battlefield than we ordinarily have. But I think my colleague Martin has hit on a sticking point that perhaps needs a little further clarification. That is, will you ever simply order us to go somewhere without explanation and expect to do so without comment? After all, we are non-combatants and do have our rights of refusal, even on the battlefield."

Emmy's audacity in disputing the right of a military person to order a non-combatant to do something brought the captain–and the general for that matter–up short. The objection struck at the very heart of the military command structure–that orders are always followed without exception and contradiction. "Compliance with orders is expected of correspondents, medical volunteers, and others when safety and pending military operations are contemplated, certainly," came the reply, "In this case I assure you that the reason for our recommendation that you do something we want to be done will always seek your willing acquiescence. If you say 'no' the matter will be closed with no retribution. Will that satisfy you?"

Emile answered for us, "Indeed, it does. I think you understand our concern and have addressed it properly. There remains only one matter that needs your attention, and I make it because I know your answer, but I want you to be aware that we are mindful of the matter as well. "Will you ever decide that the copy of the report we give you will ever be so disliked that this command will seek to have us change it?"

"Well, the report will go through the censorship process," the captain answered.

Emile said, "Of course, but I am talking about the future of the copy that comes to this headquarters. Will this headquarters, or any of its agents, try to get us to change that one?"

The general interrupted to say, "I don't see that there would ever be a necessity for doing that, but perhaps in some unforeseen circumstance, it might. My answer is 'no,' we will not do that."

"Good," said Emile. "We have taken enough of your time general, and you have given us good answers. We are always ready to be of service."

The captain accompanied us to the outer office when we exited and said, "You people are formidable and unafraid of authority. No wonder your reporting is always so good. Keep at it; I do not think the general wants that changed and will probably not interfere at all. I, on the other hand, may contact you from time to time, and I hope our meetings will be cordial." We shook hands and departed.

At the office, there was a note asking Emmy to call the same hospital where we had been treated. Thinking it was some follow-on study, she called immediately. Her call was transferred to the prisoner-patient section, where a clerk requested full identification. When Emmy had given it, was told that Major Werner Aussenfeld had been wounded in the chest and was recuperating after a difficult, but successful operation. He had given Emmy's name as a contact.

"What is the procedure for seeing him," Emmy asked.

The clerk answered, "You may see him if you wish, which may help him with his convalescence. But that is up to you. He is an enemy combatant, and you are not obligated to deal with him at all if you do not wish to. If you do wish to see him, you need to register with this office and have the permission of your supervisor or commanding officer if you are employed by the British or one of the colonial armies."

"I need to consult with my husband first," Emmy replied. I was standing nearby but did not understand what was being said on the other end of the line. She said to me, "Werner is in the hospital here with a lung wound. He listed me as a contact."

I was silent and so was she for nearly half a minute. "This is not good timing," she said. "We are newly married, and I do not want anything to upset our marriage or do anything that would call my loyalty to you into question. Even this call might be upsetting to you, so I am leery about proceeding with it at all." Most certainly she was remembering the discussions about close relations with others just before we were married. Werner's name had set that whole series of disputes into motion.

"Yet it is a problem that confronts you, and you must decide how to handle it," I said. "I don't think it's going to go away by ignoring it."

"I know that, but I want to wait until tomorrow morning to have time to think it through," she answered. "Will you be upset if I do that?"

I said, "I think that is wise. Your mind needs to play out the possible scenarios. You know I will be understanding as I can be, but there are real limits of course."

"Yes, I know that," she said.

We did not sleep together that night, as Emmy was wandering around a good part of the time, although I suppose she slept some on the divan in our anteroom. When I got up, she was already dressed. She said, "I have decided not to see Werner, but I am going to ask Emile to do that and find out whether there are things that need to be done for Werner. I will help him from a distance if need be, but as little as possible. I will ask Emile to be an intermediary and resolve whatever problems he can, but to make it clear that I will not nurse him or in any way be in contact with him."

"That's rather stern," I said. "Are you sure you want to be that distant? You are a compassionate person, and I don't want you blaming yourself later."

Emmy stamped her foot in impatience. "No, I am not a compassionate person at all! At least not in this case. He is using the wound as an excuse for getting in contact with me again and is not considerate of me or us at all. He needs to contact his wife and have her lavish her attention and love on him, not expect me to do it. I will not have a man who deserted me twice disrupt our marriage, which I hold sacred, and I will not under any circumstances jeopardize the happiness we have."

I held my hands out in surrender and said, "Whatever you say, love. I too do not want our marriage disrupted in any way and, if you think this is the way to handle this incident, I am all for what you propose. But I applaud you for talking it out with me so that we can both agree that the threat to our marriage has been "properly handled."

She pressed herself against my chest and held me for a moment. Then she said, "Now I am going to see Emile. I'll see you later at the office."

Emile is a good sort, and he willingly did what Emmy asked of him. Later in the day, he told Emmy that Werner was expected to recover with some loss of lung function and would undoubtedly be given a medical discharge from the German army. Werner had been disappointed that Emmy would not see him, but when he was informed that she had only recently married, said her reaction was understandable. He said there was no reason that Emile should visit him anymore.

After Emile reported back to us on his encounter with Werner, Emmy and I put the matter aside, although I thought about it off and on until we were once more on the Palestine front. I do not know how much Emmy thought about it, but I cannot imagine that she simply put the matter aside. I am sure she thought about it and probably all kinds of emotions rose in her over the matter. One does not have the love affairs she had with the man and not rue the outcome and even the possible future she might have had. But she hid it well from me, which was her intent in any case.

Some months later I was by myself for a period and the memory of the incident came back to me. In thinking about it I was struck by the defiant tone Emmy took, which was so unlike her behavior most of the time. After much thought, I concluded that she was answering me, when I had confessed my love for her at the American Club in Cairo, and she became aware of how serious I was about my love for her. On this occasion, she rejected a former lover and said, in no uncertain terms, "I love you, too, Marty, and here is proof of it." I got a lump in my throat, and my eyes started to well up when I understood, but I knew I could never tell her all this because it was something neither one of us could put into words.

After the breakout from Jerusalem, I saw a memo listing 'returned' prisoners and noted Werner's name on it. I destroyed it and did not even mention it to Emmy. Better to let sleeping dogs lie.

Chapter 6
The Palestine Offensive

The Battles of Beersheba and Gaza City

Military units have a pace, depending on the urgency of the situation. I remember the frenetic pulse of the Ottoman army as it moved into position to meet the expected Entente3 onslaught at Gallipoli. Also, there was the measured pace of the attacking Ottoman force at Yanbu, as it picked its way across the wilderness making sure there were no Arab traps that would turn the advantage to them. As well there was the Anzac advance on the Sanussi positions in the Western desert, which was deliberate and designed to not only win a victory, but to trap the rebels, so they would not escape and threaten elsewhere.

This was a prelude to my thoughts about my present situation, where I was traveling at a speed of about twenty-five miles an hour out of Egypt to the Palestinian border, where the British were building up forces and materials for an invasion that was designed–everyone knew it–that probably would knock the Ottomans out of the war. This effort too had a pace to it, which could be described as 'deliberate' and 'organized' but not overly hurried, lest something be overlooked. Even the correspondents–there were five of us–were part of the British concern for careful organization. We were issued uniforms, but no one told us whether they were required or not. They were without identifying patches and insignia except for the word 'correspondent' on the breast above the left pocket of most men's blouses. The outfits included floppy hats and hiking boots. There was

---

3 In this chapter it seems necessary to assign some common titles for the armies fighting on both sides. The Ottomans were fighting with the Central Powers of Germany, Italy, and Austro-Hungary. In the battles of the Palestine theater the Ottomans were commanded at key positions by German officers. On the other sides the British were part of the Entente Powers of Great Britain, Russia, and France (and later, the United States). In the Middle Eastern theater British officers had overall command, with the Australian, New Zealand and Indian armies fighting under British control. They are referred to jointly in this chapter as the "Commonwealth" forces.

no special uniform for women, so Emmy wore what the men did, although she employed a seamstress to make everything fit properly.

There was a captain of artillery assigned to see that we were taken to the staging area. There we would be assigned to specific units, all regiments, where we would get a taste of the war, but be clearly behind the lines and in minimal danger. All five of us had been in combat zones earlier, two on the Western front and one on the Russian front with Austria. Only Emmy and I were veterans of Middle Eastern fighting. The five of us had only recently met as a group and, while there was considerable respect shown to one another, we had not yet built a relationship where we could exchange information and insights with one another.

The captain, on the other hand, saw us as an unwelcome intrusion into his life. He had been on leave in Cairo, where he had drunk too much and met a licentious woman, so he was suffering from the effects of those experiences. Moreover, he was on the way back to his company, where his battalion commander awaited, who earlier had decided the captain lacked good command skills and frequently told him so. The captain dreaded the next week when he knew he would be berated, not once, but several times. Then, he had the misfortune of checking in from leave just as an officer was needed to accompany a group of non-combatants to the staging area. He regarded it as 'baby-sitting' and saw his charges as an undue burden thrust on him at an inopportune moment.

His initial meeting with us was not salutary. He roughly threw his duffel onto Emmy's camera bag, and she said with some indignation, "Captain, I have expensive cameras in my kit. I'd appreciate it if you did not throw your duffel onto it. The cameras are likely to be damaged and they are hard to replace out here!"

The captain said, with more than a little bit of annoyance in his voice, "If your baggage is so precious, then keep it out of my way." Then, to show his authority, he said, "That goes for all of you. You are not in your family's drawing room, but in a military depot, so act like it!"

Emmy, unfortunately, would not let it go. She said, "Captain, you've no reason to speak to us that way. We are non-combatants, not privates in your company, so keep that in mind. I'm sorry you drew the duty of seeing us to the assembly area, but then none of us had anything to do with your selection."

The captain grew red in the face, clearly annoyed at being called to account by a non-combatant, a woman at that, and was determined that his authority would not be challenged. He stepped to confront Emmy directly. Only I was faster and stepped between the two of them. The captain said, "Step aside!"

I said nothing, but neither did I step aside. One of the other three said, "Come on captain, let it go!" Another said, "Let's not ruin a good trip." The third one said, "Amelia please apologize to the captain. You have affronted him!"

Amelia took the advice of the last speaker and said, still standing behind me, "Captain, I am sorry to have caused you such stress. We have a long trip ahead of us. Can we not start again and try to be civil to one another? I will certainly try."

No one said anything for thirty seconds, and I could see the red begin to drain from the captain's face. I stepped aside, which left him and Emmy face to face. She said again, "Truly, I'm sorry."

The captain realized the situation he was in. If the incident was reported, he might well face military charges or, at the minimum, a severe tongue-lashing by some senior officer. He knew he had to back down. "Thank you, ma'am," he said, "It was thoughtless of me to dump my baggage on top of your camera bag. I certainly will be civil to all of you during the trip." He picked up his duffel and said, "If you will follow me, we'll see if we can find some room on this train that will give us some comfort during the trip north."

We found a boxcar that was partially loaded and spread ourselves out in it. The captain said hardly anything at all going north. The rest of the party was quiet as well. There were some brief conversations, but none of them lasted very long.

At the staging area, there was a sergeant major and two corporals to meet us and receive the five of us from the care of the captain. The captain simply ducked aside and was gone without a word to any of us. Neither did anyone try to search him out to say 'farewell.'

We were taken to Division headquarters where the sergeant major gathered us into a large tent marked 'Operations,' and gave us some 'do's' and 'don'ts.' 'Do find a trench' when alarms sound, 'don't interview anyone in combat.' Afterward, he took us to a mess tent and had us fed, and then, back at his tent, he sent us off with sergeants who had come from different units to collect us. Emmy and I were assigned to the same regimental headquarters, as we expected to be.

We were immediately ushered in to see the commanding colonel, who was an affable, tall man with reddish hair and beard. "I count my lucky stars that you two are joining us. You have been in this theater of operations for over a year and can be expected to understand what this upcoming campaign is all about. That makes my job easier, as I don't have to explain a lot about what the mission is. Since he had raised it, we expected him to tell us about the present mission. Instead, he asked about us. "Can you tell me what Ta'if was like?" he asked me.

"It was a siege, pure and simple," I responded. "We had to wait for a battery of Egyptian artillery to join us before any progress could be made. The Arabs had the Ottomans bottled up but couldn't finish the job."

"Were both of you there? I heard you were split up a good bit of the time," he said.

I continued. "Yes, I left to cover Yanbu to the north, where an Ottoman attack was planned, but it lost steam when it had to run a gauntlet of British gunboats. The Ottoman commander lost heart and retreated. Good thing, too, as the Hashemite forces were exhausted and had little ammunition left."

The colonel turned to Amelia and said, "Isn't it hard to get good photos in battle situations?"

She said, "It depends on what kind of shutter one has and the angle to the target of the photo. In the western desert, I had a hard time because I was often on a camel, but at Ta'if I was on level ground with good angles."

We were assigned to a tent with no floor but with two cots already in it. There was no room for much else, so we stowed our belongings under the cots. There was an orderly who looked after a group of tents, including ours, who was a grouch until we got to know him. He had a speech impediment and said little so that his infirmity would not be noticed. He slowly made friends with Emmy, who treated him like a younger brother.

A day after arrival, we attended a briefing for new officers which covered the state of the war in the Egyptian theater of operations. It laid stress on the past six months when the British forces, mostly Anzac and Anglo-Indian forces, had tried to drive the Ottomans out of Gaza but had fared badly in both instances. In the first attack the Australian cavalry had been successful in its initial attack on Gaza City but was withdrawn when the general's staff mistakenly calculated that the troopers would run out of water before the strike against the city was finished. The subsequent withdrawal left the troopers demoralized because they thought that victory was at hand. They were aggravated when they discovered they would have to do the exercise all over again.

The second attempt was even more disheartening than the first because the enemy knew when and where the attack was coming and closed off the point of attack successfully. Poison gas was used by the British and its allies, but winds dispersed it before it could be effective. The remainder of the operation was woefully unsuccessful. That debacle cost the theater commander, General Murray, and his chief subordinates their commands.

General Allenby, fresh off the Western Front in Flanders, was the replacement and realized immediately that the two failed attempts were due to poor staff work, inadequate location of supplies, such as water and ammunition, and a lack of coordination among field units

After arriving, General Allenby concentrated his initial effort on overcoming these shortcomings to assure that the next attempt would have better results. The briefing was intended to raise the morale of the staff being briefed and overcome the doldrums that had gripped the entire staging area after the last two failures.

The new plan called for a sweep of two divisions to capture nearby Beersheba and its water wells, to deny the wells to the enemy, and to gain their usage for Commonwealth forces. It was calculated that the attack on Beersheba would force the Ottoman units to retreat towards Jerusalem since retreating in that direction was its only option to link up with the central Ottoman force again.

After the action at Beersheba, the plan called for the capture of Gaza City, and if momentum was gained, then the expedition would move through the Judean hills towards Jerusalem. The plan seemed reasonable when it was presented, but questions from the officers attending the briefing suggested that German commanders would see through some of the assumptions made by Allied planners. There were fears that the enemy would stifle the attack before it started, as they had on the two previous occasions.

At this time, Captain Ramsing, the G-2 (Intelligence) officer whom we had met at General Allenby's headquarters, contacted us and came to talk over strategies. I had not liked him when we first met, but Emile had said he would grow on us. Fortunately, Emile was right, and we found him very knowledgeable about the campaign we were undertaking just then. He took a liking to us and spent more time with us than he needed to, considering the small errands he came about.

One day, he talked about the tactics that General Allenby wanted to put in place. "He is taking a lot of the experience from the Western Front," said Ramsing, "where they found that adding units piecemeal to forces already committed seldom worked at all, while coordination of units already engaged improved the performance tenfold. I would not have believed it, but the results here so far have been impressive. But the trenches of Flanders are closed in, while we have wider areas to cover, so we have yet to see whether that makes any difference."

"I would also add that the combination of German leadership and Ottoman fighting skills make a unique combination that may test the new theories of General Allenby," I added. "The first two Allied attacks on Gaza were repelled by the Ottomans under the leadership of German Colonel von Kessenstein, whose forte was combat operations. The present advance is being made by another German commander, General Falkenhayn who is far more experienced in strategic planning than in combat operations, so there probably will be a marked change in the Ottoman response to our attack."

Captain Ramsing laughed and then said, "I cannot agree with you. It doesn't matter which German general is in charge; the result against Allenby is going to be the same. He will whip them every time." I concluded that Captain Ramsing had a case of "hero worship," which might not hold up in actual combat operations.

"Maybe," I answered. "If Falkenhayn falters we are certain to see von Kessenstein in control again, who is accustomed to working with the Ottomans. I think the going will be tougher with him in charge. We'll see. I expect our good general Allenby has a learning curve ahead of him." Ramsing did not much like the remark but decided not to dispute me on the matter.

Emmy and I went forward with a motorized battalion and were in the third truck in line. She had a stand erected in the truck bed so she could shoot photos while we moved, which was an innovation for her. That cramped the other three of us who were assigned to the truck. The other two passengers were riflemen. No one complained, however. We all hung onto the sides of the truck as we moved speedily over rough terrain with zigzags, ditches, and potholes. At the beginning of the foray, we held our own with the cavalry unit on our right, which trotted most of the time and seemed to please the horses.

When the cavalry neared the water wells, the formation did not change at all, but the commander simply ordered an immediate charge and flew down towards the enemy guards near the wells. Instead of fighting at each well, as expected, the entire column leaped bunkers and other entrenched obstacles to encircle the entire area containing the wells. Adopting American Indian-style tactics,[4] they shot at the defenders from a moving circle of horses. The action was over within an hour, and, for their speed and heroics, the unit gained a reputation akin to the British light brigade at Balaclava during the Crimean War. It was estimated before the attack that most of the water wells would be destroyed in the action, but the suddenness of the onslaught was powerful enough that all of them were taken without damage.

During this action, our truck was parked behind a dune, and the infantrymen in it immediately formed up and attacked the nearest enemy emplacement, which looked mostly like a series of interconnected bunkers. Emmy and I hunted for an advantageous positions to watch the action, and we found one at the top of the dune where our truck was parked. I had to dig to make a revetement to protect us in case we should be fired on. It was a makeshift job, as I had no sandbags to strengthen the revetement. But no shots came our way all afternoon, probably because no fire came from our position, and the enemy did not regard us as a threat, even though we were visible to Ottoman gunners. We moved once when the battle flowed to another well beyond good vision.

We moved as carefully as we could across the battlefield, keeping in mind the infantry moves we had learned in the past year, and ended up in an Australian bunker that was engaged in a duel with an Ottoman bunker forty yards distant. While we were there, a machine gun team brought their weapon into the bunker and assembled it. After what seemed an eternity, the gun was finally made ready, and the gunner sprayed bullets into the enemy bunker, which ceased firing back almost immediately. It was outgunned. We watched as the Ottoman infantry slipped out the rear of their bunker and fled to another bunker fifty years further back.

Two men from our bunker were sent forward to make sure it was safe to move to the deserted bunker, and almost immediately, they sent

____

4 American Indian-style tactics. That is, fighting from a moving circle that surrounds the enemy, which contains the enemy, while making it difficult for the enemy to return fire against moving targets.

back an 'all clear' signal. That bunker was a small one, so Amelia and I did not go forward with the squad, but after a time, we, too, got the 'all clear' signal and moved up. It was crowded, but the view was good, and as it was starting to darken with nightfall, the green tracer bullets from the machine gun gave a clear view of the damage that the firing was doing to the next bunker in line.

We slept in place that night, and by two p.m. the next afternoon, the Ottomans began pulling back and left only a small rear guard, which surrendered when they ran out of ammunition. The Australian team we were with also were down to their last canister and, in another hour or so, would have had to withdraw themselves. As it was, Beersheba and its water wells came under Australian control.

After Beersheba was captured, our armored car made a wide sweep and came back to the original starting place in Gaza. There, we witnessed the tail end of a Commonwealth artillery barrage that had lasted all day and expended more shells than most barrages on the Western front did. It was designed to discourage the Ottoman forces and ruin most of their equipment, along with inflicting heavy casualties. It still took five days for the city to fall because the Ottoman infantry was well dug in.

Emmy and I followed the infantry into the city and moved from damaged building to damaged building and from bunker to bunker. It was an endless, monotonous ritual if one could participate in a ritual while hearing the whine of rifle bullets and the rat-a-tat of machine gun fire. We barely slept and then, only when we were exhausted, often in the open. Although we were exhausted from the campaign, as were the members of our unit, we saw them fight through to the end.

Then, as exhausted as we were, we found some wooden slats that served as a writing table and finished writing our reports, which we had written piecemeal over the previous five days. We had to wait three hours for the Division censor to read our reports. Naturally, he did not want to accept the extra copy and forward it to army headquarters as General Allenby had told us to do. Finally, however, he called and was amazed that the office did, indeed, want the extra copy. However, the censor had difficulty understanding that he was not to censor that copy but only the one we wanted to file. Moreover, he was a niggler and wanted words to change because he liked other words better than the ones I used. On the fifth change, I said, "I thought you were supposed to censor things like names of places, identifying characteristics and matters that had military significance, not word choices. A colonel happened by as I made the remark and said, "Damn, Joe, aren't you finished with that report yet. Hell, we won; what in the world do you want to hide from the public? Clean it up fast. I want to get to the beer tent before it closes." The report was finished five minutes later. He barely looked at Emmy's report. The Division telegraph operator gave us the fifth spot for sending our reports to Paris. I resolved to bring him a fifth of Johnny Walker Red as an inducement to keep our priority.

The Judean Hills Campaign

The Judean Hills were next on the agenda, and the entire army moved en masse to undertake the task. But the hills had no central route, and the enemy had spread a defensive net throughout the hills, so the entire area had to be invaded, and the Ottomans flushed out of it. General Allenby decided to use columns to do that, with each column given a specific route and assigned responsibilities for cleaning out the enemy on both sides of the route.

Immediately, there were problems. The largest one was that all columns had to leave the railhead behind and be supplied through truck and animal transport, which was slow, and the same amount of goods could not be delivered as with railway cars. Throughout the campaign, particularly as the distance from the railhead lengthened, the problems of supply increased. Emmy and I ate about one meal a day and supplemented it with the snacks we brought with us–dried fruit and beef jerky–until that ran out when we neared Jerusalem.

The weather grew colder, and the change affected the troopers who left the staging area with only summer uniforms. They had problems keeping their body heat in the nasty weather that descended on us. It began to rain off and on, with the result that uniforms did not provide the insulation that was required for moving in inclement weather. The rain also caused problems for transportation, as the roads and trails soon became muddy and, often, unusable. We wore our ponchos, not only for the wet conditions but because the rubberized material acted as an insulator that helped keep us warm.

Finding good drinking water was a continual problem, especially for the cavalry, where large amounts were needed regularly to keep the horses moving. On at least two occasions, operations were delayed while suitable supplies were located and horses were watered.

Roads were a problem as well. Most were simply age-old tracks that generations of local people had used, and they followed the contours most favored by people on foot. Since very few roads were cared for by some public authority, they were rough and rocky in places, subject to flooding in the rainy season, and hard to follow when in any sort of mechanized vehicle. A road might start with broad measurements and good footing, only to deteriorate in a mile or two into narrow, barely accessible paths or traces. The Australian military, accustomed to horse and motorized vehicle transportation, had difficulty in this terrain. On several occasions, they were unable to get their heavy weapons through and, at times, had to leave their motorized vehicles behind. They were frustrated by such obstacles and groused continually about it. When they did encounter the Ottomans, they had to use infantry tactics rather than the attacks of motorized weapons. It took time to adjust.

On the other side, the Ottomans had been surprised at Beersheba and Gaza City, having expected to drive the Commonwealth forces back with little difficulty as they had done earlier. In their retreat, the German commanders tried to build a new line of defense to protect Jerusalem and the Hijaz railhead near Jaffa. They left groups of Ottoman fighting men behind to harass the advancing Allies. But those Ottoman skirmishers faced the same problems that the advancing Australians did, so they felt isolated and deserted. They fought well in some engagements, but in others, they did not, often surrendering without a fight or retreating at the first signs of difficulty.

Most encounters were simply that, only short-lived firefights, with the Ottomans retreating or surrendering. Only in a few places were there significant battles that were contested by both sides and determined which side won an advantage. The first one was at Mughay Ridge, a site near the Mediterranean, which had at one time been a fortified area dating back in time, some said to the crusades, but more likely as a staging area against marauders and pirates later. It was a strong fortress with crenelated bastions so that stiff defense was possible against an attacking force. The Ottomans reinforced it with sandbag walls and barriers so that, even if penetrated, an interior force was to some degree protected from the invader.

Having heard about the engagement, Emmy and I arrived early the second morning of the attack on the structure when the Ottomans had already driven back a British attack and were awaiting a second charge from the Australians. It took time to do that as the Ottomans were well commanded, had ammunition and supplies, and the troops came from units not yet demoralized.

The Australians brought in artillery that destroyed the entryway in short order, and then, under a withering barrage, infantry stormed the opening, taking some casualties but gaining entrance. Once inside, however, the interior fortifications made it difficult for the Australians to advance further until communications were established by those invading with supporting artillery outside. Then, with coordinated artillery fire, the interior walls were reduced one after another to rubble, and the Australian infantry moved forward.

Since Emmy and I wore uniforms and were indistinguishable from the soldiers themselves, no one paid attention when we went into the castle with the third wave. Once inside, we found positions with good views on the crenelated sections of the ramparts and watched the Australians as they cornered Ottoman units. Ottoman resistance at that point was futile, and their natural inclination to fight on despite adversity resulted in a large number of lives lost, and only a few ended the day as prisoners. Emmy and I went into the fortification around eleven a.m., and the battle was not over until five p.m. Emmy had not had any opportunity to take pictures of the architecture, so we stayed, and I helped her do that.

While we were at it, Captain Ramsing joined us. He told me that there was another significant battle shaping up at the site of the prophet Samuel's tomb in an area near Jerusalem. He said it was built on a hill that gave the army holding it a good site for reconnaissance of the entire area and, if the Australians could capture it, would control the movement of enemy forces for a two-mile radius. He had a staff car and offered us a ride, but pointedly never told us we had to go to the tomb site. The suggestion that we go there was about as indirect as one could be, thereby avoiding any suggestion that we were ordered to go there.

The battle of Nebi Samwil lasted ten brutal days, during which the Australian troops worked their way from one hilltop village to the next, attacking Ottoman outposts. When this was completed, the Australians conducted attacks on the site of Nebi Samwil itself and had initial success, but they had difficulty holding that site. It was a problem of the right kind of weapons. Roads were non-existent, and heavy weapons, particularly artillery, were unable to get close enough to assist the ground operations. The inability to get heavy weapons into the area gave the Ottoman forces the opportunity to use counterattacks, which they did every day for over a week. Emmy and I tried to go in three times but were prevented from doing so by the Australians in command of the area, saying it was no place for non-combatants. We had to get our information about the battle from the wounded, of which there was an endless supply.

The battle of Nebi Samwil never lived up to the promise that General Allenby had for it as a launching platform for the capture of Jerusalem. So, he turned to other roads that led to the city, particularly the road up from Jaffa. Emmy and I received word one afternoon as we were relaxing and drinking tea with a New Zealand corporal, that we were wanted in a forward area near the Jaffa Gate at Jerusalem. We went there and were surprised to find the area already secured by the Allied forces. We found two other correspondents there, but when we asked about the third correspondent, we were told that he had been reassigned to cover the upcoming offensive in Flanders. There were tents for us that night and a mess nearby where we could eat. That night, we found some unoccupied tents with cots, where we slept and then enjoyed breakfast for the first time in a month. We considered these amenities real luxury.

The following day, General Allenby and a group of officials representing the various Commonwealth allies, followed by the correspondents, entered Jerusalem and found the Ottomans had decamped. We also found a city that had been through hell. There was little food, no legitimate economy, and little in the way of public services, including police. Australian military personnel were assigned to get the municipality running again. A British bureaucrat, Ronald Storrs, who had been brought along as a temporary mayor, went at his job with great zest, but his job was gigantic. I wrote two articles on the problems he faced.

In her wanderings, Emmy found her old apartment, which was not occupied, and we decided to move in for the time we were in the city, however long that might be. It was nice again to be able to bathe, sleep in a reasonable bed, and even make love. Afterward, we found a flourishing black market and got enough foodstuffs to satisfy our needs, although we mostly ate our meals in the mess tents available to military personnel.

Captain Ramsing found our happy abode and liked it so much that he was our 'guest' overnight on more than one occasion. Even though he slept on a divan with no sheets, he exclaimed it was like the Hotel Miramar in southern France. The food–simple potatoes with gravy, carrots, and cracked wheat bread–was like a tonic to him, as he, like us, had been going without much food for the previous two weeks. On one occasion, he used the last piece of bread to wipe up the remains of the gravy from an already empty bowl. "By God," he exclaimed, "One loves the simple things, you know, food, shelter, and whatever."

Ramsing said that the next target was Amman, as the general did not want to leave that city, which was a collection point for German military activity, in his rear when he went after the Ottoman forces in Syria, where he was convinced the war could be won. I asked Ramsing why he was telling me this, and he said, the general wanted someone outside official channels to understand what his motives were and "was convinced you will tell a sympathetic story." I did not know how to take that remark, whether I was a 'running dog' or a 'fair, unbiased' observer. "O, the latter, without a doubt," Ramsing replied. "Only do be careful; the general would just as soon have a 'running dog.'"

The Battle at Amman

The first two attempts to take Amman were unsuccessful, but Emmy and I were only involved in the first. The group we were with on the first attempt traveled with mules as the road was narrow and treacherous much of the way. I knew the Allied forces that were with us were in for a rough time as the roads were so narrow at points that no automobiles, let alone cannons, could get through. At most, machine guns might make it, but nothing heavier in the way of artillery. At Jericho, we encountered a city left behind by civilization. It looked like something out of the Middle Ages, with open sewers, garbage in the streets, and terrible disorder. I almost felt embarrassed for the population who had no facilities to greet us, and they were at a loss at what was happening with this army that suddenly descended on them.

We were in Jericho only a short time–two hours at the most--and then we moved on towards as-Salt, where the Ottoman forces had left just before the British arrival, with the Arab population jubilant about the matter. The Allies overnighted and then pressed on to Amman, where the German commander, Liman von Sanders, had fortified the city with machine guns and artillery pieces. The weather had been mild to that point but suddenly turned cold and rainy so that only camels could be used as draft animals and then, only with great care. Calling up troops from Madinah, who disembarked from the train at Ma'an near Amman, the Ottomans were able to fortify Amman and hold it against further encroachments. The British, exposed to the cold and the rain, decided to withdraw after besieging the city for four days.

They were followed by most of the Arab population of as-Salt as refugees, who feared the reoccupation of their city by vengeful Ottomans.

Emmy and I found the experience exhausting once again and disliked being exposed to the cruel weather. We slept together in makeshift, cramped shelters, which left us stiff and sick with sinus infections. We could not get too close to the city because of the machine guns that fired at any movement, so once again, we relied upon news of the battle from our talks with the wounded and with commanders of small units. It was sad to report another lost opportunity in the desert.

Adventures in the Transjordan Area

The second Commonwealth strike only got as far as as-Salt before it was turned back. By that time, Emmy and I, along with a camel patrol, were on our way to a point south of Ma'an on the Hijaz Railway to interview Prince Faisal, who was meeting with a British brigadier to coordinate strategy. This trip had been arranged by Captain Ramsing, who told us that Emmy and I had no official role, although it was clear to everyone in the party that General Allenby had determined we were to go. We were not ordered to go, but the opportunity was presented to us, and we did not refuse it. So, the guidelines established at our meeting in Alexandria were observed once again without difficulty. As Captain Ramsing put it, the general wanted another 'read' on the meeting than simply what his official delegation would tell him. I thought that Emmy might be chary about riding a camel again after her last experience when she had been kidnapped. But she was not.

I also thought the long trip into the desert might not be very productive of good news stories, but it proved otherwise for several reasons. First, we met Ja'far al-Askari, a graduate of the Ottoman Military College and a member of an Ottoman mission to Germany in 1910. He had been captured by the British in Mesopotamia, and since he came from the Arab area of the Ottoman Empire, he threw in his lot with the Hashemite cause. After the battle at Yanbu, he had been placed in charge of training Arab tribesmen who joined Prince Faisal's army. Al-Askari was said to be responsible for molding the tribesmen into a force that had some cohesion. We met him the first day we were in camp when the brigadier we had accompanied met in a conference alone with Prince Faisal.

Ja'far al-Askari was certainly polite and accommodating, as most professional Ottoman officers were. At the same time, he was realistic about the jobs that had been assigned to him and, especially, about making soldiers out of tribesmen.

"That is only going to happen if we take away their horses and march them around for two years, during which time we make infantrymen out of them, where discipline and tactics become their guideposts. We don't have time for that, so we must work with what we have. We must let our 'recruits,' who are not that but simply followers of a tribal shaykh, build on the skills they already have. They know how to ride a horse, they know how to charge, and they know how to use sabers and knives. Some even know how to fire a rifle from a horse, but not many."

He continued, "I have determined that we can get the best performance out of these 'irregulars' by getting them to obey simple orders with which they are familiar—' charge,' 'withdraw,' 'turn,' and 'stand.' When a unit of horsemen can follow those commands, they begin to be effective. Next, they need training in operating within a comparatively small space so that they can maneuver their horses where artillery, machine guns, and small arms fire can assist them in their fight against an enemy. This is difficult for a bedouin who likes wide, open spaces in which to maneuver, but being able to confine themselves to small spaces builds further in making them effective soldiers. Third, they must be trained not to run away at the first sign of enemy success. That is hardest of all because a bedouin relies on surprise and, when he realizes he no longer has it, believes it better to flee and fight another day."

Ja'far liked Emmy because she asked simple questions that were not always easy to answer but always got to the nub of the matter. "How do you manage 'recruits' from different tribes who have had long animosity between them because of tribal feuds," she asked on one occasion.

"Oh," he answered, "That is difficult to manage unless the shaykhs of the two feuding tribes agree that the feud has been resolved or placed in abeyance. Even then, there lingers suspicion."

I asked, "I have heard that some camel riders are adept enough to manage machine guns mounted on the camels' backs. Is it effective?"

"It takes time to train the camel to accept the noise and the shaking, and it takes time to make the rider effective at operating a machine gun, even while he steers his camel to get to his targets. We have not trained such units, although they do have considerable prospects for the future. We are now working out tactics for the inclusion of small units into our overall battle plans."

Emmy asked, "You now have motorized trucks, cars, and specialized equipment. Do Arab tribesmen take naturally to those inventions or are there difficulties?"

Ja'far laughed lightly and said, "It's not too hard to teach them the elements of driving, but they have no concept of what speed is called for on different kinds of surfaces. They tend to go as fast as they can and run into things as a result, such as rocks, mud, and mounds of sand. They also abhor formations and seek always to be first in line. They seldom understand that the functions of different vehicles often determine their respective places in formation."

Eventually, we went to a drill field where the matters we had discussed earlier were being addressed. The group we watched, about twenty-five horsemen with their mounts, went through a series of commands and did them well, except that the 'stand' order was the hardest to execute. The horses and the riders preferred to be in motion.

At a second exercise field, we witnessed live-firing exercises where riders were firing a gun from the sitting position on a horse. They were not accurate at all, but Ja'far said this group was only in its second day on the range and better shooting could be expected in another day or two.

In the afternoon Prince Faisal asked to see both Emmy and me, which surprised me, as I thought he might disregard Emmy's presence because women are not given much public role in Arab bedouin society. But the note asking us to see him specifically asked for her to attend, and when we entered his tent, he made a point of greeting her. Faisal looked tired, not simply from the meeting in the morning with the brigadier, but 'campaign, tired' as if the long days and nights of fighting in the cause of Arab liberation were taking its toll. "There have been changes since you were last with us at Yanbu," he said to me.

"Those were trying days and nights," I answered. "I was unsure that you would triumph, but the bedouins answered your call and stopped the enemy. You wore out the Ottoman troops in the 'wilderness.'"

"True enough," he answered. "Since then, we have driven out the Ottomans from the entire section of the Hijaz, as far over as Aqaba. and brought all the tribes into one great union." He turned to Emmy and said, "Your husband is one of the most steadfast men I have ever met. He had opportunities to leave us when we were fighting at Yanbu, but he never considered it. The only time he left was when the battle was over, and he received word that you were injured. His loyalty was to you immediately! Treasure him!"

The remark impressed Emmy, as she had not expected a discussion about me, or at least that is what she told me later. "Yes," she responded, "We have been to many places, side by side, but at Yanbu, we were separated, and I was occupied at Ta'if. I know that loyalty is considered a great virtue by bedouins, and I think that the relationship between Marty and me is somehow similar to it. We vowed earlier this year that we would not be separated at work anymore, and so far, we have lived up to that commitment."

Then he surprised her again, as she did not think he would raise the issue of a family. "What of children, my dear lady? Will there be little ones eventually?"

It was an obvious question to ask, so Emmy answered with ease. "But of course, dear Prince. As soon as the war is over and we return home,

I will become pregnant and await our first child. I want two; Marty has no set number in mind. Do you approve, Your Grace?"

"Yes," he answered. "My wife will certainly ask when I see her next. I think she will like your answers very much."

Then he switched subjects and said, "Good lady, do you think the year 1918 will see the end of the war here in Palestine?"

"It would be today," Emmy answered, "if I had my way. But you ask whether I expect it to be over in Palestine in a matter of months. Sometimes, I think it will last another year because the Ottomans are strong when they have German commanders and supplies, but at other times, I think it will end very soon. Watching the surrenders and wholesale retreats that we saw in the Judean Hills gave me hope it would be finished before the end of the year."

"Of course, I am a Muslim who believes God ordains all things, so my opinion is not really of great issue." The prince was careful of his religious beliefs as he chose an appropriate answer. "Based on the strength of the tribal support for my father's cause," he said, "I think it likely they will be the key factor in pushing back and even destroying the Ottoman forces in Palestine. Yes, I think the war will be over before the end of December. I do not know about the war in other places. I lack good knowledge of other theaters."

We ate an evening meal with the British brigadier, who headed our expedition, along with his two aides. As no one else was present, it was natural to speak English. The three of them had said little to us on the trip from Jerusalem, and as I sat down to eat, cross-legged in a matting, I thought that Emmy and I were in for a period of silence until we could comfortably eat and excuse ourselves. But I was surprised. The brigadier immediately said to me, "I understand that you have been with us since the Battle of Beersheba. Is that right?"

"Yes, Amelia and I struggled through the entire campaign to Jerusalem."

"What were your memorable moments?" asked the higher-ranking aide, a lieutenant colonel.

I answered, "Beersheba was interesting because of the fighting. Amelia and I had ringside seats, sharing a dugout with a squad of Aussies who brought a machine gun in to manage a particular tenacious group of Ottomans. It took over a day to root them out, but the Aussies finally got the job done. Watching tracer bullets in the dark is an experience."

Amelia added, "Mughar Ridge was interesting since it was an old fort at one time, and the Ottomans had transformed it into a modern citadel, which had to be opened like a tin can of fruit and gone through like a woman combing her hair. There were defensive walls everywhere that had to be recognized and dealt with one by one. I was surprised at the efficiency of the Aussies in doing that."

"You two have been busy," said the brigadier. "I commanded a regiment of Sepoys to act as a reserve column if it was needed, but it never was, so we moved up through the Judean Hills after the fighting was finished. Then I was seconded to the general's staff because General Allenby needed someone who could negotiate, and I have had some experience doing that in Mesopotamia, where negotiations went on all the time."

Once engaged in conversation, it was hard to stop, and we spent over two hours talking with one another and became momentary friends. We would go in different directions in a day or two, but for those few hours, we could be collegial.

.

The following day, Captain Lawrence arrived at camp after an absence of several days, during which he was destroying a section of the Hijaz Railroad. He joined our dinner group the following night. He seemed shy at first, perhaps because of the brigadier and his first aide, both of whom outranked him. He followed the old military dictate of 'in the presence of a senior officer, never speak until the senior officer addresses you personally and then answer him as concisely and clearly as you can. Then again, remain silent.' But I did not think the rule applied to me, so I said to Lawrence. "You disappeared at Yanbu after I met you, so we did not have a chance to talk with one another. I understand you have been busy since. Anything interesting you can tell me, knowing I'm a journalist? I'm sure the brigadier would like to hear about those adventures as well. You don't mind, do you, brigadier?"

The brigadier replied, "I only get to know any of Captain Lawrence's exploits from official reports, which are stripped bare and only slightly interesting. I would, indeed, like to hear from you if you don't mind telling us. We are dinner guests together, so we can be informal."

It was still difficult to get Lawrence to be spontaneous, so Emmy asked a series of questions designed to get Lawrence talking. Then, the conversation followed, with everyone participating. Lawrence talked about negotiations with other tribes and their suspicions about the Hashemites, who he held, was not altogether up front about their goals. He told about tearing up railway lines and about minor scuffles with Ottoman railway guards. Late in the evening, he even made observations about Arab nationalism, which he found 'incompletely formed' and 'nascent' rather than actual.

He said, "The local Arabs will fight against the Ottomans, but only because they are pledged to help the Hashemites, not because they feel any kind of loyalty to the 'Arab' cause. They don't even know that concept." The brigadier agreed with him and cited his own experience on the Mesopotamian front as illustrative.

The Lieutenant Colonel's aide opined that "the British ought to move fast then if we want to take advantage of the Arab unity that exists since it might evaporate overnight if both of you are to be believed." Both nodded their heads in agreement.

"Do you suppose," I interjected, "that any of the tribal shaykhs might be inclined to encourage Faisal to ignore his ties with the British and use his new equipment and the solidarity of the Hijaz tribes to go after Ibn Sa'ud and other holdouts?"

Neither Lawrence nor the brigadier suddenly seemed to have nothing more to say and ignored the question. The brigadier ended the session by saying, "Good conversation, Lawrence. We must do it again."

Lawrence responded, "Thank you for your frank expression of views, sir. It was informative and enlightening."

Emmy withheld comment until we were in our tent when she poked me in the ribs and said very softly, "Hey, I think you are on to something! You're almost as good as a senior international correspondent with those penetrating questions."

"Keep it up with the wisecracks, lady, and I'll leave you here for induction into the harem," I whispered.

On the way back to Jerusalem, I rode alongside the brigadier for the first day. He had something he wanted to say but seemed reluctant to raise the matter. Finally, in the early afternoon, he said, "Was that a lucky guess about a diversion of forces to advance Hashemite claims in other parts of the peninsula?"

Now, I am enough of an egoist to know that I could not deny the assertion because I have a certain reputation for clairvoyance, and I had made a reasonable assumption about what I knew of Arab politics. But on the other hand, I dislike bragging, so I sidestepped the question. "It's an assumption anyone familiar with the Arabs could have made. It was simply me who brought it into the conversation. It could just as easily have been anyone else in the group."

"Well," said the brigadier, "It's one of the questions I was instructed to specifically ask Faisal. Allenby is deeply concerned about a pullback by Faisal at this point, feeling that the balance of forces in Palestine right now is at a tipping point. The Ottomans were not in good shape, but the German command and German units still made it a formidable force. We are only now getting our Anglo-Indian units through training for the offensive that General Allenby intends to launch soon. It would be very 'iffy' if Faisal and his Arabs were not involved."

There was silence for half a mile, which is a long time when riding a camel. Then the brigadier continued, "I have told you something confidential, but I have permission from the general to make it known to you. I expect you not to use it in your next news article."

"Of course not," I said, "I know the importance of the matter and will not betray your confidence, even without your warning. When it is not important any longer, I will matter-of-factly use the material. At that time, I expect no opposition from the general or you."

"Understood," he said.

I waited a second and then asked, "What answer did Faisal give when you raised the matter with him?"

The colonel looked at me and then said, "He denied it, which is to be expected."

We were halfway back to Jerusalem when a fast-moving rider came up from behind us with a message from Captain Lawrence. It was in the form of a note and read:

> Sir:
>
> At an early morning council, Prince Faisal decided to move against Ma'an. The Prince asks that you and your party return to witness the key battle tomorrow or the next day.
>
> Lawrence

The Battle at Ma'an

'Maan' referred to the railway stop on the Hijaz Railroad, which was a well-fortified station. It served as an outlet for Ottoman forces coming down the railroad to control that section of the countryside and to supply the forces that operated out of Madinah. Maan had been attacked two months earlier by Hashemite forces, but the attack had been blocked by a staunch Ottoman defense and by extremely bad weather. Ja'far al-Askari had been the Hashemite commander then and would be again.

We returned and arrived at the Faisal camp, where the news was announced that the same tactics were used as in the first battle. The opening moves had already been made. At points several kilometers out of Maan, both north and south, Arab raiders overcame the guards that were posted there and tore up the tracks. Then, Hashemite guards were put at those points to prevent Ottoman crews from repairing the damage. With Arabs occupying the territory around the entire site, Maan was effectively sealed from the outside and could get no reinforcements. The Ottoman force located at Maan was then isolated.

In our absence from camp, a French artillery force had arrived to assist in the siege of the city, but it had limited ammunition, enough for three days of fighting. The French commander knew who I was and that I spoke French, so he invited me, with Emmy, to visit him in his tent that evening. He greeted us cordially when we arrived and even had a bottle of wine with him for the occasion. It was from a Maronite vineyard near Beirut and had a nice aroma. We talked about its qualities while enjoying the first glasses, which allowed us to get to know one another. Emmy understood that part of the French conversation well.

We turned to the work of the French force in that region. "We are here, of course, to assist our Arab allies, who are going to need help in reducing this fortress city. They cannot do it without artillery. We are glad to help."

"But you are a rather strange group," I said. "You are a small force with limited infantry and cavalry. What is your real purpose?"

"We are a monitoring group," he said. "French forces in this region are on the coast protecting the peoples, mostly Christians, from the Ottomans, who go on rampages from time to time against non-Muslims. We have been sent up here to help keep the war going against the Ottomans so that they stay away from the coast. As well there are French interests to the north, where we would prefer the Arab forces not go. Mostly, they are areas that the Allies have said would go to the French after the war. We will not fight the Arabs if they go there, but I will inform my superiors in Beirut of Arab transgressions if that occurs." Emmy's French was not strong enough to take all this in, so I had to translate for her.

She said, "Captain, which mission is more important: assisting the Arabs or monitoring their presence." I translated.

He was not abashed in his reply. "Monitoring, of course." Neither Emmy nor I were surprised.

The bottle was soon empty, and we all knew that the morning would bring a battle, so we shook hands and departed. The captain had been more revealing than he wanted to be, but now we had a clear idea of his priorities.

The first morning, the French artillery opened with a barrage against the highest point of the landscape just north of the city, and al-Askari's infantry made an all-out attack. The Ottomans were ready, and the battle for that city sector lasted all day, with the Arabs finally gaining control. At the end of the day, I found myself on a camel near the brigadier, and we exchanged comments about the battle. The brigadier said, "They finally did it, but I would have expected faster results with the artillery support they had. On the other hand, the Ottoman infantry is reminiscent of their fighting in the Mesopotamian campaign where they give up ground at a considerable cost to the attacker."

I agreed, so I replied, "Tomorrow will tell us a lot, I'm sure, as the next logical objective is the railroad station, the key to the entire city. It won't be easy, as the Ottomans will put up an even stronger defense than we saw today."

He said, "Yes. Much depends on the ammunition stores they have in the city. I suppose it's a lot, as they have been expecting this attack for a long time."

Later, in camp, the Arab shaykhs came and went and were in high spirits from the fighting of the past two days when two outposts and a strong point had been taken. They saw only another day needed to finish the job. Even Prince Faisal was infused with their optimism. Emmy said to me, "They don't have that much to crow about with today's results if they were watching the same battle as we were."

I agreed.

The following day, the early part of the battle went to the Arabs, who advanced across three of the four lines of trenches that the Ottomans had established. The French artillery was useful, but then ammunition supplies ran low so that the rate of use was lowered, and by mid-afternoon, everything had been expended. The final line of trenches was not breached by the Arabs. Night came on with the Arabs only halfway to their goal. It was apparent that the machine guns and small artillery in the hands of the Ottomans were keeping the Arabs from advancing.

However, the next day saw the Arabs stymied again. Without French artillery to clear the way, it proved impossible for the Arab infantry to make any more gains through the trench lines of the Ottomans. In late afternoon, the Arab cavalry made a last charge and then departed for their own homes, in effect deserting their infantry comrades.

On the fourth day, the residents of Ma'an rallied to the Ottomans when they realized that if the Arabs won, their homes would be sacked. With over 200 more fighters from the general population, the Ottomans counterattacked and drove the Arab infantry out of the trench line altogether. The battle was effectively over. By that time, the Arab headquarters had decamped as well, and al-Askari marched his infantry away to fight somewhere else. The second battle of Ma'an had ended the same way that the first battle had, with the Ottomans still in control of the city.

The British headquarters group, with the brigadier as its commander, left as the last lines were breached, and as we left with the group, we did not see the last phases of the battle. There was little talk for the rest of the day as everyone digested what had happened. That night, we camped on the edge of a small village and bought a chicken and some eggs from one of the residents, which we ate along with the rations we were carrying. It was strange food, all lumped together, but edible, nonetheless. After the meal, the brigadier, his senior aide, Emmy, and I talked for about an hour, going over what we had witnessed.

"The Arabs are just not very good fighters," said the senior aide. "They quit easily and never seem to get past normal difficulties in a battle. Even with the artillery gone, if the cavalry had stayed, they might still have won. But they left without regard for their fellows in the infantry. That's no way to run an army."

The brigadier said, "It's probably because they have no sense of obligation to one another, something a modern army teaches its trainees. You identify with one another, and you do not leave your compatriots to perish on the battlefield. The Arabs don't seem to have grasped that yet. They are only loyal to their families and clans; greater relationships have a very loose hold on them."

Emmy said, "But you have got to hand it to the Ottomans again. Everyone says they are living on borrowed time, but they keep coming up with small victories, even without German leadership. This battle shows their resiliency and supports the view about whether they ought to continue as a nation. They are so unlike the Arabs. They do have a common identity."

I said, "But it will not be enough to save them. No, what I saw the last couple of days was two people who are going to be losers in this war. The Ottomans are in decline and are living on borrowed time. The Arabs are on the rise but don't have the ability yet to be the winners."

We talked for a while longer and went to sleep. Jerusalem was still a day's journey away, and we were anxious to get back.

When we arrived in Jerusalem, Emmy and I found that Captain Ramsing had moved into our apartment and claimed the divan for his permanent sleeping space. We certainly could not complain, as we had no ownership of the apartment, but he caused us inconvenience. It was two a.m. when we arrived, and we both knew we had to work until early the following morning, completing our reports. We shooed Ramsing into our bedroom and went to work. I finished at nine a.m., and Emmy, with photos added to her report, took until nine-thirty. Then we left for headquarters to find the censor, who was late that morning and was not in the mood to work when he arrived.

He decided we needed harassing and started in on Emmy first. "Why were you in Prince Faisal's camp? That is a restricted area, and you had no specific permission to go there."

We did not want to check with General Allenby's office, knowing that at this crucial phase in planning for the upcoming campaign, the general would not like to be disturbed. He was right, for I called and got one of his aides, who was irate about being contacted when he was preoccupied with the upcoming campaign. I listened to the tongue-lashing he gave me and then explained as quickly as I could about the censor's insistence. "Put the bugger on the line," the aide said.

I listened and could hear some of the conversation, which said basically that the general decides who goes to Prince Faisal's camp, and he had decided that two newsmen needed to go there. "You barely need to censor the reports as what they have to say is suitable for the public." Then he added, "If you haven't already done so, get a clean copy to send on to this headquarters."

Having that matter cleared up did not placate the censor, who was annoyed at being reamed by the aide to the general, so he believed we were the perfect foils for getting his revenge.

He got into editing my report, which was way beyond censoring, so I finally threatened to call the general's aide again. He reluctantly put his initials on the report. Fortunately, Emmy had her reports read by another censor who was aware of what was happening in my case and decided that challenging anything was apt to backfire on him. He initialed Emmy's report long before mine was done.

The Syrian Breakout

Back at our apartment, we found Captain Ramsing still there, waiting for us. "I know both of you want to go to bed and rest, but I have things I must tell you. This afternoon at five-thirty p.m., there is a briefing, and it is by ticket admittance only, meaning it is a very exclusive group. I have tickets for each of you. The general request that both of you attend. Further, at five a.m. the next morning, the campaign for Syria begins, and you need to be at the 3rd Australian Mechanized Battalion for a ride. They are a spearhead division heading for the coast and intend to go along the coast to the Anatolian border. The supposition is that a fast, lightning-like raid will crack the Ottoman lines, and they will melt away before us. We anticipate taking prisoners and Ottoman soldiers fleeing ahead of us."

"Aren't you a little optimistic?" I asked.

"I don't think so. Reserve judgment until you attend the briefing this afternoon."

Emmy shooed him out the door, as we had had no sleep for two days and were exhausted. He left only reluctantly, wishing to tell us more about the upcoming campaign.

The briefing was confidential. Participants were warned that the details of the attack could not be discussed openly with others for forty-eight hours when the plan had either succeeded or failed. From what we could see of it, it looked like a sure winner. It postulated a fake move towards Amman as if Allenby was determined to take that objective before moving elsewhere. Using lots of dummy housing, equipment, and cardboard cutouts of people, it was intended to mislead General Liman von Sanders, the German commander, into focusing his main strength to blunt the attack on Amman.

The main thrust was to be a two-pronged attack up through Syria, one aiming for the coastal areas and the other going straight through Damascus. The two prongs were to use cavalry and mechanized units so that speed would disrupt the Ottoman defensive lines. The infantry would fill in behind but be backed up to consolidate areas already gained, not take new territory. Emmy and I left the briefing optimistic about Commonwealth prospects.

It was a chore getting to the 'jump off' places the next morning. We had been told to bring all our gear, but much of it would be sent to us later by truck, but we had to have it there that morning long before five a.m. Everything was ready to go at four thirty a.m., and the battalion commander had us on the road fifteen minutes early. As we were headed for the coast, the battalion commander said he wanted to see the sea before we stopped for our evening meal.

We saw the Ottoman defensive lines around Jerusalem as we passed through them, but we hardly gave them any attention at all. They would be handled by the infantry, which already was coming up the outsides of the road we were using. They had machine guns and small cannons, so we believed the Ottomans were in for a real test later in the morning.

In mid-morning, we were forced to halt when an Ottoman unit threw up a barricade to stop vehicular traffic. The commander of our unit merely brought up a field piece we had with us and fired about twenty rounds into the barricade, which disintegrated before our eyes. The twenty-five Ottoman infantrymen who were tending the barricade took off running as the barricade fell to pieces. A lieutenant wanted to form up a party to capture the fleeing enemy, but the commander, a major, said, "Not today, Lieutenant, we've got more important things on our mind. Leave them for the infantry, which will get here tomorrow."

By evening we were on the coast and waited for other units in our column to join us. Four more companies came in during the evening, all as jubilant as our own company was. We ate well from the stores we carried, and we slept beneath the vehicles, which made me sad that I no longer had the comfortable bed we had enjoyed in Jerusalem.

For the next five days, we repeated this process. The further we went, the more fleeing Ottoman soldiers we saw because the defensive lines had been broken. Word had gotten back that there was nothing to stop the Allied advance.

When we reached the Anatolian border, we parked, dug in, and made a large holding area for prisoners, which we began to fill the following day. Emmy and I found a railroad station that had telegraph facilities, so we were able to file reports. It was a satisfying experience, as there were no censors around for us to check with first. We knew that later, we might be called to account for not holding our reports until the censors found their way up to us.

Two days after arriving at the Anatolian border, our commander received orders to have a vehicle drive across the country on secondary roads and enter Damascus, where Emmy and I were to be detached. That trip was lonely, as we encountered very little vehicular traffic and very few Ottoman troops at all. As soon as we arrived in Damascus, we unloaded our gear and were placed in field tents, which were just as cramped as those we had stayed in during the buildup to the Gaza campaign. Probably, they were the same tents. The batmen serving the tents, however, were not the same and, in fact, were lazy and ungracious, which made the three-day wait that we endured hard to bear.

Emmy and I found the other correspondents. The one that had been sent off to the Western Front had returned, so the five of us were together. We celebrated our reunion the first evening by going into Damascus, where we found a restaurant that was operating. The food was sparse and not good, but the ambiance was fine. There was even wine to drink, which helped us overcome our fatigue and made us talkative. We discussed our adventures and found that no one had experiences like the others. They were all unique.

No one liked the censors, and most found working in uniform to be inhibiting. "I don't care if I have to find my food. I'm not doing it again," said one reporter who had missed Jerusalem but had been in both Amman campaigns. Moreover, none of the other three had anything good to say about Commonwealth commanders they had met who were short with them. They regarded correspondents as a nuisance rather than a tool they could use. Emmy and I kept quiet about our relationships with officers.

It was the third day that General Allenby arrived, which upset the camp we were in, as the members of his entourage needed more tents than had been erected. The afternoon was concerned with that new reality as new lines of tents were constructed, some doubling up was done, and some of the former denizens were sent elsewhere. Most importantly, the new arrivals brought news of the campaign, which was unbelievably successful. The ruse at the Amman front had worked to perfection and had nearly captured the German staff, but it had gotten away at the last minute. The Ottoman front, north of Jerusalem, had folded and had little chance of reorganizing itself, as its leadership was gone. That left individual soldiers and small units adrift, and they were so isolated that they chose to surrender as the only alternative to annihilation. The fast-moving columns of the Commonwealth forces had shredded the Ottoman defense, and the Ottoman army was not able to reconstitute itself.

The next day Prince Faisal arrived and led the way into Damascus. He rode in on a horse, while Allenby, behind him, used a staff car. The two leaders met twice, and, afterward, held a press conference, which surprised everyone. A spokesman for the British forces gave a battle summary, beginning with the statement, "The enemy army is in tatters, and it only remains for us to remove it from the field." He said that finding facilities for all the thousands of prisoners that were being processed was putting a strain on Commonwealth forces, but that it was a better problem than having those soldiers loose and still fighting.

A second spokesman gave a summary of the discussions between Allenby and Faisal. He noted that during the war, confidential agreements had been made that affected the political conditions of the Middle East. He said that an agreement with the Jewish representatives had produced the Balfour Declaration, which permitted the Jewish people to immigrate to Palestine and establish a Jewish home there. Great Britain would oversee that territory until the home was established.

The spokesman also said that an agreement had been made between the British and the French. The French were to control Ottoman territory in Lebanon and Celicia, while the British would gain control of Mesopotamia. As well there had also been negotiations between Sharif Hussein of the Hashemites and the British about Syria and the Hijaz, which were to be honored, but Sharif Hussein's claim to be 'king of the Arabs' was seen as an aspiration, or as hyperbole, and not to be regarded as an actual claim. I was surprised that the press conference revealed so much of what had been unannounced earlier and wondered about the strategy of such revelation.

There were ten correspondents. In addition to our group, there were two Arab correspondents, a Greek reporter, and two Italians. For the first twenty minutes of questions and answers, these five outsider reporters dominated the news conference, all making the case for more territory to be given to the nations they each represented. They were quite raucous about the claims, and the news conference was called to a halt because of the unruliness.

Then, we five correspondents attached to the British army had our chance. Our questions centered on French claims, British claims, and the Jewish national home. None of the questions were unfriendly but merely sought further clarification of what might happen with these arrangements in the future.

The encampment lasted five days, and two more press conferences covered little new ground. The Jewish National Home became a major topic of conversation, with a great deal of worry about bringing Jews from so many places around the world into a single society. Interestingly, no one talked about the Arab population that already occupied Palestine and whether there would be any opposition on their part. That difficulty was to come later. Slowly, the press conferences began to drift over into the problems of governance that the British were experiencing in trying to bring order and services to the people of the area.

Other than the press conferences, there was little to do except wait for the daily issuance of bulletins from British army services. The most important ones noted the progress of rounding up drifting Ottoman soldiers. Those drifters posed a safety threat to the local population, as they were turning to theft to feed themselves. A second set of bulletins tracked the flight of the German units that had commanded the Ottomans in Palestine and were now headed towards Anatolia. There was no attempt to stop their departure; they were merely shadowed until they left the Syrian theater of operations.

Emmy seemed out of sorts, and I knew something was on her mind. I asked her what was bothering her, but she put me off. Then after the meal one evening she said she had something she needed to tell me. We took a walk out beyond the tents, where we were alone, although others used the area as well for privacy.

She was silent for quite a while, but I knew better than to hurry her when she was thinking through a problem. I thought it might have something to do with Werner but told myself that it was unlikely. I could only wait and let her tell me in due time what the problem was. Trying to hurry her was going to do no good. Finally, she said, "I think the war is over, don't you?"

"Well, it certainly is here in this section of the world, and I think it's only a few more weeks before the Ottomans leave the war altogether. I don't know about the war in Europe, but it looks like it's winding down as well."

"So, I won't be a quitter, if I go home now?" she asked.

"No, you won't, but I don't think you would have been earlier either. You've been out here a long time." I paused and asked, "Do you want to go home?"

She said, "But I don't think I have a choice. I'm pregnant as all get out. Morning sickness, hardening of the breasts, and the whole thing. I don't think living like we do is the best thing for me to go through while I'm pregnant. I think Fort Mill, South Carolina is a better option."

"I drew her to me, kissed her tenderly, and said, "Well, if it's a girl, you know her name has to be Naomi?"

"Yes," she answered, just a little exasperated. "I know that. You've told me a hundred times, at least." She was silent for several seconds in my embrace, and then said," So you're okay with all this? You want me to go through with it?"

"Hell, yes, girl," I said, "Your clock has been ticking. It's time for you to do what women are expected to do. Besides, I want a daughter named 'Naomi.'"

"I hadn't expected this just now," she said. "Ordinarily, I would wait until we go home when recalled at the end of the war. However, since I am pregnant, I feel good about it. I'm glad you see it that way too. I am surprised at the support you have just shown. Somehow, I did not expect that. Your reaction puts a very positive spin on the entire matter, and I can rest easier than I did the last two nights when I was fretting about it."

We decided we would inform the *Tribune* headquarters in Paris the following day. I wanted to do that in a unique way, so I sent the following report:

Conceived in Jerusalem on its liberation day, a likely girl to be named 'Naomi Rose Caruthers-Mintz.' The child's mother, Amelia Pamela Caruthers, now a senior international correspondent for the *Tribune*, will return to her home in Fort Mill, S.C. to prepare for the birth. Her father, Martin M. Mintz, also a senior international correspondent for the *Tribune*, will remain in the Middle East for another six months to fulfill his contract and then will join Amelia to wait for the birth of little Naomi. Selah.

There was an immediate congratulatory reply from headquarters in Paris and the process for getting Emmy home was set in motion. The *Tribune* printed my report on the front page the following day. We did not lack congratulatory letters after that.

Chapter 7
Changing Professions

The Armistice and Its Aftermath

As I predicted, with the end of the war and, especially with Emmy's departure from the correspondents' ranks in the Middle East, most of the 'juice' of being an international correspondence drained away. It was not that I particularly disliked my assignments, for news is news and has considerable appeal when one gathers it. But without Emmy there, the evenings were long, and I missed talking with her about the thousand and one things that occupied our lives.

We were both in Alexandria when she made her farewell. There were not a lot of people there, just Emile and his staff of three, a representative of the *Tribune* from Paris who came to Cairo especially to say goodbye and to sign Emmy to a contract for a published collection of her photos and articles. Surprisingly, Captain, now Major, Ramsing was there and was as haughty as ever. Two of the correspondents who had been with us in Palestine were on leave in the Alexandria area and decided to attend as well. We had champagne and cake with white frosting, which proved to be quite good. Our celebration was not long, less than an hour, as Emmy's ship was scheduled to sail at eleven p.m., so we had to have her on board by nine-thirty. The party was generally upbeat, but everyone knew that it was ushering in a sad era. The wartime employees would soon all be leaving, since the war was over, except for the announcements of its demise.

I planned to get Emmy on board her ship and then catch a freight train hauling military goods north, immediately afterwards. I did not want to stay in Alexandria without Emmy; that would have been far too depressing. There were no hitches, and we both departed on schedule.

At Damascus, the discussions of who was going to rule which parts of the now moribund Ottoman Empire were in full swing. By decree, General Allenby divided the Syria-Palestine region into three parts ruled by the British, French, and Arabs, respectively. No one was against that division, but all sides quarreled over which areas belonged to which zones. The haggling was interminable, and I quickly lost patience with the discussions that went nowhere. The only news was that the decisions of yesterday were no longer valid today. I did not think my readers wanted to read about such indecisiveness. To pass the time I garnered interviews with General Allenby, a French commander then in Damascus, and Prince Faisal.

All three were happy to oblige me for interviews, perhaps seeing the time with me as an excuse not to be occupied with the endless arguments over the new land divisions of the Middle East. All three were exceedingly cordial since I spoke with everyone in his language when they could be expansive and say things freely without concern for proper translation. The French colonel who I had never met before, was especially surprised by my ability to handle French. He became almost human in his remarks about his duties at Damascus, which were rather troubling to the British and the Arabs.

The interviews were well-liked by the editors in Paris and there were suggestions that I get more of them, but the names I proposed, all second-line officials, were not known by the editors, which constituted a veto of sorts. Nonetheless, I said I would stay alert to interviewing other personalities when opportunities arose.

Then came the Lemnos conference where the temporary Ottoman government entered negotiations to end the war with British and French officials. Major Ramsing arranged for me to travel with the British delegation, and to be accommodated in quarters of my own near the conference site. There were only two other correspondents there, one from France and the other from Athens, Greece. The three of us met briefly before the opening session to identify ourselves with one another but afterward had little contact. I no longer had to submit my reports for censorship, but still made sure that a copy was always sent to Major Ramsing. It was obvious he expected to get them.

There were few enough observers so most of the meetings were open to whoever wanted to attend. Mostly I was the sole observer because the meetings were slow and ponderous since so much translation had to be done between Turkic, English, and French. On two occasions I was conscripted to do translation work, when regular translators were not available because of other duties. This was especially true when the conference broke down into committee work.

It was an undisputed surrender, so the basic terms were agreed on quickly enough. The Dardanelles waterway was to be opened, its protective forts turned over to the British and French, and the minefields removed. The Ottoman army was to be demobilized except temporarily, prisoners in Entente's hands would remain there until they could be transported back to Constantinople. All naval vessels were to be surrendered to the British and French, and the communication and transportation systems were to come under Entente control.

All Austrian and German units were given one month to vacate the region and return to their respective homelands. All Armenian prisoners were to be sent to Constantinople and placed under the protection of the British and French It was implied that there would be an accounting for the atrocities committed against that minority group. The political dimensions of the war's end were put off to a meeting of the peace conference to be held the following year.

Still, even when everything is generally agreed on, it takes time to translate that understanding into a written document, that will be read the same way in three different languages and different parts of the world. So, there were often disparities that had to be reconciled, verbiage that needed to be unraveled and made plain, and general understanding made exceedingly explicit. All this took time and what was decided in the first two hours of the first meeting dragged on for three more days as the documents were carefully constructed. The conference was given the name 'Mudros Conference' for easy reference to the agreements it set forth.

Afterward, I traveled to Constantinople to witness the implementation of the Mudros Conference agreement. I secured lodging in the correspondent's hotel, where I had stayed when I first went to the city in 1914. The old name sign was gone, and the hotel had a new one, 'The Metropolitan Hotel," but other than a new entryway and lobby, little on the interior had changed. It still had leaky faucets, grungy carpets, and flaking paint in the hallways. Importantly, the international telegraphic service was still operating, which was one of the main attractions that drew businessmen and government officials to the hotel. The service at the telegraph was still 'superior,' and it was easy to send a message from there. The first message I sent was to Emmy in the United States, which stated:

> emmy stop at old hotel constan stop witnessing implementation cease-fire accords stop not much changed here stop different atmosphere howeveer stop are you and Naomi well stop misss you very much stop love stop marty

I spent three weeks moving about the city witnessing the implementation of the accords. General Liman von Sanders received me very cordially, and we talked about the Palestine campaign. He believed, that if the Ottoman campaign had been undertaken a year earlier, it might have been successful enough to reach the Suez Canal and change the nature of the war entirely. I agreed that the war would have been different but contended that the Ottomans were never going to put together enough strength to capture the region, as witnessed by the difficulties in ever holding the Arabian Peninsula and Egypt even before the war. The general would not sit for a formal interview but had no objections that I use his comments in a press article.

I tried to locate Enver Pasha but discovered that he had fled the city before the armistice and had traveled across Europe to Berlin where the German government had granted him and his fellow Ottoman leaders political asylum. Now that Germany had surrendered, his destiny was unknown, but it was speculated by some that he might return to Constantinople. I doubted that, as his style of leadership was generally discredited among the Ottomans, the Turkic faction, and the minorities. Many wanted the Ottoman Empire to continue, but they certainly did not want Enver Pasha and his Committee of Union and Progress (CUP) to lead any government formed in the post-war era.

Midway in my stay, the office in Paris wired me that they had dispatched a woman photographer to accompany me during the remainder of my stay in Constantinople and my return to Damascus. She was to spend some productive time with me and learn to be a field photographer. She was then to move on to Emile's office in Alexandria. She arrived with lots of cameras and equipment, and I placed her in my hotel. She was about twenty-five years old. She had worked at Paris throughout the war hoping along the way for a field assignment, but she had never been considered for one. She was excited about this opportunity.

The new photographer's name was Sadie Bronstone. She was blonde, with her hair worn in ringlets, about five foot three, and well proportioned. She was British and spoke upper-class English that bore marks of an elite finishing school. She was relatively self-assured and went about her work with quiet competence.

Shortly after she arrived by train, I took her with me to the fortress area of the Dardanelles to witness the destruction of the minefields. She immediately grasped what was going on and took an array of photos that showed clearly what was being done. We went into one of the bunkers that had just turned over to French troops, who were a friendly lot, and they joked with her about all the cameras she had. She spoke with them in Parisian street French, which amused the soldiers a great deal. She said she had picked up that lingo to get around Paris during her two-year sojourn there. Later in the day, we saw the remnants of the Ottoman fleet which had just been turned over to a British gunship. She got a good shot of that as well.

She spent most of the evening developing the film and getting everything ready for transmission. I helped her the following morning with descriptions. They were sent and she waited impatiently until an acknowledgment of their receipt in Paris but was disappointed when no response came with it saying the work had been done to their satisfaction. I told her not to expect too much the first days she was in the field. It took time for the Paris office to know what to expect and to evaluate what sort of a job a new fieldhand did.

The following day the work was heart-wrenching because it centered on the assembly of Armenian refugees, who had undergone terrible experiences at the hands of Turks. Most of them had been starved, many were disfigured from harsh treatment, and all of them had signs of psychological impairment from bad treatment. Units from hospitals in Europe had been sent in to handle them, but the medical facilities were too sparse for the number of people that had to be treated, and it was apparent that many were going to have to wait days and weeks before being given attention. Meanwhile, they were being put up in warehouses and tent hospitals, but there seemed to be shortages of those facilities as well.

Sadie grew more and more emotional the more we saw, until early afternoon when I took her away from the scene. She cried all the way back to the hotel in the horse-drawn carriage that was a normal means of transportation because of the shortage of automobile gasoline. I took her to my room and let her rest on the sofa and, by that time, she was almost inconsolable. Finally, about seven o'clock that evening, I had her straightened out again. I took her to dinner and then sent her to bed in her room.

The following morning, I told her she could not go out with me again if such a scene were repeated. "I realize that you saw a heart-rending scene yesterday, but this war has produced far worse, some of it not over fifty miles from your offices in Paris. You have got to harden yourself to such suffering, because there is nothing you can do about it and your job is to tell others, through your photographs and descriptions, the horrors you are witnessing. You have to be in control of your own emotions to do that."

She sniffled as I told her this judgment of her behavior, which she did not want to hear. "Today," I continued, "you are going to see something else that is not pleasant to see. Prisoners of war will be sent here for processing. Most of them will have been mistreated, and many will be in bandages and on crutches. You will see those with missing limbs and bad facial wounds, so prepare yourself for what you are about to experience. There may even be basket cases." She was crestfallen and had tears streaming down her face when I got to this point in my lecture.

As difficult as it was for me to scold a young reporter experiencing gross human suffering for the first time, I understood that she had to conquer her emotions, her fears, and her righteous indignation about it. I said, "I will not interrupt my work today to bring you back here as I did yesterday. Moreover, if you cannot bear it, I will put you on a train for a trip right back to Paris, because I do not have time to deal with such foolishness." She left the table that we eating at and went to her room, presumably to get herself up for the day's work. A half-hour later, when I was in the lobby ready to leave, she joined me, with somewhat red eyes, but with a determined look on her face.

The prisoners of war were in worse shape than I thought they would be. Bandages were scarce, and rags had been used in many cases to cover wounds, and some patients had their wounds visible to viewers. Broken legs with only splints and no wrappings were common, as were bullet wounds where the bullets had been removed and some sort of medicinal salve had been smeared over the opening, leaving the hole visible. Facial wounds were largely untreated and grotesque. Moreover, it was seemingly unending.

Sadie blanched when she saw the first group of survivors. During the first three hours, she withdrew three times to compose herself. But each time she came back within five minutes and went on searching for worthwhile pictures, talking with the patients and snapping pictures. About noon we became separated, as I was interviewing prisoners with stories to tell, and that took me in a different direction than Sadie who was with the general population of the wounded. It did not occur to me that I should have been by her side even though the assignment was a difficult one.

 Somehow that afternoon she sent a message, without my knowledge, to her mentor-editor in Paris, who called me that evening by telephone. It was a miracle that the phone even worked because there were ordinary service disruptions. After all, the system had been turned over to the British and French, but it did. The caller asked whether I needed to make the work so graphic that Sadie would have trouble with it. I was unsympathetic, saying that Sadie had asked for her 'dream job' and now had to endure the hardship that went with it. "She can go back to Paris if you want that, but I am not going to make anything easy for her, whether she stays or not. She is here to assist me and I expect her to do it. If she can't, she leaves."

The editor said, "A little patience goes a long way. Can't you work her into the difficult jobs gradually and let her do less demanding work for a time."

I said, "We don't have a stack of 'easy' and 'difficult' jobs that we can choose between. We deal with what comes our way and some days it is horrific, as the last two days have been. Tomorrow may be less demanding, I don't know. Sadie must adapt to what faces her, just as I do."

The editor said, "O, you have some discretion, I am sure of it. You have just decided to throw Sadie into the worst of it to prove she cannot do the work, probably because she is a woman. I do not appreciate your approach at all, and I will see that you are reprimanded." The editor-mentor was on her high horse and wanted her outrage dealt with by high administrators.

'Confrontation' is not something I like, but I do not back away from it. I said, "No one in your office has ever complained to me about how I treat my fellow reporters, and I don't expect it to begin now. Send a message up the line for a reprimand for me if you want but spare me any lectures on how I ought to treat my fellow reporters. I do not ever abuse them. Why don't you call my wife in the United States, who did the same job that Sadie is doing now, and see what she thinks about it."

Two hours later, I got a telegram from the lead editor; it said:

> marty stop I have received complaints from both sadie and her sponsor about the work with refugees and prisoners of war which evoke strong emotional responses stop sadie is not ready for such fieldwork stop absolutely no blame attaches to you stop her sponsor had no permission to interfere in your work and has been told to desist stop send sadie home as soon as your schedule permits time to find her transportation stop sorry you were shackled with this unintended responsibility stop ch. ed

I went to bed without replying to anyone. When I awoke in the morning, I went to the dining room to eat breakfast which was something that looked like cream of wheat, except it was browner and less tasty. Wars produce such deterioration in food. Sadie joined me and said, "Where are we going today?"

"I'm going back to the mine-clearing exercise and expect to be there most of the day. You are going to pack, as I am going to get you a ticket for a train leaving this evening. Paris recalled you last night. I passed the telegram over to her."

A frown appeared on her forehead as she read. "I did not mean I wanted to go back to Paris. I just want to have a little more consideration when I am obviously in distress over what I see, that's all. I do enough work that you should not want to get rid of me, don't you think?"

"It doesn't work that way, Sadie," I responded. "You complain to your mentor, your mentor complains to the chief editor, and the chief editor does not want to hear about the whining of a young woman who doesn't want to adjust to the conditions of the fieldwork she has been assigned. The chief editor did not consult me, as she does not want me to make exceptions for you. The editor decided the matter, not me. She is going to always assist me because I produce quality work, day after day. She sees you as someone given a chance to learn, not to upset things. So, eat your lovely cream of wheat, and then get ready to vacate this amazing city."

Half an hour later when I came through the lobby to get my taxi to go to the Bosporus, Sadie was sitting there with her field clothes on, her cameras on a cord, and film tucked into her cargo jacket. She stood as I approached her and said, "I want to go with you. Won't you please let me have one more day here? You can send me back tonight if you want, but I want to be here today to continue what is probably the most memorable moment of my life."

I said, "Come on then. We haven't got all day. Remember no whining or I'll leave you in the middle of some god-forsaken street." I climbed into the closed carriage. She threw her gear onto the seat on the other side and climbed in as well."

"Today is Friday," I said, "What does that mean? Do you know?"

"It's the day of worship, so probably all the businesses are closed?" she replied.

"Well, you are partly right," I answered. "Most people work until prayer time, then the men go to public prayer, and then decide not to go back to work for the rest of the afternoon. They spend the afternoon in coffee houses discussing whatever the topic of interest is that week. This week it's probably the nasty peace that's been foisted on them. Then tomorrow is a leisurely workday, and Sunday is the official day of rest. Got it?"

"I think so," she said, "So we have to hurry to catch anyone working because it's going to be a slow afternoon and weekend."

"We're going to get some photos of the mine-clearing, and, perhaps, talk with some British or French officials on site. Afterward, we can duck into a residential area to see whether we can find Muslims at prayer and take some unobtrusive photographs. Do you think you can be unobtrusive?"

"I'll certainly try," she responded.

At the Bosporus, there was one mine sweeper at work and not working at all fast." There were no officials on shore and the artillery bunkers were closed off with big signs that said in Turkic, "Entry will not be permitted."

"We may as well be in Germany," I said. "Even Ottoman signs are translated straight from German." We drove along the Bosporus some ways and noticed that several ships, most of them cargo ships, probably with a foreign registry, were waiting for the mine clearing to be finished so that they could sail directly through the Dardanelles to the Black Sea. Their merchandise would probably end up on the black market in Romania, Ukraine, and Russia.

We turned around and went back into the city proper, where we were in time to watch men gather for prayer in a mosque. There were enough that they spilled out into the street. I signaled to Sadie to take some pictures and noted, with satisfaction, that she did do it unobtrusively. Maybe the woman's attitude was changing a little bit, I thought.

We stayed until the service was over and, the men scattered along the neighborhood streets and alleys. Then I signaled the driver and ordered him to take us to the Topkapi palace, the official residence of the padishah, the titular ruler of the Ottomans. We spent two hours by the great public buildings–Saint Sophia, the palace, the Janissary parade grounds, and the Sublime Porte[5]. Sadie was agog at the magnificence of the buildings. I made her take several pictures of each from different angles.

Then we traveled to the Sea of Marmora where we located a fish restaurant, and had some fish roasted over an open grille. We ate slowly and drank some local wine. I forgot about the misery of being separated from my wife and suspect that Sadie forgot about the bad spot she was in with me regarding her internship, then we traveled back to the hotel. It was seven p.m. so I said. "Time enough to write a letter or read a little and go to bed. Be up at eight a.m. as I have a project for you that will determine whether you go back to Paris on Sunday or stay with me for a while longer. It will be difficult, so don't think you are going to have an easy time of it." I left her standing in the lobby.

---

5 Saint Sophia was originally a Byzantine cathedral, later under the Ottomans a museum; the Topkapi Palace was the residence of the ruler (padishah); Janissary parade ground was a showcase for the elite infantry of the early Ottomans; and the Sublime Porte was the ornate administrative building for the central Ottoman Administration.

There was a letter waiting for me from Emmy, so I went to my room and read it. It read:

Dearest Marty:

Little Naomi kicked me today. Can you believe that? I think that she is going to be a spunky child, which I know you will adore. It is strange to be home and go to my room and realize that I am not the single young woman who occupied it before my great adventure with you in the Middle East. I look back on all the traveling we did and can hardly believe we did it with such ease and self-assuredness. I suspect that doing it again would not be the fun it was when it was fresh and new for us.

The trip over Lisbon was not too bad, although I was still plagued by early morning sickness and then was ravenous afterward. There was an elderly couple who knew who I was and had read the announcement that was in the *Tribune* about my pregnancy. They were solicitous and spread the word to others about who I was. It was nice to have a group of friends to share the trip with.

Mother is hinting that the matter of Naomi's church affiliation should be opened for her input, but I have put a lid on it and told her I will go live with my parents if she insists on doing that. That frightens her, as she is leery of Aunt Bea's reaction, especially since she lays great store in what Aunt Bea says.

I saw your pal Janet Everett in Charlotte again, but when she saw me, she crossed the street rather than speak with me. Now there is a woman that I wonder about. How in the world did you ever become her pal? I know you told me it was simply that you lived close to one another as children, but, Marty, couldn't you tell then that she was trouble?

Sleep well tonight and remember that the time will go quickly enough so that you soon will be crossing the Atlantic yourself. Then we can be together to welcome Naomi into the world.

Oodles of love, your Emmy

The following morning, I met Sadie for breakfast when cornmeal mush was the meal of choice (the only choice). It was better than the cream of wheat served the previous day. We ate in silence, and as we were drinking our ersatz coffee, I said. "I want you to do some creative work for me today. Get some of your most troubling photos of the Armenians and superimpose them on the shots of the magnificent buildings we took yesterday. Don't be sloppy. Don't be syrupy. Don't be condescending. Be an artist. I'll see you at three p.m., and the results of your work will tell me whether you go back to Paris or stay with me." I got up and left.

I spent the morning searching for the activist journalism group that I had encouraged two years earlier and found three of them, but they were no longer functioning as an organization. They told me the group had disintegrated the previous year, largely concerning a split in the organization over whether to keep the Ottoman tradition alive or to move over to a Turkic identity. The split reflected the greater schism among Ottoman intellectuals nationally, where the same debate occurred. All three were pleased to see me but did not feel that it was a good time to get together for further talks as the near future was too uncertain.

I then went to the *Herald* newspaper and found that the editor was still there. He was pleased to see me and said that he often wondered what became of me. He said when the *Tribune* was appearing in Constantinople it was sort of a golden age, as thought flowed rather freely, even if censored somewhat, and politics had not yet become sullied enough that one lost hope. He said the cases of the Greeks and the Armenians were a sin that the Ottomans would probably never live down. "Even I am now ready to throw my lot in with the Turks. The Ottomans have been guilty of too many atrocities and have shown too many shortcomings." We parted with sadness and neither of us suggested a future meeting. It seemed too unlikely to happen.

I arrived back at the hotel and found that Sadie had completed the assignment I gave her. I looked at her work piece by piece. "Too artificial," I said of the first piece and threw it aside. "Too maudlin," I said of the second attempt and threw it after the first one. "This one doesn't show any match or any relationship," I said of the third in the series and threw it after the first two. Numbers four, five, and six I accepted. Number seven I tossed and number eight I accepted.

With big tears running down her face, Sadie said, "You are too picky. There is nothing wrong with two or seven. Not if you take eight, as you have." She was upset with my draconian judging but tried not to show it. She apparently couldn't control the tears. I hardened my heart and went back to judging.

"All three are borderline," I said, "You are right. I'll toss number eight as well. That leaves us with three out of eight. Now tell me, Sadie, do you think that the juxtaposition of the photos enhances or destroys the shame and degradation of the photos of the Armenians? Or doesn't it make any difference?"

"It makes a difference, believe me," she said. "To see such suffering and poverty of spirit against the backdrop of such magnificence tells a better story than the bald picture of the atrocity," she said.

"Good, we'll send the three photos tomorrow. So tonight, I want you to work on some descriptions. I'm tired of doing your work, so I'll leave that job for you. I would have thought you would have learned how to do that job better in Paris." Without any pause, I said, "There's a chicken restaurant near here, so you can join me at seven p.m. if you want to eat with me. There is some gunky and spicy sauce they put on it, so go easy on it, or you'll be up all night. See you then if you are interested."

I then went to the telegraphic desk and wrote a telegram for Paris.

chief editor stops trains filled with returning german and austrian soldiers stop no chance to send sadie back to paris just now stop she will have to put up with the job for a few days more stop perhaps she will cease whining in that time stop regards stop marty

At the restaurant that evening Sadie thought the chicken was the best she had ever eaten, and I had to agree that it was unusually succulent and tasty. However, she fell in love with the sauce and, even though I gave her another warning, she put it on her chicken with reckless abandon. Consequently, beginning at five the following morning she did little other than sit on the stool in the bathroom and evacuate the meal she had enjoyed so much. She was not finished with that chore until late afternoon and then, went to bed to rest. It was Sunday and I had nothing planned in any case.

On Monday we spent the day watching German soldiers load their gear on railroad cars and prepare to depart for Germany. Sadie got a lot of pictures, and, of course, a lot of comments from the German soldiers. I interviewed two who knew French and one who was well-versed in Turkic. Sadie and I coordinated our photos and stories and were pleased with the result.

The next day we worked again with the Armenian refugees since a new group was brought in, this time from rural Syria, where they had been transplanted. They were less haggard than the group from several days earlier, as they had lived on subsistence farms and were out of the way of vengeful Turks, even though they had initially suffered when they were resettled. Again, Sadie and I coordinated our stories. I felt she did well at this type of work, rather than when she freelanced. And so the week went, as we covered group after group as they transited Constantinople, or Istanbul as the Turks were beginning to call it again.

On the next Saturday, I got a phone call from the chief editor in Paris. She said, "I assume the trains are still full of returning Germans so it will be impossible for Sadie to return. If you feel she is not too big a burden, I suggest you take her with you to Damascus, as I know you intend to go there this week. From there she can go to Alexandria as planned and return to Europe via boat over southern France. How does that sound?"

"All right," I said. "In the meantime, I think Sadie has picked up enough skills that we can consider her internship in the field a success. I notice you are using her photos regularly and I think she is beginning to be creative and inventive, so that she will be a good field photographer if she stays with it."

"Yes, thanks to you," the editor said. "But I have something else that needs to be discussed. The newspaper is cutting back on its overseas reporters because the war is over, and such broad coverage is no longer needed. We intend to leave one person in the Middle East who will do a lot of traveling, very much like you did back in 1913. I need to know whether you want that position or not. We prefer you to stay but think maybe your family situation will persuade you otherwise."

"You have it right," I said. "I want to get a university teaching position in the Carolinas as does Amelia and leave overseas reporting behind. What are we looking at as an end date for my job? The sooner the better."

"One of the young men who filled in for you when you were married, has expressed interest in returning to the Middle East. Emile thinks he will do fine. He can be there at the end of January. How does that fit with your plans."

"Wonderful," I said, "If I were in the military, I would make a 'short-timers stick' which notches a stick each time a day goes by. Let's plan on it."

The Saga of Sadie and Alfred

Sadie and I traveled to Damascus on the Hijaz railway on Christmas Eve day arriving about five o'clock in the afternoon. We checked in to an out-of-the-way hotel, just outside the government district, and found that my mail had been forwarded from British army headquarters where my last address had been. I had requested that this be done before we left Constantinople. There was an invitation in that mail for Christmas dinner at four p.m. the following day. I showed the invitation to Sadie and said, "Do you have some sort of a dinner frock with you."

"No, I haven't," she said. "I guess I can't go." She sounded disappointed.

"Well," I said, "Damascus has some fine women's shops, with styles right out of Paris. I expect that has held despite the war. Let's take some time tomorrow morning to see what's available. Now I've got to get my evening suit cleaned and pressed before then and see if I can find some medals to pin on my breast to appear like the military swells who will wear all their campaign ribbons and medals. So, you see, we both have problems with what to wear."

There was also a letter from Aunt Bea, which read:

Dear Marty:

Your mom and dad are pleased that you will be returning to the U.S. in early February, although they are at a loss as to why you didn't insist on coming home for the holidays. After all, you have missed them throughout the war. I rejoice that Amelia is with us and she will come to Hickory for Christmas Day celebrations with the family, over the objections of her mother, I know for a fact. But her presence is important because not everyone has seen her since she got home, and the women all want to discuss her pregnancy with her. A few even want news of you, even though they all read your articles nearly every day in the *Tribune*, which they have delivered especially, as it is not ordinarily available in this region.

The end of the war was like letting the air out of a balloon. It's flat and a little stale this year as all the excitement dies away. I can only imagine that doing a daily grind of reporting is even worse, as before you had the excitement of operating just behind the lines and having adrenaline course through your arteries and veins all the time. Well, you can soon substitute that experience for being a college professor and dealing with the scintillating comments of sharp students. At least I hope you become the professor you always wanted to be, although your father seems bent on introducing you to the furniture business. Don't let him persuade you to do something you don't want to do.

Be careful as your days in that mysterious part of the world wind down. We all want you home safe and sound.

Love, Your Aunt Bea

The following day, with the advice of the hotel owner's wife, we found the proper shop to get the afternoon frock for Sadie. The shop owner herself came to assist us when she discovered the bill was to be sent to the *Tribune* office in Paris. She said she had often passed the building while she was a fashion designer apprentice in France before the war. She brought forth three dresses—one blue, one red, and one black, all of which looked lovely on Sadie. Ultimately, Sadie chose the black one, and then the woman brought the accouterments— fashionable shoes, black silk stockings, elbow-length gloves, a fine mesh veil, slip, corset, garter belt, and underwear. Sadie grew uneasy as the goods mounted and worried, she was overspending. She said, "Maybe I can do with my underwear,"

"But, Mademoiselle," said the owner with a sly, side glance at me, one never knows how the evening ends and one wants to be prepared for the most serendipitous ending possible." I broke up on that remark and said, with a laugh, "Go for broke, Sadie. The accountant at the *Tribune* is going to have a heart attack over the cost in any case; a few more francs is not going to placate him at all." When Sadie was completely outfitted, she was taken to a hair salon two doors from the shoppe and a stylist washed, tinted, and groomed her hair to perfection. It was shorter with no ringlets, and, consequently, she appeared more mature than she ordinarily did.

Then the woman went to work on my suit and did some minor restyling on the lapels and adjusted the trousers in-seam so that the slight bagginess that was there beforehand disappeared. She took my junior skeet championship medal and made it the center of two more shooting medals that made an elegant display for the suit itself. Then she provided a white, pleated shirt, over which she placed a wide cravat of navy blue with a reddish stone stickpin. She threw away my belt, snipped away the front belt loops, and provided red and blue suspenders that might be seen if my coat was unbuttoned and loose. As the final touch, she provided a collapsible top hat.

We were in the shop for two hours and had word from the owner that the new clothes would be delivered to the hotel by 2 p.m. "Why would you do such a wonderful thing for me," asked Sadie when we were in the motor taxi again. "You could have left me at the hotel while you went to the dinner. I would not have thought you ill for doing that. After all, I am just a lowly intern."

"No, you're more than that, Sadie," I said. "You are my team partner just now and you share in the good and bad the adventure brings. I could not in good conscience leave you in your room, while I was off enjoying myself at a military dinner. Besides, it's Christmas and we all deserve to be with other people on that special day. I hope it will be one that you remember for a long time to come." We then took an hour's drive around the high spots of Damascus and ended with a short visit to the metal goods area, where we saw some well-designed metal trays that would pass for art in many wealthy homes.

The late afternoon dinner was an enjoyable experience. First, I received a very warm welcome from General Allenby in the receiving line, and he congratulated me on my successful trips to Mudros and Constantinople. Second, Sadie, who had been afraid she would be a wallflower because no one knew her, was swept up after the receiving line by none other than Major Alfred Ramsing himself, He became her escort for the evening, introducing her to important officers throughout the assembly and rationing out her dances when that started late in the gathering.

It was a buffet dinner, followed by a round of greetings, jokes, in-house humor, and some ceremonial hi-jinks common to the regiments of the British army. I went through the serving line with one of the other correspondents I had known at the beginning of the Palestine campaign, and we talked then and for a while afterward about our adventures. He had gone into Amman on the second Jordan attack and was amazed at the fighting ability of the Ottomans under German leadership.

Later I talked with one of the negotiators at the Mudros conference, and we compared notes on some of the other figures at the conference, particularly the French counterparts. As we were speaking one of those counterparts recognized us and entered our conversation. A most interesting conversation in French occurred, in which the clearest version of the French aspirations in the Middle East emerged, which corresponded exactly with the earlier Sykes-Picot Treaty of 1915. Our *ménage trois* broke up when the two military officers decided what they had learned from each other and obliged them to report immediately to their senior officers.

I was left alone but soon found myself with one of the few women there, the wife of the new military district commander of Cairo, who had once met my wife and wanted to know the latest news about her pregnancy. That brought three other women to us, and we talked about the small number of women present, which they were sure would change, now that the war was over. They all wanted to know about Sadie and my relationship with her. I winked and said, "For god's sake don't tell my wife!" which made them laugh, and then I explained her real role. They agreed that Alfred Ramsing was the best escort she could have for the evening. After that, the dinner party broke up and I made my way to the door, stopping to talk with several people on the way out.

At the door, Alfred and Sadie were waiting for me. The captain said, "With your permission, sir, I would like to take Sadie to an *apres-partai* at the general's home. It will last past midnight, I am sure, because there will be dancing. Sadie knows all the latest steps. Do you mind, sir?"

"Of course not, major. Sadie is an adult woman and can make such decisions on her own. I only ask that someone escort her back to her hotel. I don't want her out on the streets alone." I would have liked to whisper to Sadie what the shop owner had said about 'serendipitous outcomes' but, then again, I figured Sadie was old enough to make that decision on her own as well.

I was assured she would be escorted back to the hotel, as I knew that would happen in any case. I had only requested it as a formality and the answer was given to me as a formality. At the hotel desk, I left a note for Sadie saying that the following day was one of 'rest and recuperation.' I figured Sadie would not be ready for work in any case, and I wanted to catch up on my sleep as well. We had been working hard lately and deserved a day off.

Sadie was already at breakfast two days later, when I arrived to find that bacon, eggs, and toast with marmalade were featured. "Everything is good except the bacon," she said. It tastes like pressed wood."

"It probably is," I responded, "but eggs and marmalade sound wonderful. How was your party the other night?"

Her cheeks reddened a little and she said, "Alfred is a good dancer, so I had a fantastic time. We danced until nearly two and then he came back here and spent the night and most of the next day with me. Do you mind? I figure you are going to find out anyway, so I thought I would tell you upfront."

"Well, you see the shop owner was right about the underwear," I said. She was a little puzzled at my statement, apparently not remembering the incident. So, I said, "No, I don't mind at all. It's hard to find someone to relate to in this line of work, and, when you do, it's best to take advantage of it."

"Do you miss your wife that way," she asked. "I got to thinking it must be hard for you not to be lonely."

"It was bad when she first left. After all, we had been together for several years, but even then, there were some absences. But this time was depressing at first. Now it's not too bad, but, fortunately, it's not terminal, so it's not something you have to worry about." Then I changed back to the original topic. "Do you like Alfred?"

"Yes, I really do," she answered. "He seemed a little standoffish in the beginning, but he grew on me as the night went on. He has asked to see me again before we leave for Cairo. Do you think that will be possible?"

"From our perspective, I would think you could do it a couple of times. But I don't know his schedule."

"I guess I am surprised by your attitude concerning this," she said. "I thought that you now have the best argument for sending me back to Paris and that you would jump at the chance to do that. So, are you going to send me back?"

"No," I answered. "I never wanted you sent back. I wanted you to face your fears and conquer your emotions so that you could do your job. I did not think that pampering you was going to get the job done. It was Paris that asked for you back. I made excuses so that you would not be sent back until you had a chance to prove yourself. You seem to be doing all right. I have no plans for getting rid of you, and certainly not for enjoying a young man you seem to like."

We turned to our work schedule. I said that we would spend at least three days in Damascus to learn whether negotiations among the British, French, and Arabs were proceeding or not. If not, then we would move on to Jerusalem, because I wanted to look at some of the Jewish projects that should now be booming. I said, "I want to see the impact of the Balfour Declaration on the population of the region. Today I would like you to get some photos of the headquarters building and see whether we can get some group photos of the various staff. We may be in luck, as most officials love to have their photos made."

However, in the reception area, there were two men in dark suits waiting to see me. I recognized Shimon Erfan immediately but did not know the other. I said to Shimon, why didn't you join us for breakfast? They even had eggs today. Mine were over-light, but they made boiled eggs for others. Incidentally let me introduce you to my colleague, Sadie Bronstone.

Shimon was happy to see me and embraced me. "This is Rabbi Horowitz, and we are part of a delegation hoping to meet with the military officers holding meetings in Damascus. We don't want anything to go awry with the Balfour Declaration. Can we talk about that for a few minutes, or are you in a hurry?"

"No, of course not," I said. "We have plenty of time. Do you want to talk here or in a conference room?"

"The conference room would be better," he replied.

In the conference room, Shimon said they did not yet have an appointment with General Allenby or anyone else and were hoping I could help them with that. I said, "I'll certainly try. Are you free this morning?" When he responded that he was, I said to Sadie, "Sadie, be so kind as to call Major Ramsing and tell him what has transpired here. Mention that the two gentlemen would like to meet with General Allenby at the earliest opportunity. Can you do that for us?"

"Of course," she said and disappeared from the room. She returned ten minutes later with the response that the general had a clean schedule and would meet them at ten a.m." Sadie's new relationship with Major Ramsing was paying dividends already. We then spent another fifteen minutes talking about the discussions of the Balfour Declaration to date. I said, "There has been mention of it and the British have repeatedly stated that it is now a tenet of their administration in Palestine, but no specifics have been mentioned. Neither the Arabs nor the French have said anything about it but have both sought details on what form the 'national home' would take.

"Good," said Shimon. "That makes our job easier because now we can present some basic formulas for their consideration without having to undo what was done while we were not at the table. We will also be seeking permanent representation. What do you think the response will be?"

"I don't suppose that will happen, because this a meeting for three military forces and does not meet regularly. It's ad hoc and not exactly a political entity," I said, "but probably they will allow you to have a permanent representative at the site, who they can consult when matters come up dealing with the Balfour Declaration."

"Well, we'll push for something a little more meaningful," he said, "but, I am glad you gave us the warning." The Rabbi so far had said almost nothing. But at this point in the conversation, he asked, "Do you sense positive or negative attitudes about the Jewish national home."

"Mostly neutral," I answered, "but the wording of the communique is matter-of-fact and positive. There is no question about its acceptance, only its implementation. I would say, however, that the entire scheme is seen in the context of British colonial control of Palestine. You may have some feelings about that, as it allows Great Britain a veto over everything." Shimon curled his lip slightly at this remark and the Rabbi twisted his head and shook it slightly. I had no idea what those gestures meant, probably unsureness about what confronted them.

Sadie and I were not invited to the meeting, but a short statement was made afterward before the five correspondents who were present in Damascus at the time, which was made to accommodate us. The statement merely said that the delegation had arrived and had made contact. It would shortly meet with representatives of the three powers and conduct initial discussions on the establishment of a Jewish home in Palestine."

 Major Ramsing talked with Sadie for a moment alone afterward and asked her to thank me for getting the two members to them in such a timely manner. "If they had contacted the French or Arabs first, it might have been a disaster," was his comment. He also asked her whether they could have dinner together at eight p.m.

"Will we be finished with our work by then?" Sadie asked, obviously about her prospective dinner date with Alfred.

I responded to Sadie with a question. "How efficient are you with filing your reports?"

She said, "Believe me, I will be done early tonight. Thanks."

We were in Damascus for a full week because the Zionists used us as a sounding board and as a point of contact. Through Sadie, via Major Ramsing, all sorts of contacts were made, especially with the French. My contacts through Prince Faisal were important on the Arab front as well. Faisal's willingness to use me in this respect was, at first surprising to me, until I realized that the Arab community had few other contacts that they could trust. My tenacity at Yanbu had made a deep impression, so my attempts to contact their delegation were always met favorably. As it turned out I acted as a go-between of the Zionist delegation with senior members of the Arabic delegation, and they met in my hotel suite twice in private sessions, which were generally cooperative.

At the same time, we were also talking with the two Zionist leaders, who wanted us to visit their new projects in Palestine and give candid assessments of their worth. One was at Hebron, where it was featured that settlements there could incorporate the holy shrines of the patriarchs. Another was in the coastal area just beyond Tel Aviv which would build on the cooperatives (*kibbutz*) already established. A third would be centered on the area near Gaza City, where landlords seemed specially anxious to sell their property. The fourth, and final choice was in East Jerusalem, in the old city, which might be difficult because of its history of long-term Muslim residents but was regarded as essential if Jerusalem were to become the capital of the Jewish home. Shimon and I had breakfast together twice to formalize the list. At the second meeting, I informed him that there had to be some stories coming out of these visits or there was no deal.

"You are mercenary, do you know that," he told me. "Don't you do anything for the good of a cause?"

"It's your cause, not mine," I answered. "You wouldn't even contact me if you did not want something from me, so don't give me this mercenary crap." He shrugged and said, "Okay, okay, I get it."

Eventually, we threw in three more locations to confuse the issue and make it look like a random list. I was also to report it as a regular article, but not present it as a feature article about Zionism. I agreed to that as well, largely because I had no reason to do otherwise. Zionism was not such a hot topic among the general readership of the *Tribune* just yet.

As the time grew shorter before we went to Jerusalem Sadie brought in special news regarding her relationship with Alfred Ramsing. It seemed that Ramsing mentioned her in a letter home to his mother, who said Sadie's name was familiar and, on checking, she found that the two grandmothers had been best friends at finishing school together. The mother felt that this girl was worth knowing based on family ties and wanted her to hop across the channel and visit her when she returned to Paris. Sadie also said that Ramsing himself was due for rotation back to London, probably with the G-2 section of Army headquarters near London. They both thought that contact between the two of them would be possible in the future, which they both wanted very much.

Sadie did not neglect her work, and never procrastinated in the evening to get away to see her lover. In an off-hand moment, General Allenby said to me, "That girl of yours has handcuffed poor Ramsing. He still does his work superbly, but he's never up for a game of cards or some billiards in the evenings. Too bad, as he is a good chum at male get-togethers. However, it's nice to see him courting a lovely girl for a change, and he likes this one. Incidentally, where do you find them, Marty? First Amelia and now Sadie." It was the first and only time the general referred to me by my first name.

We started our tour in Jerusalem with a visit to the new mayor, Ronald Storrs, who told us more than we wanted to know about the city's problems. More to the point, he also told us about how he intended to remake Jerusalem into a cosmopolitan city, reflecting the glory of the three great Western religions. He stated his belief that the upcoming election of the new mufti of Jerusalem would give the city a chance to revitalize the role of Islam in the life of the city. He felt that the Christian patriarchs of the city needed to rethink their antagonistic policies towards one another and act in friendly concert. As well, he hoped the various sects of Judaism would show unity as they created the national home. It all sounded like more hope than probable reality.

The presumptive heir to the mufti position was a young man of the Husseini family–Mohammad Hajj Amin, who had been in the Ottoman military during the war. His family had been prominent in many important positions over the previous century. He, like Storrs, wanted a renewed Jerusalem. He wanted a rethinking of many subjects, such as the pious foundations that funded mosques and charitable works, He also wanted land reform addressed as well, so that landowners could not sell away the rights of their tenants. It sounded good, but not well thought out yet. Perhaps we were too early with our interview.

There was no single Jewish leader yet, as we well knew, and the two patriarchs of the Christians were leery of meeting with us as we were not well known to them. We felt they were missing an opportunity, but they said they were willing to wait until the situation clarified itself.

Our tour of the sites on the list given to us by the Zionists in Damascus took nearly a week, although it allowed us to see much of the city and adjacent countryside. There was little doubt that the land was relatively fertile, but that it had suffered severely because of the war when labor was short and little had been grown. It had not yet begun to recover. Coupled with an abundance of absentee landlords living in Syria and Lebanon, the process of reinvigorating the agricultural base was daunting.

The Jewish initiative had a golden opportunity to take advantage of this rural deterioration and was ready to do that. Many of the landlords living in Syria had been contacted and were willing to sell their land. They always said that the sharecroppers (*fellahin*), who occupied the land, would retain their rights, but never specified this in writing. After all, it had never been written out; it was an oral understanding. I immediately saw difficulties, because the Jewish purchasers were not going to be too concerned about oral agreements made years before with no substantiating documents.

Our review led us to the conclusion that the sites at Hebron and Tel Aviv were the best bets, while others were less encouraging for one reason or the other. Special attention was given to the Old Jerusalem site because of its strategic location and the strong identification of the city with Muslim interests, which were probably as strong as those of the Jews for the city. Our conclusions predicted great difficulty in gaining access to that territory.

I called Shimon to tell him the results of our visits, which he found disappointing. "You are too pessimistic," he said. "You need the fervor of a convert to give direction to your investigations."

"True, true," I said. "We have had this conversation before, so I won't repeat my viewpoint, which you know only too well. In any case, listen to what I tell you as assessments and move as you see fit. In nine out of ten cases, you will ultimately move in another direction altogether because you have to take advantage of the opportunities that present themselves."

"Well, Marty," he summarized, "No one can accuse you of being duplicitous, which cannot be said for many others we have met in our travels. Thanks a lot for your efforts. I appreciate them even if I don't always seem to be."

In the third week of January, we spent two days in Amman trying to assess what was to happen there in the new alignments of the Middle East. The city itself seemed to be in limbo. There was a strong Turkic element, mostly connected with the old administration, which very much wanted a restoration of the old Ottoman governance and style of rule. On the other hand, there was a more volatile element emanating from the backcountry that reflected the values of bedouin society and wanted change in governance that would reflect Arabism and desert ways of life. Ours was not a positive assessment, as it offered no definitive conclusions on which way the future would develop for the population there.

Knowing that our next destination was Alexandria I declared another day of rest and recuperation and allowed Sadie to travel to Jerusalem for a last meeting with Ramsing. She was touched that I would do that for her. "Think nothing of it, sweetie," I said, "After five years I'm tuckered out and need a little downtime. Enjoy yourself."

I think that was the end of my tour as a correspondent, as I gathered no more information after that date and only tied up loose ends. I do remember coming to the end of a long task, but I was satisfied and in no way perplexed. I spent the evening reviewing my notes, looking for material that could still form articles to be turned in to Paris for publication. I found ten of them and finished them before I departed the Middle East.

I hoped Sadie might come in before I went to bed so that I would not be concerned about her, but she did not appear before breakfast when Ramsing dropped her at the hotel. While she was in her room changing, he came to the restaurant and wished me a good trip home. He said, "You've been generous in giving Sadie time to see me and I appreciate it, especially yesterday when you might have moved on, but you didn't. We had a proper goodbye, but I hope the two of us will connect when I am reassigned to London two months from now. Thanks for allowing us to make our cases to one another. I am positive about the future, and I think she is too."

We did not talk about our work together. It would not have been appropriate since our minds were on him and Sadie, and no one wanted to detract from that central point. He excused himself and left. Sadie came in ten minutes later and sat down to eat. She was not surprised to find mush as the only breakfast available. Our only conversation was my remark, to wit: "Today we head for Alexandria. Let's hope it's a gorgeous day."

Farewell in Cairo

We came into Alexandria on the train, only to find that Emil had decided to relocate to Cairo again, where the agency would now have its headquarters. So we took another train there the following morning, and, apparently, for old times' sake, we were put up in the same hotel where Emmy and I had first met and where Emil had offered me my job as a reporter.

The new office was located some distance away, but we found it easily. Within half an hour, Sadie was detached from me and given her own office, which put her in contact with the other staff members. When I left for the afternoon, she was busy discussing her first photo project with Emile. She did not even pay attention when I slipped out the door.

I went to a small outdoor bookstore near Al-Azhar University, where I found an unabridged copy of Tolstoy's *War and Peace.* It was just the book to read on the sea voyage home that would pass the time of a lonely passenger. I did this, despite the advice of an undergraduate friend, who once confided to me that he had never met a person who had read *War and Peace,* who did not brag about it and be obnoxious. I decided I was already guilty of such transgressions, so it did not make any difference.

The following day, I stayed at the hotel and splashed around in the swimming pool, something I hadn't done for four years. I hadn't lost my swimming ability, but I found myself less than graceful with my overhand crawl and backstrokes and decided I needed to get to the pool more often after returning to the US. I was joined at the pool by a representative from the *Tribune* in Paris, whom I had expected later in the day. Over beer at a table in the pool area, I signed an agreement to edit two volumes of my newspaper articles made over the past several years and to accept royalties for them. He also gave me a check for $1,000 as a bonus and a request to consider coming back to either Europe or the Middle East if there was a large-scale, newsworthy peace conference in the next few years.

Concerning my bonus cheque, I said that I was surprised that the cost of Sadie's frock and accouterments, as well as my updated suit had not been deducted. The representative laughed and said that I certainly had splurged, and the accountant had made some caustic remarks about it, but the chief editor had said, "I'll bet the little minx wrapped some influential official around her finger wearing those glad rags, and we got more than the usual stories as a result. Consider it an investment."

"It was a hell of a lot less expensive than the cost of the armed guards we used in the Hijaz," I said." I thought someone might fume about that."

"The accountant was on the verge of raising it as an issue until Amelia was rescued by her guards, even though she was beaten. The investment in security was then seen as a necessity, although you never used them again."

I changed out of my swim pants to ordinary working clothes, after which the representative and I had a four-star lunch with two martinis. Afterward, we walked off the alcohol we had consumed and then went to the office, where there was a small farewell party for me featuring the champagne and cake with white frosting that had been displayed at Emmy's farewell earlier in the year. It was a low-key, sober goodbye without tears, to my relief. I caught a train later that delivered me to the Ionian Princess one hour before departure time. When I undressed for the evening, I found a note that had been put in my jacket pocket. It was from Sadie and read:

> Dear Marty,
>
> I thought you were arrogant and unsympathetic when I met you, but you grew on me. I discovered that you were a real mentor who made me produce quality work and face cruel reality a lot better than I ever had. Perhaps, most importantly, you showed that you had real understanding for a young woman as she went through her first love affair and did not get in its path, even though you easily could have. I will always remember you for those things. I think (and so do the editors) that the *Tribune* is losing one of its real stars with your departure.
>
> All the best, Sadie.

On the trip across the Atlantic, I did read most of *War and Peace* but put it aside the final two days when a group of fellow travelers asked me to explain the Middle East to them. I ended by giving a series of discussion sessions on the subject. I was met at the New York docks by a representative from the *New York Times* who asked again whether there was any chance I might join their group of international correspondents, as the grapevine had it that I had been released by the *Tribune*. "We don't want to be left out if you are changing companies," he said. He was disappointed with my answer.

I slept most of the way to the Carolinas and was met at the Charolotte train station by Aunt Bea and Emmy, still carrying Naomi. We drove to Fort Mill for the first night back, and I knew I was home again when Emmy crawled into bed and nestled against me as she had so often done on our long, often dangerous journey across the Middle East. We both slept soundly, content to be together again.

Chapter 8
Dissertation Travails

Preliminary Moves

When I arrived home in Hickory, N.C., I found a letter, about a week old, waiting for me. It was from the dean of graduate studies at Winston- Merritt University, who explained that he was new to the job and that there had been considerable disruption in graduate dissertation work during the war. He mentioned social disruption, the absence of people serving in the armed forces, and other factors too numerous to mention. He noted that he had reorganized the faculty and begun a recruiting program to bring standards back to where they had been earlier, if not to, indeed, improve on those standards. In particular, he noted that rules for dissertations had undergone a complete overhaul that would improve the quality of those writings, and some, undoubtedly, would become monographs.

The letter went on to say that all this had affected my dissertation work. He noted that all three members of my dissertation committee were no longer with the university, as the chairman had died, and the other two members had been summarily retired. He noted I had contacted his office five times since January 1915, asking for information about the status of the draft submitted in August 1914. He stated that a form letter had been sent each time to my home stating that the dissertation was still under review and that the committee would be in touch as soon as the review was complete. In retrospect, the letter stated, it might have been better if a more formal reply had been sent giving explanations about the cause of the delays.

It was also stated that the case was complicated by the death of the committee chair in 1915, and no one else on the committee had stepped forward to continue the work of the review. The copy that the committee had been working with at the time was bundled up with other possessions of the expired chair and sent to the archives of the university. It had recently been retrieved when it was decided that further action on the case needed to be undertaken.

To finish up this very overdue matter, a new committee has been named consisting of three new, very dynamic professors who could be expected to bring the matter to a successful conclusion with a minimum of delay. They were Dr. Barklay Froehlich of Psychology, Dr. Clyde Evers of English, and Dr. Byron Pennyworth of Modern Studies. All were adjuncts in the Department of Middle Eastern Studies based on some research on the Middle East they had done. I noted, with some dismay, that not one of the three had been at the university long; all were untenured, and they were not Middle Eastern specialists.

The letter stated further that the committee had located the submission, reviewed the notes and glosses made by the previous committee, and decided none of it made any real sense. Since the rules for dissertations had changed the preceding year, and the document did not reflect the new guidelines, it was determined that the manuscript should not be accepted and that the candidate should begin the process at the starting point of all new graduate work by submitting a new proposal. It was suggested that a new subject be chosen, as the committee members did not much care for the existing subject matter, finding it outside the scope of what they regarded as 'a good subject for academic research.' The committee suggested the finishing time should be extended by a year to the applicant's clock for finishing his graduate work.

The letter urged me to contact the new committee to discuss the matter and get further clarification. The letter stated that 'Time is of the essence since the 'clock is ticking' on my eligibility and something should be done 'sooner rather than later.' I contacted the telephone number listed on the letterhead and was told that no appointments would be made with the committee until the beginning of the Fall semester, some five months hence. When I tried to explain that I did not have that amount of time to wait, I was told to write a letter explaining the situation, and someone on the committee would respond when time permitted. We call that 'the right hand does not know what the left hand is doing.'

Enough is enough! The committee had my revised dissertation for over four years and never responded with any kind of meaningful clarification, and now refused to meet with me for another half a year. I called my father and told him the story. He was sympathetic and immediately called the chairman of the university board and expressed his outrage. The chair said the board did not like to intervene in academic matters, and he was inclined to side with the school of graduate studies. Dad immediately put a hold on two checks amounting to Ten Thousand Dollars for a new library wing. The director of research called later that day to inquire about the hold and, when it was explained to him, said that he would make inquiries, but was sure that there was some misunderstanding that could be cleared up. The director asked that in the meantime the hold on the money be released. My father refused to do that until the matter was resolved.

Later in the day, I received a call from the dean of graduate studies, who had sent me the letter in the first place, saying that such tactics as withdrawing badly needed funding from the university were uncalled for and would not be countenanced. Under no circumstances would he yield to such blackmail. He hung up without letting me speak. I was mystified as I did not know about my father's contacts with the university.

I let my father know about the call and he telephoned four other big donors to the university and told them the story. Together they agreed to 'lean on' the university officials to have my case reviewed. The president of the university called my father to say that he had been out of town when the hold on funds had occurred and was only now learning about the case. He was sure that something could be done. He suggested that I come to the university two days hence when he would have principals in my case together to explain the matter to me more fully. The president then asked that my father remove the hold on the funds so that the university would have access to the money.

When my father informed me of what had transpired, I called the president's office and an aide talked to me about the case. I said I would not come unless given some assurance that the dissertation draft, I had submitted was on the table for approval. He said the best that could be expected would be that I could prepare a new dissertation with an additional year added to the period I had to complete the dissertation. I told him I already knew about that offer and found it 'unacceptable,' since the university was at fault for keeping me waiting so long. He replied that, if that were my response, there was little more he could do, since the matter was handled by an academic department where the president's authority was limited. He wished me well in 'future endeavors,' whatever that meant. He broke off the call.

I told my father about the call, who said that the university officials needed a lesson in taking responsibility. He immediately contacted the five U.S. representatives near the university, plus the two U.S. senators from North Carolina. My father and his friends had given generously to their many election campaigns. All immediately telegraphed support for my case and strongly suggested that meetings be held with me immediately. The two senators mentioned in their letters to the university president that the renewal applications for three federally funded science projects at the university were under review, and their approval of those funds would depend on the way my case was handled.

Two days later the president of the university called me and said that there had been some internal action on the matter that somewhat changed the overall picture. Two senior faculty members in the Middle East program had learned about the status of my dissertation and were alarmed at how the matter was being managed. A resolution was passed in the faculty meeting held to discuss the issue, that, since it was the department's fault that the matter was not handled expeditiously, no disadvantage should be laid on the candidate. It stated that the submitted dissertation draft should be reviewed immediately and that a different committee should be appointed.

The department chair vetoed the resolution, so the two senior faculty members took the matter to the faculty senate, which held an emergency meeting on the matter. There was outrage about the matter. It was agreed that committee appointments were the prerogative of the department chair so that matter was not disputed. On the matter of the submitted dissertation draft, the faculty senate decided that my original submission should be reviewed, but that the meeting should be chaired by the president himself. Hence, the president said, a new meeting was scheduled for two days and that my dissertation draft would be the first item of discussion.

The Examination

So, I went to the university at the time arranged and met with the committee. Only two members were there, the third member was in Italy, Dr Pennyworth, studying the impact of the war on the Italian Alps, a boondoggle if I ever heard of one. Dr Froehlich, the chair of the committee was barely as old as I was but was a pompous man of perhaps five foot three, with a balding head, wire-rimmed spectacles, and spoke with a fog-horned voice. When he spoke, his superior attitude came out of him like the great oracle of Greece: loud, baffling, and extremely narrow in viewpoint. I did not like him from the start, and I resolved that he would bear the brunt of any attack I made. The other member, Dr Evers, was a tall blonde man with blue eyes and a dour outlook. He looked like he was ready to give in before we even started, sensing, perhaps, that the committee had stepped on a land mine.

As he was instructed to do, the president of the university began the session. He had brought two members of the board of trustees with him, as well as three assistants and several deans and department chairs. They all sat on one side of the large table in the board of trustees meeting room, and I sat on the other side by myself while the president sat at the head of the table. The president said, "We are faced with a real crisis here, and I lament that the matter has pushed its way into projects and programs the university sees as vital to its functioning."

My father, sitting at a chair on a side wall of the room where observers generally sit, interrupted at that point. "John," he said, "you promised you would not pontificate, explain away, caterwauler, or delay these proceedings. Let's get to it."

The president wiped a little sweat from his upper lip and nodded to my father. "Yes, of course," he said. The only item on the agenda is the draft dissertation of Martin Mintz, a candidate for a Ph.D. in Near and Middle Eastern Studies. Do I hear a motion on the dissertation?"

There was no motion, so the department chair spoke from the other side of the table, saying, "I contacted Dr Pennyworth, the third committee member, this morning by phone, and he has agreed to make the motion of acceptance." Without a pause, the dour member of the committee seconded the motion."

"Let us move to discussion," said the president. "Barkley," he said to the chair of the committee, "you can have the first crack at the document. You have read it, haven't you?"

Barklay coughed, cleared his throat, and took a sip of water. "It is at best a pedestrian piece of research and writing that fails to meet the standards of the department. That is all I want to say." He whipped off his glasses and polished them vigorously with a large handkerchief.

The president looked at me and signaled me to respond if I wanted to. "Excuse me, Dr. Froehlich," I said, "In what way is my research inadequate?"

"It relies heavily on Ottoman newspapers written in Turkic, documents and papers in Arabic, some Yiddish and Hebrew studies, and a mishmash of other materials that are unknown in our library, or, for that matter to any of us. There is no way the veracity of those documents can be examined. The number of English-language works is limited to only a few works, all secondary."

"Yes," I said, "You are right about the use of foreign language works, which are called 'original research' in academic parlance, Dr. Froehlich. They are materials from the Middle East, which is not strange since the dissertation is written for that department. They are all identified by title and source and can be checked by any other interested scholar. I have never known a dissertation's sources to be checked, although there probably are cases."

I continued, "I have here, and I lifted a book for others to see it, your dissertation on pre-Freudian dream sequences where there are forty-five documents, all in German and French listed, incidentally without completed attribution. Moreover, your transliteration of German words to English is sloppy at best and wrong in a fourth of the cases. I have marked up this copy to show the errors in your workmanship. I'm greatly surprised that your committee let you get away with such slip-shod work. I also checked to see whether there were any copies of your research in the library of the university where you did your library work, and there were not. I only found two in the New York Public Library holdings. If your sources are not checked, why should mine be?"

Dr. Froehlich interrupted. "A graduate student did the notations of my work, so they are hardly my responsibility and are inconsequential in any case. But I speak and use those languages, and my reputation is such that I do not need to be checked. You have no such accreditation. How do we know you have the sort of language mastery necessary to read and understand these works."

"Well, Dr Froehlich," I said with a short laugh. "How about I read you a couple of clips from two books on my journalistic journeys through the Middle East? The first, on page 25, says, "It is rare that we have a journalist who knows Arabic as well as Martin Mintz does. His articles sparkle with dialogue from people of all strata of life in the Arab world." That judgment comes from a leading professor of Orientology at the University of California. The second, on page 17 of my most recent compilation of press reports from my days at the battleground of Gallipoli, states: 'Who else but Mintz could meet daily with common, illiterate Turkish soldiers and understand their concerns as he relays them to us in his book. He even wrote letters to the parents of soldiers on the soldiers' behalf and taught them to sign their names, usually in a scrawl.'" That one was written by the editor of the series, an erudite French scholar with privileges at the Sorbonne." I paused.

"I think I have answered that question to everyone's satisfaction," I concluded. Now let me ask you, Dr. Froehlich, why do you dislike my writing so much? What in the world is the matter with it?

"To begin with," Dr Froehlich said, "You use short sentences, usually simple words and short paragraphs. Dissertations should be works of art, with flowing sentences, using similes and tropes when possible, and showing that the author has a sense of artist in him."

I laughed and said, "You will excuse me Dr. Froehlich, but I was under the impression that a dissertation was an exercise in examining a subject in the candidate's field and explaining it to a group of professors in that field. The instructions of the university do not mention anywhere 'tropes' and, unless the dissertation is on art, one is certainly not expected to be an artist. The question a member of the examining committee needs to ask is: "Does the language used convey the knowledge of the material that has been examined or not." But to add some fuel to the fire of controversy, let me quote your dissertation. I knew the matter of tropes would be raised as it is a favorite of examiners who can't find substantive issues to raise. I looked in "Dream Sequences" and found only one on page 100 and that was more of a mundane comparison rather than a trope. Since it used 'like,' it is a simple simile." I paused for effect.

After a few seconds, I continued, "As well, my sentences usually run between 18 and 27 words; yours 11 to 30 unless you use semi-colons, which I very seldom do as they confuse people, rather than inform them while your sentences are over 60 words. The essence of good writing is whether it conveys meaning and I certainly know mine does. I am not sure I can say that for the sentences with semicolons in your dissertation. I turned to the president and said, "I think I have answered those complaints well enough. I am ready for the next set of questions."

Froehlich was boiling by this point. He interrupted and said, "See here, Mintz, I've had enough of your charges. You are being examined, not me. My dissertation was judged as 'superior' and was put forward for a prize. Who are you to pass such negative judgment on it?"

I responded, saying, "Be civil, Dr. Froehlich. I have addressed you by your title. We are not in the army, where addressing one by their last name is permitted, nor are we at a European university where the practice is the same. I am a recognized journalist and still carry the title of 'senior international correspondent,' which deserves at least the polite title of 'Mr. Mintz' when you address me or refer to me. As for examining the errors of your dissertation, Dr. Froehlich, I am merely pointing out that you don't practice what you preach, and you need to understand that your charges against me don't always hold water."

The president turned to Dr. Evers, the other committee member, who looked 'out of sorts' and a little more than scared. He drank some water, and fumbled with some papers in front of him, while he kept his eyes on the center of the table, avoiding those of either the president or me. Finally, he said, in a barely audible voice,' "Unfortunately the volume of work I have had to deal with lately has been extreme, and I have not had an opportunity yet to read enough of the dissertation to be able to formulate meaningful questions. I will 'pass.'

The president merely said, "Mr. Mintz, have you anything to say on this matter."

"Only this," I said, "the honorable committee member has missed a golden opportunity to learn something from a graduate student that he was assigned to assist and mentor. He has had a long time to read the study and has provided me with nothing at all. One wonders what this committee did with the time my dissertation was at the university. I would recommend that Dr Evers be dropped from the committee if he does not wish to participate fully."

"We'll take that under advisement, Mr. Mintz," said the president.

The department chair spoke at this point. "If I may, President May, I have a question from the absent committee member. He thought the section on the Jews of Palestine did not fit into the model of the other groups that were examined. He recommends that the section be dropped from the study, as it hardly contains any thinking that the major Jewish congregations in the United States and Europe recognize and support. The groups the candidates included mainly use Yiddish, the barnyard language of low-caste Judaism, not Hebrew which is the language preferred by the chief writers and intellectuals of Judaism." I knew immediately that the committee member had not read the draft, merely opened it by chance to the section on the Jewish commune, and decided to make a bold statement to falsely show his familiarity with the document. But I didn't care about that 'common sin' of academic review, I had enough with his statement to make a good rebuttal.

I responded. "Barnyard language of low-caste Judaism! What a judgment to make on the several million people who speak it every day! Wow!! I am flabbergasted! I can hardly believe that a professor at a major university would make such a crass and damning statement about people who have done nothing that merits such condemnation. Talk about arrogance!"

The chair knew he had made a poor choice of words and cringed at my rebuke, the audience murmured, and one person let out an embarrassed laugh. I waited until the audience settled itself, expecting the president to intervene, but he did not. He was silent and stared at the far wall. So, I continued, "Who is to say what is to be included and what is not, other than me, the architect of this study? I have located a group that is relevant to the examination of new trends in the Middle East and have provided evidence of its contribution. As for the language it uses, if I was writing about the Pennsylvania Dutch, I would be compelled to use their lingo, not that of the educated elite of German settlers near Philadelphia that have advanced educations. It may seem strange to give credence to the old shibboleth, *"The kuh hat uber die fence gejumped und die cabbage gedamaged,"* but I would be wrong not to use such language in a study about them, for that is the language they use every day and has the understanding to them. The same is true about the Yiddish speakers in Tel Aviv."

I paused, feeling sure that the president would intervene, but then I realized that my indignation at the unkind and highly judgmental remarks of the department chair gave me leeway to carry my remarks to whatever conclusion I wanted. Realizing this, I said, "Regarding Yiddish sources, I had the assistance of an orthodox Jewish scholar, a Sephardim, from Basel, who was a member of the Zionist organization negotiating with Ottoman authorities over the increase of Jewish settlement in Palestine. He certainly could be expected to know whether the Yiddish group in Tel Aviv was legitimate or not as advocates of change."

I paused for a sip of water and then continued. "Not only did he help me with the Yiddish translations, he pointed out the significance of the writings, and how they related to the standard yearnings and goals of the entire Jewish diaspora in creating a new Jewish Home in Palestine. He found the use of Yiddish more than acceptable. I explained that in footnote 51 on page 160. The committee member doing important work on the impact of the war on the Italian Alps did not get that far with his reading. He is so overworked with his research program." A titter ran through the audience. "Perhaps you could send him a graduate assistant to help him out."

The president finally said, "Mr. Mintz, please do not use such sarcasm here. We assume the best motives of our colleagues. The entire audience nearly broke up on that remark. Things were not going so well for the academy, so the president called for a recess.

We met again four hours later. This time the meeting was held in a small auditorium and there was considerable press coverage as well as students and professors present. Everyone was waiting for more vitriol from me, the challenger, against the crusty defenders of the academic citadel who had tradition and authority on their side. But it did not turn out that way, and the meeting was anti-climactic. The defenders of the academy folded from the beginning.

The president again chaired the meeting. He said, "Before we return to the examination of the manuscript, I have two announcements. First, the membership of the committee has been changed to reflect the absence of one original member and the inability of another to participate fully. Dr. Froehlich remains chair and his two new members are Dr. David Steiner, Professor of Jewish Studies, and Dr. Harry Wustenfeld, Chair of the Department of History. Both are familiar with the candidate himself and with his academic work since he took courses from the two professors. Both have had several hours to read the manuscript.

"Second," he said, "There will be a reception in the anteroom after this session is finished, followed by a press conference in this auditorium, one-half hour after the beginning of the reception.

"Now let us return to the manuscript. Dr Steiner, will you start the next round of questions, please."

"Delighted, President Bohrmann," he began. "Marty, I spent the morning reading your fine dissertation draft. I could hardly put it down once I had started reading it. Your writing is gripping and, you tell a story like you never did when you took my classes. Your time as a foreign news correspondent in the Middle East has given your writing an edge it never had earlier. As to the subject matter, your coverage of the new projects in the Sudan was, especially riveting. In your travels, did you have any chance to run across Ottoman Jews who favored or objected to the Yiddish Jews you mentioned?"

"Twice," I said. "With mixed results. One older gentleman, who carried a book by Averroes with him, said that Jews from elsewhere should be careful when they enter the Ottoman Empire, lest they upset the arrangements the Ottoman Jews created over centuries. He felt the Yiddish group posed a threat to the consensus that existed regarding Jewish rights in the Ottoman Empire, where considerable toleration had been obtained. The other case was with a young Jew in Aleppo, who had attended an advanced institute on irrigation, who said the Ottoman authorities ought to loosen restrictions, so all Jews could worship at the Western Wall in Jerusalem. The young Jew, however, added that such arrangements were not important so long as Jews had access to education, even as he had." I added as an afterthought, "If I publish this dissertation as a book, I will include those anecdotes."

"Thank you, Marty," Dr Steiner said, and then to the chair, he said, "John, I have no further questions."

"Then let's turn to our last committee member, Dr Wustenfeld. "Harry, what do you have for us."

Harry Wustenfeld was ready. "Marty, Marty, Marty! Why are you busying yourself with such a narrow landscape as the near and Middle East? We've talked about this before. You need to see these areas in a much broader context. But since you have been overly narrow, we'll stick to what you've done, which is a lot. "Tell me, has the work of Muhammad Abduh and his Muslim modernists had any impact outside the Middle East?"

"Yes, I answered," realizing that he had thrown me an easy question. "The pilgrimage, as you know, is the great disseminator of ideas in the Muslim world. There is evidence that the ideas of Abduh and his disciples have found their way through the pilgrimage to Central Asia, to India, and, especially to Southeast Asia. The transfer has raised new issues of identification of non-Arabs with Arab Islam, so it has not been easy but is nonetheless telling. New mosques, new books, and new institutions have risen in all the areas I mentioned as a result of the spread of Abduh's doctrines."

Before I could proceed further, Harry Wustenfeld interrupted and said, "That is what I wished to hear. Thank you, Marty." He turned to the president and said, "I am finished."

The president turned back to Dr. Froehlich. "Do you have further questions for the candidate?"

"I pass, President Bohrmann."

The President asked whether I had any concluding remarks. Now, I am not dumb, and I can read a situation well, I could see that any vote of a reconstituted committee would favor me. Why prolong the ordeal? "No," I said, "I'll forego the pleasure."

"I call the question," said Dr. Steiner.

"The president said, "The question stating that the dissertation draft submitted by Martin Mintz be accepted, has been moved. All in favor say 'aye.'" Two voices said, 'Aye.' No one voted against it, and one voice voted 'no vote.'

Dr. Steiner, however, was not finished. He said, "In the interest of unanimity among faculty and to remove any doubt from this process, I ask that the chair call for a vote of 'acclamation' of the members."

The president said, "I like that motion" and, looking directly at Dr. Froehlich, said, "Lots of things hinge on a motion like that, so I hope all members will see the advantages of such faculty concord." I wanted to tell Froehlich to take the deal or his career at the university was over, but he was stubborn and, when the vote was called, he voted against a unanimous vote of acceptance.

I learned later that an investigation into his credentials was launched by the university, and all sorts of irregularities in his research were uncovered. He was removed from his assistant professor's position with its tenure track and was given charge of a university research project in Psychology. He disappeared from the university a year later when he was offered a job elsewhere.

The committee member in the Italian Alps resigned after returning home and not being able to show any progress on his supposed studies. He faced a reprimand and loss of his place in the tenure-track system. Dr. Evers, the member, who had not read my report, resigned as well when he faced a reprimand. Finally, the department chair, who had started all this incompetence, resigned as chair and, after three months as a regular faculty member, chose to go to another, less prestigious university as a regular faculty member there, hardly a promotion.

The reception went well, and all my former professors congratulated me. A few students, who knew I was a noted journalist, asked for an autograph. The president and his staff did not stay for the reception but were seen meeting with my father and several board members, presumably about restoring grant money to the university. I did see the president at the press conference, where he was the perfect diplomat assuring everyone that reports of a rift between the university and its donors were a minor bump in the road that was already fast on the way toward being remedied. I was not asked a single question, and I might as well have been invisible.

Dad told me that evening, when we ate dinner at the University Inn, where we were staying, that re-institution of the donated funds was not automatic, and other complaints were being raised before new arrangements were made. Even the federal government, sensing an opportunity to intervene in the work of its projects on campus, raised several issues, especially the heavy absentee rates of some of the key researchers, who seemed to have too many outside interests. Dad said the complaints were coming in slowly but steadily and probably would for the next six months. The university had received a clear wake-up call.

The following morning, I took the train back to Hickory and was met at the station by Aunt Bea and Emmy, who now was quite large with little 'Naomi,' Emmy said, "Somehow, it would have saved me a lot of trouble if they hadn't approved the degree, since you will insist on being called 'Doctor' for the next six months.

"I looked her straight in the eyes and, with a big grin on my face, said, "You bet your bottom dollar I will!"

Aunt Bea groaned at the remark, and Emmy said, "The baby has kicked me again."

Retrospect

I have been given the task by the editors of the *Tribune* to write a celebratory article marking the awarding of the 1919 Pulitzer Prize in Journalism to Amelia Caruthers Mintz and Martin M. Mintz for their outstanding wartime reporting from the Middle Eastern Theater of the Great War. The entire publishing and editorial staff, reporters, photographers, and others in the *Tribune* organization join me in congratulating our two stalwart correspondents, who labored with few complaints in the inhospitable climate and terrain of the Middle East for five long years to report almost daily, on the conditions facing the opposing forces and the dreadful consequences on all those who were involved. Their courage, coolness amid harsh conditions, and insight into the people involved stand as exemplars of what we wish for in journalists but only seldom see attained at such a high level. They have our admiration for a job well done and our good wishes on the day of their recognition for high achievement in journalism.

I met both Amelia and Martin on the same day in Cairo in early 1913, at a private party given by Cynthia Mintz, the mother of Martin. I am slightly abashed to admit that I 'crashed' the party to meet Martin, who, I was told, had good writing skills and had just completed advanced courses in the Arabic language. I met Amelia as well and learned that she was a master photographer with awards in two national competitions. But I left the party without inking either one to a contract, as they were involved in their first meeting with each other, which seemed to consume both of them so that there was little room for mundane journalism just then.

But my luck returned a few days later when I convinced Martin to join me on an excursion through the Near and Middle East to establish press centers and to interview prominent people. It took longer to bring Amelia abroad, but that was done by my colleague Boris Deckar. Through his efforts, she joined the excursion two months later. Both gained readerships early in their reporting careers. Martin did it with his description of a fair at a saint's tomb in a Nile village, where the circumcision of small boys was undertaken. He contrasted the festivity of the fair with the anguish of the little boys, as they became full members of the Muslim community. Amelia did it with her photos of Jewish pioneer families in Tel Aviv with happy children and mothers feeding chickens, kneading bread, and working in a communal garden.

Their early work together featured the photos of Amelia accompanying the interviews of Martin, as they met mayors, generals, religious leaders, high-ranking officials, and, importantly, ordinary people. Readers waited impatiently to see who the next person would be that received the attention of this duo with such insight into human character. When the war began, their relationship changed. They served near one another but were no longer a team, so the electricity that was so apparent in their earlier works diminished. Instead, we had two reporters with advanced insights into the subjects they covered. Amelia turned to the conditions of the Ottoman citizenry and then to the plight of minorities, which produced articles that touched the heartstrings of the *Tribune* readership. Martin centered on the military happenings of the Ottoman theater, most notably the Gallipoli campaign, where he spent over ninety nights on the front lines. His reporting on the thoughts and attitudes of ordinary soldiers was poignant and revealing of their souls. For the last years of the war, they were in the Egyptian-Palestine region, where they became a reporting team again, only they shared the writing chores and illustrated them with Amelia's photography. This final metamorphosis produced a mature product that revealed the impact of war on a major part of the Middle East. Their reporting from the western desert alone resulted in a great increase in the sales of the *Tribune.* Their coverage of a meeting in the desert between the British agent T.E. Lawrence and Prince Faisal revealed the inner workings of policy formulation among players in the Middle Eastern region. The reporting of that event verified that various sides in the conflict had vastly different hopes for the future after the war ran its course. When the end came in 1918, the two of them stood as the consummate reporters of Middle East war news.

Their relationship went through trials and tribulations, of course, but they always remained close colleagues and friends. Other men and women appeared on the scene as love interests, but none lasted more than a short period, so the underlying romance between the two always simmered beneath the surface. Ultimately, they decided to devote themselves to each other exclusively. In 1916, they became engaged, and in 1917 they married. In late 1918, as the war in Palestine came to an end, Amelia became pregnant. That ended the reporting team as Amelia returned to her home in South Carolina to await the birth of their daughter, Naomi. Martin finished out his tour reporting the end events of the war in that troubled area of the world.

They both decided that foreign journalism was an adventure that had run its course in their lives and that, with the end of the Great War, they would turn to other challenges. Martin recently obtained his doctorate and intends to go into college teaching somewhere in the Carolinas. Amelia took a position as Associate Professor of Art at Winthrop College, where her photography skills were to be featured in a new course of study. Undoubtedly, their resourcefulness and insight will be just as important in their new careers as they were in their glory days later in the Middle East. We all look forward to their new contributions.

On a personal note, I would say that I served as a mentor to both at different points in their career, even as Boris Decker did. One must understand that they were initially raw talent that needed refining and molding so that their initial instincts on getting the job done were tempered with an understanding of human nature that allowed them to work with other people with a minimum of friction. Boris and I were the heavy lifters in that transformation, and they, themselves, responded with dedication and a spirit of cooperation so that all of us can be proud of the professionals that emerged as a result.

It is satisfying and rewarding to see two of us reach the pinnacle of our profession.

Emile Bowdoin

The End, at least for now

Glossary

Anzac– Combined Australia-New Zealand armed forces

Balfour Declaration. A 1916 announcement by the British that a Jewish national home would be established in Palestine at war's end.

Bedouin – nomadic people of the Middle East

Caliph– Islamic ruler of the first rank

Chadur – Head and shoulder covering for a Muslim woman

Commonwealth – Former colonies of Great Britain who had graduated to the level of autonomous nation-states but still recognized the King of England as sovereign

Central Powers. The alignment of powers during this war, which included Germany, Austria-Hungary, Bulgaria, and the Ottoman Empire

CUP Committee of Union and Progress– Ruling elite of the Ottoman Empire in World War I

Effendi– Sir

Entente Powers. The alignment of powers during the war included Great Britain, France, Italy, and Russia. Later, the United States entered the alliance.

Ferengi- Stranger

Harem– Place for women in a Muslim household

Hijaz – Arab area to the south and east of Palestine. (Today's Saudi Arabia)

Kibbutz – Jewish agricultural commune

Levant – Geographical area of Syria, Lebanon, Palestine, and sometimes southern parts of Turkey

Sanussi – militant groups of Egypt and Libya favoring traditional forms of Muslim rule

Sepoy– Indian soldier (without regard to religious community)

Shaykh– Tribal leader; leader of a mystical group

Suq– Arab marketplace

Zionism– Ideological Jewish movement promoting Jewish return to Palestine

Historical Note

Istanbul is Constantinople, the capital city of the Ottoman Empire. In these volumes, it is Constantinople because the Ottomans wanted that title to emphasize that their empire owed something to its predecessor empire, the Byzantines (330-1453). This was part of the effort to promote Ottoman identity rather than the more narrow identities reflecting solidarity with ethnic, racial, and religious communities.

In the same way, the empire is Ottoman, named for the dynasty descended from Osman (reigned 1299 to 1323/24). Its greatest expansion was during the reign of Sulayman (the Magnificent) (reigned 1520-1566). The last ruler of consequence was Abdul Hamid II (reigned 1876-1909). The popular title of the ruler was *padishah* (emperor), although, officially, he was the Sultan-Caliph, a combination of two ranking titles of Islamic derivation. Historically, the Ottomans have been called 'Turks', which was the major ethnic group in the empire and the leading supporters of the dynasty. Arabs were strong supporters until World War I when they were broken off through revolts and dismemberment of the empire. "Turks" is only used in this set of novels when someone refers to the ethnic group, not to be regime. Of course, the Turks (with the Kurds) were the largest of the surviving groups at the end of World War I when all other groups were stripped away for new nations in the region. The rump group took the name Turkey.

In this book, eight historical personages have been incorporated as characters. Their actions and words are intended to reflect their real-life positions on those matters. They are T.E. Lawrence, British military operative; Prince Faisal bin Hussein of Mecca, Arab leader; Prince Abdullah bin Hussein, Arab leader; Gertrude Stein, British author and intelligence agent; Hajj Amin al-Husseini, Grand Mufti of Jerusalem. Ronald Storrs, interim mayor of Jerusalem for the British military government, and General Sir Edmund Allenby, British commanding general in Palestine and Syria.

There are innumerable histories of the Ottomans, a few good and a great many bad ones. Two of the best are found in Hodgson's *Venture of Islam*, 3v.(Chicago, 1961) and *Cambridge History of Islam* 4v. (London, 1970). For the period of World War I, three more recent volumes were used. Eugene Rogan, *The Fall of the Ottomans* (New York, 2015); Michael Provence, *The Last Ottoman Generation* (London, 2017), and Kristian Coates Ulrichsen, *The First World War in the Middle East* (London, 2014)